needing to fall

RYAN MICHELE

Cathy –
Sometimes we need to
fall in order to
Rise!
♡ Ryan Michele

Needing To Fall by Ryan Michele

Editor: C&D Editing (http://cdediting.weebly.com/)
Proofreader: Silla Webb
(http://tinyurl.com/AlphaQueensBookObsessionAS)
Cover Designer: Melissa Gill at MGbookcovers
(http://mgbookcovers.wix.com/mgbookcovers)
Cover graphic: Shutterstock

This book is intended for mature audiences only due to adult situations, sex, and violence.

**Warning: This book covers many tough issues—including, but not limited to, depression, anxiety, post-traumatic stress disorder, and abuse. It is a very highly charged, emotional read. Please note: depression, PTSD, and other issues covered in this book take different lengths of time to combat—some take a lifetime. In this book, time is skewed and sped up to flow with the story line.

This book is dark. It deals with tough issues that many of us don't talk about because we're afraid of being exposed and cut open raw, but to heal, we must lay it out there. We must go there to find our sunshine and hope like hell that we do. Depression and suicide numbers are on the rise, and we need to be aware.

Table of Contents

Dedication

To those of us who have seen the dark, lived it, been sucked so deep in the sticky tar we thought there was no hope. The pain was too much to take, too much to live with another day, only to find that small ray of light that gave us purpose to climb up. It gave us strength, gave us the hope we thought we would never have. This book is for us. There is light; I have seen it. Even though I never thought I would, I did. It was dull in the beginning, and it wasn't easy to achieve, but it was there. Reach out, take ahold of it, and rise.

Need Help? Are you or someone you love in need of assistance? Please seek it immediately by contacting your physician. Here are some contacts. There is help.

YOU ARE NOT ALONE.

Suicide Prevention Lifeline 1-800-273-TALK
https://www.afsp.org/preventing-suicide/find-help
https://www.nimh.nih.gov/index.shtml
http://www.suicidepreventionlifeline.org/getinvolved/locator
http://www.ptsd.va.gov/public/where-to-get-help.asp
http://veteranscrisisline.net

Chapter One

The door creaked, and then not so silent footfalls hit the hardwood floor. I closed my eyes tightly, praying he would go away and not hurt me. Unfortunately, I didn't believe in who I was praying to, because He had never helped me before, so why would He start now? Why would He care about a kid like me, who no one wants, one cares about, no one gives a damn about. A Nothing. Exce Drew, the boy in the next room who had always cared. Ho didn't want to wake him, didn't want him to know. m.

Drew was all I had in this world. I couldn't survive ithout I only had two more years before I could get out ore years anyone looking for me. Two more years to be leg and I was O-U-T: out. Two years, and Drew and I could get on with our lives, far away from here.

The footsteps came closer, and before I could breathe, he was above me. I didn't see him, but I could feel his slimy heat. I hoped he would think I was sleeping. I hoped he would go away.

Hope was something a girl like me should never have, because it never came.

His hand trailed up my leg, my flesh rising with bumps of resistance from his touch. It was the Eww factor times a thousand. I wanted him nowhere near me, not even breathing the same air as me. Regardless, I had no choice. I never did.

"Reign." His voice sang with humor, and if I wasn't mistaken, slurred from too much drink.

Mr. Peterson had a problem with that, but I had never said a word, not wanting to stir any pots. I had been in enough foster homes to know it was always best to keep my mouth shut and mind alert.

"Reign," he said again, but I feigned sleep while clocking his movements next to me.

When his hand glided up the inside leg of my shorts, my body 'ent ramrod straight. I tried to stop myself from the movement yet 'dn't. In turn, I gave myself away.

'. Peterson pushed my shoulder hard, laying me flat on my ' my eyes sprang open.

and h. you were awake." His face was sunken in, eyes droopy, d back. What really caught my eye, though, was the smile on his face: devious, cunning.

On instinct, I gripped his wrist, trying to stop him.

I had been fighting for everything I had since I was six years old. Fighting was in my bones from top to toe, even though I told myself not to. Although I told myself to keep quiet, I couldn't help myself. Some things were so engrained they never went away.

He full-out laughed, thinking my trying was a joke. "You think you're gonna stop me? No, you're gonna take those little tease of shorts off and fuck me."

My stomach rolled and bile rose in my throat. This wasn't the first time Mr. Peterson had come to visit, and I knew it wouldn't be the last. I hated it, but he always ended up playing the one card he knew he had on me.

"Please don't," I begged him, knowing he would do whatever he wanted and my words meant nothing to him, but I always felt the urge to try. He didn't care about me or Drew. We were paychecks to him and his wife, and I was a toy to him.

He ripped his hand out of my grasp and began to pull my shorts down my legs. "You little slut, you know you want it."

I fought, my instincts not letting me stop.

His hand came down hard across my face, and pain speared through it before red hot fire followed. My eyes burned with tears from the force as he tore the shirt from my body.

"You fucking little bitch. You want it hard? I'll give it to you hard," he said as I began to kick and use my long arms to hit and nails to scratch. "You want me to go next door and do this to

Drew?"

My movements seized like my mind had finally caught up to my body in that exact moment. Cold ice seared my veins like a physical pain.

Mr. Peterson always threatened to hurt Drew; that was the only way he could get me. The only way I would stop fighting him, the only card he could play to get what he wanted. And the entire time Mr. Peterson did what he wanted to me, I thought of Drew and how I was protecting him, because he was the only one who mattered.

The door to my room flew open with a hard crash, hitting the walls and shaking them. Somehow, I got enough strength from the panic to get out from under Mr. Peterson and jump from the bed, my heart pounding.

"What the fuck!" Drew screamed loud enough to wake the entire house.

I scrambled, trying to find something to cover my nude body as tears spilled over my eyes and down my cheeks. I never wanted anyone to see me like this. No one ... but especially not Drew. Never, ever Drew. I never wanted him to see me as Mr. Peterson did: a slut, a whore.

The pain on his face sliced through me like a razorblade. I felt more than exposed. I was turned inside out. Drew's face twisted then, his upper lip curled, eyes narrowed and hooded, and his brows came together. He was disgusted at the sight ... of me.

I felt worthless, ashamed, and completely shattered. I could have died in that moment and disappeared from the face of the earth from his one look at me. I was utterly gutted.

"You fucking piece of shit!" Mr. Peterson growled, standing up and pulling his pants up.

Drew went after him, clenched fist in the air, ready to make contact with Mr. Peterson.

"No!" I screamed as Mr. Peterson punched Drew so hard in the stomach I could envision each molecule of air pushed from his body in a gush. Then Mr. Peterson kicked him in the legs, pushing them out from under him and making him fall to the ground with a hard thud.

I ran to Drew, driven to protect him. I threw myself on his body, shielding him, but Mr. Peterson picked me up as if I weighed nothing and threw me across the room, which slammed me into the wall, narrowly missing the sharp edge of the dresser. I choked down the agony my body felt. I needed to breathe and stay focused.

Mr. Peterson stood just as Drew got to his feet, and in Mr. Peterson's hand was a gun. I didn't know where it had come from or how he had gotten it. All I knew was that it was pointed directly at Drew. At once, time stood in slow motion.

I screamed, knowing I couldn't get over to Drew, knowing this was going to end badly.

As the shots went off, Drew fell to the ground in a heap, his bones like noodles, giving him no support. His green eyes locked on mine as the metallic scent of blood filled the room. I wanted to rush over to him yet feared moving. The bile from my insides churned, filling my mouth. I tried choking it back, but it burned.

Drew made some strange, gurgling noises along with some moans. Pain like no other speared me as I watched the spark that was my best friend in the entire world, my everything, slowly die in his eyes.

I woke from a sweat so cold I could have had icicles forming on my nose. I rubbed my fingers together, the nightmare so real I could still feel Drew's blood between them. *No.*

I grabbed the gun beneath my pillow and threw off the blankets, looking around the space: white walls, chair in corner, and dresser against the wall. I moved to the first door, opening it and tossing on the lights. The bathroom had no one inside, just the standard toilet, sink, and shower. It didn't slow my heart rate, though. Nothing would until I knew the house was safe. Next, I checked the closet, finding it empty. Windows locked. I opened the door to my room, flipping on the lights to the living room/dining room/kitchen, checking all the small areas and finding nothing. The sliding glass door and front door were locked, undisturbed.

Not until everything was checked did I let out a sigh, and it wasn't of relief, because that never came. Never. To never feel safe at twenty-one years old was pathetic. Living in this apartment for four years and still being so scared all the damn time was pathetic. I couldn't stop it, though. I couldn't make it go away. The fear that they would all come back for me, find me, was too intense, so much so it was almost blinding.

I was forced into therapy when I was younger. That was what the foster care system did when they struggled to get a foster kid settled anywhere. They sent us to therapy to learn better coping skills.

I didn't need someone to listen and twist my mental state. I just needed to survive until I could get out. I'd learned the hard way never to speak about what went on in the homes I was sent to. I was who I was.

But after running away five years ago, it was beginning to get ridiculous. Nothing had happened to me since I moved here. I was safe. I should have nothing to worry about, but damn if the nightmares didn't keep plaguing me, the unease riding me hard every second of the day.

I knew I wasn't going back to sleep. Therefore, I pulled out my cell and typed: *You awake?*

Not seconds later, the response came.

Be over in a sec.

I'd met Andi two years ago at a waitressing job I still had. I was so damn closed off—hell, still was—but somehow, her happy-go-lucky spirit broke through to me. I didn't know how, but her little ray of sunshine, no matter day or night, was the only thing that kept me sane. Andi was my positive in the midst of all the negativity.

A knock came to the door, causing my heart to pound at the sound. Checking the peephole, I was partially relieved to see Andi. The other part wouldn't be relieved until she was behind the door and it was locked so I knew she was safe.

I threw open the door, grabbed her arm, pulled her in, and locked the door, all in one practiced swoop.

"Reign, you have got to relax a little," she said, tossing her purse on the chair then plopping herself on the couch.

She had on sleep pants that had little, brown dogs all over them and a blue hoodie. Andi was what most guys called beautiful with long, golden hair that had a slight curl, and big, blue eyes that showed compassion I had only experienced one other time in my life. I was pretty sure that was what pulled me to Andi two years ago. Her eyes were never fake or clouded over.

She wasn't out to *fix* me, and she never looked down on or pitied me. Every day for months, she would strike up conversations, but I wasn't in a good place at the time. Hell, I was never in a good place, yet somehow, with her persistence and kind smiles, I opened to her, letting her in inch by inch.

Deep inside, I needed to believe Andi was true, so each day, I let her in a little more. It took six months, but she finally whittled her way in, filling me with sunlight I so desperately needed.

I fell down on the couch beside her. "Can't." She knew this. We'd been over it continuously. Nothing would ever change.

Andi reached over and grabbed my hands, pulling me so I had to turn my body sideways to face her. You would think this small touch was easy for me, but it wasn't. It was gut wrenchingly painful and took what seemed like forever to allow.

After gathering everything we needed, Andi and I sat in the far back corner table of the diner with a shit load of sugar, salt, and pepper bottles to fill, and like usual, when the place was slow, Andi was rambling on about this and that. She never had a quiet moment.

One would think this would be annoying, but for some reason, it wasn't to me. I actually liked it.

The way she talked about simple things, like watching the sun rise and its beauty, put a new spin on the dreary, gray world I lived in. I didn't buy into what she was saying, but it was a nice thought.

"My nana was wonderful. She taught me how to make peach cobbler. Sure, I was only seven, so I don't remember much about how to make it." She talked as if I were listening to every word, and I was. I wanted to hear her good stories, because I didn't have those in my life. I didn't really know they existed until Andi began her "talks" with me. Now, I sucked in every one of them like I was dying of thirst, dying to find something good in this miserable excuse of a life.

"I do remember her laugh and smile and how she'd scrape off the measuring cup with this flat thingy like it was the most important thing she was going to do all day, such precision and pride in what she was doing. Then we'd wash the dishes together." She looked up from her salt container. "I was still short back then." She giggled, and I liked that sound, too. It was another thing that had only been in my life when Drew had been there. A sound many took for granted, but Andi gave it so freely I let myself enjoy it for just a bit.

"We'd make these big bubbles and then start throwing them at each other." She laughed full out, lost in her memory, her joy.

Her hand came out and landed on mine. I froze and stared at her hand like it was poison that was seeping into my pores. She couldn't touch me. No one could touch me.

It took me merely a second to get my shit straight.

I ripped my hand away from hers, making the smile that was on her face disappear. It felt like a kick to the gut. I wanted to feel bad for doing that to her, making her feel like that, but I couldn't breathe as the panic took over and my throat closed, suffocating me. I inhaled, but nothing was getting in my lungs. I was choking ... on air. Then I was coughing on it violently.

I gripped my throat, and Andi came near me, reaching out to me to help, but I shook my head profusely and scooted back into the booth as far as I could, needing space.

"Reign, it's okay," she cooed like I was a small child, and in that moment, I was. "I won't touch you. I'm gonna move back over to the other bench, but you're gonna have to breathe for me."

I nodded as she moved out of my space, her frightened eyes never leaving mine for a second.

I watched as the two lone patrons in the diner looked at me like I had every screw loose in my head. Little did they know they were right. I did, and those screws were all I had left.

I sat on the cushy vinyl and closed my eyes then took three huge breaths. This time, the air went in, and my body began to relax. When I opened my eyes again, Andi was staring at me like she didn't know what to do with me. Hell, I didn't know what to do with myself, but Andi was so damn patient, not pushing when she knew I couldn't be pushed.

"You okay?" she asked, and I nodded. "You need anything?" This time, I shook my head. "Girl, you scared the shit out of me."

She heaved out a big breath, and I knew in that moment that Andi was a keeper.

Her touching me took months and months for me to allow. Andi suffered through many of my freak-outs and didn't let the fact that I acted like I was burned with acid every time she touched me bother her. She was so damn patient. She kept at me until I felt comfortable enough for her to even embrace me, which I did eventually.

"Reign, you can't keep living on no sleep." I wanted to laugh, but she continued. "You're young, and you were dealt a shit deal to start your life, but you're free now. You're free to live the life that you were intended to have."

Flashbacks of Drew hit me like a heavy weight, pulling me down like cinderblocks tied to my ankles in the ocean, drowning. I would never be free to do anything.

"If they catch us, we are in serious shit," I warned Drew as he pulled my hand through the door and out the back of the school. If our foster parents found out we didn't go straight home, I was afraid of what they would do to us.

"Mr. and Mrs. Peterson have an appointment at four. They won't be back until at least five or five thirty, so we have time," Drew tried reassuring me, but I couldn't help the fear that crushed me.

I didn't want them to be angry at us. I didn't want to suffer the consequences. Mrs. Peterson was good with her fists, but not as good as my biological father was. Mr. Peterson took his anger out on an entirely different level, and I wanted neither.

Still, I followed Drew. I would follow him to the end of the earth as long as he was there by my side. After knowing him for two years, he was my best friend, my only friend, my everything. He was the only thing that mattered.

He led me through the bright green grass, which was the color of his eyes, and out passed the football field, gripping my hand the entire time. I loved the small tingle just from his touch on my skin. He led me to a secluded area behind the far part of the field where he pulled me under a large tree then stopped and turned to me. His body was so close to mine I felt his heat on my chest.

That feeling in the pit of my stomach began as I lifted my hands to his chest and looked up into his eyes. They were telling me something, but my mind was so foggy from being this near to him that I couldn't think.

One of his arms drifted around my back, tugging me closer to him. The other came up and cupped the side of my face. The gesture was so tender I had to fight back the tears threatening to spill out.

"Reign, I'm getting you out of here. I know we planned on waiting until we were eighteen, but I'm getting you out of that house."

My stomach fell. I didn't want him to know what was going on at night in that house. He couldn't know, could he? I never knew for sure, because he never said, and I wasn't about to ask.

"We don't have anywhere to go," I told him, something we already knew. Between that and the fact that the authorities would come looking for us, we had to stay in their house. Together.

How damn lucky was I that Drew and I had gotten into the same foster home and met? I felt like the heavens were finally listening to me and helping me, that someone up there gave even the slightest shit to put us together.

"I'm figuring it out. Six months, Reign. We're out of here in six months. Sooner if I can pull it off."

My eyes widened, panic clenching my heart. "What are you doing?"

"What I have to in order to get us both to safety," he told me, but before he could say any more, his lips came down on mine. Although it wasn't the first time he had kissed me, it was still so new I gave in to it completely, letting my mind and body only focus on Drew.

"Reign!"

My name being screamed snapped me out of my thoughts. I blinked away the memories and focused on Andi, who was mere inches from my face, her eyes gleaming with sorrow. I hated when she got that look for me. I didn't need anyone feeling sorry for me. Ever.

"Thank God," she whispered, pulling back and giving me space.

I scoffed. "You know I don't believe in that." I didn't. How could I when He took away the only thing that was ever good in my life? How could I when whatever was up there didn't take two minutes to protect me in my entire life? How could I when my life was something I didn't want to live in? How could I when the sliver of hope He gave me in Drew was ground into dust and blown into the breeze?

Her hands tightened on mine. “Have you ever thought of going to his grave and telling him good-bye?”

I ripped my hands out of her grasp and pulled as far away from her on the couch as I could. If I could have made my legs work, I would have certainly gotten up and run as far away from her as I could. However, seeing as my legs were nothing but noodles, I simply sat there, staring at her, dumbfounded, my breath taking a vacation from my lungs.

She moved closer, my pulling away having zero effect on her. “Honey, I’m not saying this to hurt you. I just think it could help you. You never got to say good-bye.”

Tears streamed down my face. There was no point in trying to hold them back, because they would fall, regardless. Ugly sobs threatened to break from me. My chest was so tight it felt as if ropes were around me, squeezing the life out of me, the coarseness of it shredding my insides.

It was true. I had never said good-bye to Drew. The moment Mr. Peterson dragged Drew’s lifeless body out of my door then shut it was the last time I laid eyes on him. When I tried to follow, Mr. Peterson pointed his gun at me and threatened to shoot me, too. I wished he had. Then I could be with Drew and not rotting in a life that meant nothing to me. The pain would have melted in that moment, instead.

For the second time, I said, “I can’t.”

After Mr. Peterson came back, beat the shit out of me, and told me he was dead, I packed everything I owned, which was next to nothing, and ran away. I couldn't look back; it hurt too much.

For almost a year of my life, I drifted. Each moment of those days, I wished Drew and I would have just run away, not caring where we would go or what we would encounter. Then he would at least be by my side, and I wouldn't be so alone I couldn't bear it.

Not once since his death had I ever thought of going to Drew's gravesite. Some sick, twisted part of me didn't want to let go of those last moments I saw him and replace them with him under the ground. I couldn't help what rolled around in my head.

It was demented to think seeing him die before my eyes was more comforting than seeing him buried. It was almost like, if he was buried, all the memories I had of him would be gone, too. I would lose what little I had of him even more.

I shook my head. I couldn't think of this.

"No," I said on a choked sob.

"Honey." She rubbed up and down my arm, trying to comfort me, but for the first time in a long time, her touch felt like sandpaper scraping my skin, so I pulled away.

"I think it'll be good for you to say your good-byes. It will help you close this door of your life so you can go on living."

My head snapped to her. "You think I want to be like this? You think this is fun? I hate my life. Hate it! I wish that asshole would have taken *me* instead of Drew or even with him, but he didn't. Going to see Drew buried six-feet under isn't going to make any of this go away. What if I don't want to close the door on that part of my life? It's like closing the door on Drew. I won't do it!" If anything, I thought, it would bring back too much, and then the already deep pit I was in would open and suck me fully in. But maybe that's what I needed. I needed to fall and just be done with everything.

"No. You were given a second chance."

What?

"What!" The word came out full of rage and accusation. "You think this life is my second chance? You've got to be shitting me!" I jumped from the couch, my legs getting their function back due to my need for space from Andi. The room felt as if no oxygen was in it, and I was suffocating from lack of breath. The panic, the anguish, the emotions all consumed me in a rush. I felt as if I were under a powerful waterfall as the pounding flow crashed over me, pinning me down, keeping me helpless under the water. The weight of the emotions was drowning me.

She stood and followed me, obviously not getting the hint. "Reign, it is. You have a chance to live a life that you were meant to. Do you think Drew would want you to live in this hollow forever?"

As if the air in the room wasn't strained enough, her words were a sucker punch to the gut. The room began to spin, and I gripped the chair in front of me to steady myself.

"Breathe," Andi instructed.

It took everything in my power to make myself do that small task because what she said was true. Drew would hate what I had turned into. He would be disappointed in me, and that was one thing

I never wanted. Ever.

As more tears spilled, Andi wrapped her arms around my body, and I went willingly, crying on her shoulder.

After what felt like forever and was probably an hour, I was all cried out. We moved to my bed where Andi easily climbed in beside me. She lay with me, the sounds of her even breathing lulling me into a restless sleep that left me waking groggy and aching.

Would I ever know what real rest felt like?

Chapter Two

Two weeks of waitressing during the day and tending bar at night kept me busy. Two weeks of thinking about nothing but what Andi said that night I fell asleep in her arms after crying. I didn't want her to be right. I didn't want what she had said to be true. I didn't want to say good-bye. Then it was final. Then it was over. Then what would I do? Nothing would change in my life. I would still miss him every day. I would still mourn him. What would going to his grave prove?

The sad thing was, in my gut, I knew she was right. I didn't know how I knew; I just did.

"Reign." A deep voice from across the bar called my name.

I turned and my nerves sparked to life. They shouldn't. I had called Trey in for help. He was a regular in the bar, and he was also a man who knew how to get information.

Stupid me. I tried googling Drew Lewis' name but got nowhere. Thousands of searches popped up, and looking through each one became too much for me. None of them were my Drew, so I sucked it up and pulled in Trey.

"Trey," I greeted, wiping down the bar then grabbing his usual longneck, popping the top and placing it in front of him.

He winked, and I just barely stopped myself from rolling my eyes.

"You wanted me." He would think I wanted that considering he went home with any woman who would spread her legs for him. Sure, I had an abundance of tits and ass along with long, dark hair, which were great for tips, but I kept everything sexual about myself locked up tight. That part of me was totally shut down.

The bar wasn't busy, as it was still early in the day. Luckily, no one was within earshot. I needed to get this over with before I lost my nerve. It was all or nothing.

I pulled a small slip of paper from my back jeans pocket, along with one of only three pictures I had of Drew, and slid them across the bar.

"Presents?" Trey said, not looking at the papers.

I swallowed deep. "I need a favor." I knew it was going to cost me. What it was going to cost, I didn't know. I didn't have much to give.

"And what would that be?" His brow lifted, urging me to go on, but I didn't want to. I wanted to just forget the whole damn thing and go home. I wanted to yet didn't.

"I need you to find where someone is buried."

Bringing his arms to the top of the bar, Trey crossed them, leaning in. "Where someone is buried?" he questioned. "Normally, I find people who are alive, darlin'."

I let out a gush of breath. If I wanted him to help me, I had to tell him everything, which was not something I wanted to do.

I inhaled deeply and rattled off my time with Drew so quickly one would have thought I was an auctioneer, like on that TV show Andi made me watch all the time. Trey's face didn't change, but from his attention, I could tell he took in everything I said. No emotion played anywhere on his face, though.

When he didn't say anything, I prompted, "So?" I fought myself to keep the emotions at bay. In the last few minutes, I had shared more with Trey than I had shared with anyone except Andi.

He leaned back and whistled low. "Fuck, woman. I had no idea." His eyes filled with the start of pity that I didn't want or need.

I balled my fists. "Don't. Don't feel sorry for me," I demanded.

He just shook his head then picked up the picture and paper, not letting whatever he was thinking come out of his mouth. "You've always been a hot, little thing."

I didn't know what to do with that, so I stayed quiet while he looked at the picture. It was one with both Drew and I standing in front of Mr. and Mrs. Petersons' house. The foster liaison took it and gave us each a copy. She never explained why she took it, but neither of us asked. It was covered in fakeness, though. Smiles: fake. Happiness: fake. Everything: fake.

We stayed that way for a long time—way too long—until he finally broke it.

"I'll do it."

I wanted to feel relief yet didn't. If anything, it only amped up my anxiety.

"But it'll cost ya," he finished.

This wasn't a surprise.

"What?"

A devilish grin came across his lips. "I'm keeping that in reserve."

Reserve? Who does that? I guessed the shady guy I was asking to help me.

"Fine," I agreed.

He stood from the seat, tapped the bar top twice, and was gone.

I was a nervous mess.

***

Three days went by, and each time the door opened to the diner or the bar, my eyes shot to it, expecting Trey to come in at any moment. Nothing.

What I didn't expect was the knock on my door at ten-thirty at night on my day off from the bar.

I checked and double-checked the peephole, seeing Trey standing there. I shouldn't let him in. I didn't know him enough to actually trust him. Hell, there was only one person on this planet I trusted. What if he hurt me? *You went to him, Reign. Pull your shit together.*

I straightened my shoulders, chastising myself. Andi was so right; I needed to pull my shit together. I sucked in deeply and opened the door.

"Hey, what's going on?" I greeted as if him being in my personal space was no big deal at all when, in fact, I wanted him gone in that instant.

"We need to talk," he said, not waiting for an invite. He just breezed on by me like I wasn't there.

The space inside my safety net felt tight and claustrophobic.

"Come on in," I grumbled, shutting the door and locking it. If he were going to hurt me, locking the door meant nothing. Still, it was a habit, and who knew who lurked outside?

He turned abruptly. "He's not dead."

The vast void below me opened up and sucked me into its abyss at his words. I felt as if I were floating down to the gates of Hell, burning as I went.

"What?" was the only word I could muster as the dredge of emotions spiraling out of control pulled me under.

"Andrew Lewis; twenty-one; foster care, the same time as you. Records link him to a Mr. and Mrs. Peterson, but they were sealed. He was shot five years ago, stitched up, and thrown back into foster care, but he went into a group home for boys. He was banged up pretty good, so it was more of an in-house hospital. Got out at eighteen, had odd jobs, and landed a good one at a business firm. He worked his way up from the bottom and owns his own house in Newport about five hours from here."

I reached around, trying to find something to sit on. I was sure my legs were going to give out on me at any moment. The wobble they kept doing was sure to have me plummeting to my ass.

I sat in the hard chair, almost missing it, and scrambled to right myself. I held on to its base for some sort of balance, my world shifting on its axis. I wasn't sure what to make of that.

Trey held out a paper to me, and I stared at it like it was a poisonous snake that would kill me with one bite. I didn't want it. There was no way Drew was alive and never came to find me. No way. I couldn't believe it.

Trey shook the paper in front of my face, making that annoying noise. Somehow, I grabbed it and clenched it in my hand, but I didn't look at it. I didn't want to know what was written on it.

It just couldn't be.

"You're sure?" It had to be a sick joke.

"Reign, I'm good at what I do. It's true."

My hands shook uncontrollably, and my body soon followed. Trey took a step toward me.

"Stop. Don't," I barked out. I couldn't handle his touch right now. Normally, I couldn't take it. Right now, I really, really couldn't. All of this was too damn much.

I ran with everything I had to the kitchen counter and searched for my phone, typing as I clumsily held it, almost dropping it several times.

Come here now, I typed, sending it to Andi.

I needed her like I needed air. I needed a light in the dark. I needed someone to grab on to, something to hold that was real because this … This just couldn't be real.

"Go," I told him.

While he could call in whatever favor I had to do for him, he must have seen the look on my face or taken in my body language, because he got the hell out of there. He didn't stick around a second longer.

I raced to the door, locking it just as a rushed knock came.

I checked and swung the door open to a wide-eyed Andi. I pulled her into my arms, initiating a hug from her for the first time ever. I needed her. I needed her to be my rock since I couldn't be it for myself at that moment. I needed her strength because I was falling.

I heard the door close and then lock. Then Andi's arms wrapped around me as she walked us over to the couch where we sat still in each other's arms. She just held me, waiting until I was ready to talk. It took a while until I could, but Andi, as ever, didn't push me. She simply waited with the patience of a saint.

"He's alive." The words were completely disheveled as they came from deep in my throat.

"Who's alive?" she asked.

I didn't tell her I was having Drew checked out, because I didn't know if I would go through with going to see him. Having Andi disappointed in me wasn't something I liked, so I wanted to avoid it at all costs. I also didn't want to be pushed.

"Drew."

At his name, Andi's comforting arms tightened and her body stilled. She gasped, "What?"

I had told Andi everything about Drew, so she knew how much I loved him with everything I had. She knew every little, minute detail about our time together, including the crushing feeling his death had on me that I continued to carry around.

I pulled away, swiping the tears and snot covering my face. "I had Drew checked out by a guy I know from the bar. He found him, and he's alive."

"I…" She faltered. "Can you trust whoever this guy is that he's telling you the truth?"

My heart kept tripping over itself. "I don't trust anyone but you. However, he has no reason to lie." I shook my head back and forth, trying to make sense of all of this, some of this, any of this. I had seen Drew's life end. I knew I had.

"I don't know what to say." She relaxed her arms yet continued to hold me. Tears spilled everywhere, and by the time Andi pulled me back, her shirt was soaked. "What are you going to do?" she asked hesitantly.

I gave her the paper. "His address."

She looked at the paper. "Are you going to go see him?"

I shrugged. At that moment, I didn't know what I was going to do. All I knew for sure was, once again in my twenty-one years of existence, I was knocked away from any familiarity of knowing myself.

"I'm going with you."

I didn't respond. I didn't know what to say.

The night was spent with me crying in Andi's arms. The way she held me as I sobbed for the man I had loved all my life showed me to the core what kind of person Andi was. She didn't waiver or lessen her grip on me at any given time. I felt comforted, soaking up every minute of it.

I felt Andi's body relax as she fell asleep. Me? I did not. I couldn't. Too many thoughts were crammed into my head. First, was it really true that he was alive? If he was, did he remember me, think of me? Why didn't he come and find me? I would have found him had the roles been reversed. Through all of this, I cried and cried, letting all those thoughts overtake me.

I woke with a start, having passed out from the tears. I looked around the bed, seeing Andi still fast asleep, curled in a small ball. I had only slept maybe an hour. Every cell in my body was telling me I had to get to Drew. He was alive on this planet, and I had to get to him. I had to see him.

I slid out of bed, dressed, grabbed the note with the address, and flew out the door.

The only thought that kept on repeat through my head was, *He's alive. He's alive. He's alive*. I couldn't help smiling at that. The boy I loved was alive, and I was going to see him. Nothing else mattered, because today, I would see him. Today, I would get to experience a small bit of joy for once. I would get my small splash of hope.

The five-hour drive went by in a flash, consumed as I was with my nervous energy. When I got to the address, though, I had major second thoughts.

I shouldn't have come. I shouldn't have entertained the idea. The idea was better than the actual vision burned in my eyes, never to be scraped away.

I sat it my car, staring at the house my GPS had led me to. It was a one-level with some type of greenish worn siding around it. It wasn't new yet wasn't old, either. The home had flowers and bushes around the front and sides. It had a *Welcome* flag hanging from a pole by the door. It was a home for a family, a home I once daydreamed of building with the very man who owns it. The house felt like that, like a home, a happy one.

I had been there for hours, just staring, sure the neighbors would see me and call the cops on me, but so far, so good. I couldn't stop staring at the house. Could Drew really be inside there? No, this was all some sort of sick joke. It had to be.

That was when it happened.

A small, blue car came from down the street and turned into the driveway. I was parked far enough away that they could see my car, but not really make me out inside. I wasn't sure I wanted to knock on the door. Hell, I didn't think I could.

The car came to a stop, and a beautiful woman with long, straight, blonde hair got out. Her body was perfect, not a blemish anywhere. My stomached rolled, hoping the thoughts swirling in my head were wrong, so very, very wrong. This just couldn't be.

She walked over to the back door and opened it. A little boy with dishwater-blond hair cut short, small shorts, and a shirt with a dump truck on the front got out of the car. The smile on his face radiated for miles.

The front door to the house swung open, and a man exited the door. He had dishwater brown hair, a lean but muscular build, and he was tall, so very tall. It wasn't until his face lit up in the most perfect smile that it hit me like a ton of bricks coming down on my chest.

Drew. He was alive. He was here. Not dead.

The grip on my steering wheel became painfully tight as tears began to well up in my eyes.

Alive. Here.

Drew bent down as the little boy ran into his arms. My breath left my body as every synapse in my head forgot to fire. He was alive, and he had a little boy. Same hair and I would bet my life they had the same green eyes.

I had thought Drew had taken my heart with him when he died in front of me, but that was a lie. This right here was ripping my soul and what was left of my heart out of my body.

He was alive, and he had a little boy … without me.

I watched as Drew stood to his full, healthy height as the woman walked right up to Drew, and he wrapped his other arm around her and kissed the top of her head. He had a woman who was not me.

He smiled at them both, love pouring out of him, and I broke. The images burned with hot irons into my retinas, searing, branding their spots forever. My insides twisted so painfully I had to wrap my arms around my stomach as fresh tears skidded down my cheeks.

It was official. I had … nothing. There was absolutely nothing for me to believe in. It was ironic that I had wished over and over for Drew to be alive, and he was. It had come true. But the cost was me, because seeing him alive and happy was like watching him die all over again. Only, this killed me more than watching the life drain from his eyes. This destroyed me, and I fell deeper.

I couldn't wrap my brain around it. He was here, and he never came back for me. He never looked for me. He never…

The tears turned into sobs, but I couldn't tear my eyes away from the only guy I had ever cared about. The only one who ever gave a shit about me in my pathetic life. The one guy who made plans with me to get away from the life we were living and be free. The guy I saw my future with. The guy I dreamed about at night and watched the light leave his eyes over and over on replay. I relived his death every time I closed my eyes, yet he was alive and happy without me.

Everything inside me hurt. The tears became so bad I had to shut my eyes. It was physically impossible for me not to. I didn't want to take my eyes off him, though. I feared this was all a dream and he would disappear, so I fought it. The sad thing was another part of me was hoping this was a dream and I would wake up so I didn't have any of this etched in my head. With all these conflictions, I had no direction.

He was going on with his life, moving on, when here I was, a pathetic excuse for a human, stuck back in time. Me, here, crying over something I had lost so long ago. The hurt was too much, and I had to cry. I could feel the hole beneath me opening up, and there was no way to stop it. All those years of loss were for … nothing, and now they had turned into something I didn't know how to process.

When Drew pulled the woman in for a tight hug and whispered something in her ear, she pulled away, smiling up at him. Then the three of them went into the house, Drew never letting go of either of them.

This had to be a joke. It had to.

I sat there for hours, unable to wrap my head around what I had seen. I wondered what they were doing inside. Were they having lunch together, watching TV, or was Drew playing with his kid? The more I thought, the bigger the hole beneath me expanded.

When the door to the house opened again, the little boy came running out faster than a shot. Drew and the woman were on his heels. Drew turned around and locked the door then walked with the woman to the car and got in the driver's seat. I watched as the car sped off down the road, but I was rooted to the spot. I sat there until night fell, unable to force myself to go. I sat there until my cell rang, snapping me back to the present, knowing there was only one person on this planet it could be—my saving grace.

"Yeah?" I answered softly.

Andi's voice came across the line. "You okay?" She knew exactly where I was without even telling her. That was how well she knew me.

"No. I'm nowhere near okay."

Chapter Three

I didn't know how I made it home. I didn't even remember driving, but somehow, I got there. When I pulled up to the complex, Andi came barreling down the sidewalk like she had been waiting for me. I was a zombie and could barely walk to her. I didn't have the strength.

"Oh, baby," she said, wrapping her arms around my body and holding me up.

Lone, hiccupped whimpers came from my throat. I had already cried so much during the drive home. I didn't think I could do more, but I was wrong. The dam collapsed, and I fell to my knees. Andi tried to pick me up yet ended up falling to the ground, as well, my weight being too much for her.

Weeks passed in a blur of tissues and emotionally exhausted sleep. I asked for time off from both of my jobs. After all, I couldn't move from the bed, let alone go to work. The diner fired me after a week, and Judi called from the bar yesterday saying she had to fill my spot. Now I had nothing there, either, but I didn't care. Rent was due last week, but I didn't have the money and got an eviction notice three days ago. Good thing I knew how the system worked. I had a good two to three weeks before I was actually forced to leave by the cops.

I didn't know what I was going to do. I didn't care to try to figure it out, either. I was too lost in my head to make any sense of the world, so having a roof over my head or bills paid wasn't on the radar of giving two shits.

I wasn't sure what was worse: watching the boy you love die before your young eyes or finding out five years later that he was alive, happy with a woman and a child, and now a man.

I *should* have been a bigger person and thought "At least he's happy. He deserves that. I'm happy for him." Nevertheless, I couldn't be that bigger person. I couldn't feel that happiness for him, not when I ached so badly inside. I wanted him to be hurt, too, not carrying on with his life like I had never existed, like I was a blip on his screen as he continued his happy life.

As the days dragged on in one continuous loop, the hurt turned into anger and then back into hurt. I couldn't stop it, didn't even try. The dark hole I had been trying to avoid for years since Drew left me the first time finally fully sucked me under. I let it consume me, eat me up, and swallow me whole. I was surrounded in a thick, dark cloak of pain and despair that nothing could cut through.

I had thought I was alone before. With my mother and father being the assholes they were and then all of the foster homes never great, I had only had Drew. I had only had him for two years, and those were the best two years of my life. Even if I was doing things I wasn't proud of, they were the best because I had someone. I had someone I could turn to, talk to, and count on. I had my person, and I had never once in my life had a person.

Part of me wished I had never had it, never had him. Then I wouldn't know what it was like to lose it twice now. The ache burned so deeply in my soul and the pain rolled and gained momentum from day to day, building, digging, and embedding itself into my soul.

"Eat," Andi said at the doorway of my bedroom.

I groaned and turned slowly around in my bed, staring at her holding a cup. I didn't want to eat. I didn't deserve to eat, not when other people out there needed it. I was just a waste of space in this world. They should have food to live, not me.

Andi being Andi, I knew she wouldn't give up, but I didn't want to give in. Like everything else, it was pointless.

I regretted giving Andi a key to my place. One, for this, and two, because I never knew for sure if she locked the door after she came in. Having that worry in my head drove me farther down the rabbit hole that was becoming my life. I wanted to get up and check the doors and windows. I wanted to make sure everything was locked and secure, but I couldn't make myself get out of bed. Still, that compulsion rode me hard, suffocating me.

When Andi rolled me over onto my back, I didn't fight her and used the little bit of strength to help her.

"Drink," she ordered, holding the lukewarm chicken broth to my lips.

I tried to drink it, but it kept catching in my throat, causing me to cough, gagging on it. Andi didn't stop, even as my stomach rolled from the liquid. She kept at it until I drank every bit.

"Good. Want to shower?" she asked, sighing as I threw the covers up over my head.

"No."

Andi was the only thing keeping me alive at that point, something I lay in bed all night, thinking about.

I couldn't do it anymore. There was absolutely no reason for me to carry on like this. Having Andi care for me wasn't living. I was a burden on her, just like I was to my biological mother. I didn't want that for Andi. She of all people deserved better.

The black hole became deeper as I sank into it willingly. My entire life I had been a disappointment, a disgrace, a nuance, a punching bag, a sex toy … alone. Me, myself, and I. And I didn't like either of those three people. Each one of them was shitty. I didn't deserve to be here, didn't deserve to breathe air.

The light that Andi shone on me was fading to the point where it was lost. It was so far away it was unreachable. There was no coming back from this. There was no revival. There was nothing. *I* was nothing.

As I sat on my bed, my feet touching the floor, the heaviness of the cold metal sat in my hand. The gun was so weighted it felt as if it were all my emotions swirling around in my head, now sitting in my hand and under my control. For once, it was under *my* control. This was the one tool I could use to make everything stop, to make everything go away, to make *me* go away.

It was my answer to end the pain.

I stared at the shiny, silver metal as flashes of Drew's vacant eyes flashed through my head. The pain of that hit me all over again, but the gun could take it all away, even the good of when I saw Drew again and the bad of finding out he had a son and a woman.

Who would care? I mean, Drew didn't care to find me; he had moved on with life. He certainly wouldn't miss me.

The burn in my chest only grew as the thoughts raced through my head, and I realized how fucked in the head I really was. I never really had a shot in this world from the moment I was born. I was never anything. I was and always would be nobody. I let some guy fuck me over and over again while thinking I was protecting Drew. I made things work while I was on the streets. Every, single fucked up thing I did was to survive a life that I should have disposed of years ago. The world wouldn't miss me.

The only one who would was Andi. She was everything I was not. She had the ability to push through all the bad and be strong when everything crashed around her. She would survive and be better since I wouldn't be holding her down.

I, on the other hand, couldn't. I was drowning in darkness and losing what little I thought of myself. I had held her back, making her think she had to take care of me. She needed to be free of me, free to live her life without me and my fucked up existence.

I needed it all to end. I wanted to disappear, vanish, leave this life, not feel anything anymore, make everything whirling in my head stop and quiet. I needed to fall. I needed to succumb to the losses, to the unanswered requests, to the wishes not granted. I needed to fall into the pit of emptiness and make it all go away, to find a sliver of peace.

"What are you doing!" Andi screeched, making me jump as she bore down on me, not stopping until she was at my side and the gun was in her hand. I didn't even have time to struggle, which would have been futile, anyway, since I was so weak.

"Give it back."

Her brows were knit between her angry eyes as I spoke, her long hair pulled back in a ponytail so tight it made her look madder than I had ever seen her. The fury pulsed from her in thick waves.

"That's fucking it!" She opened the clip on the gun and pulled all the bullets out. Her hands didn't even shake; she was in full control of the weapon.

I didn't even know she knew how to do that. I had never seen her with a gun in my life. I was taught on the streets by a guy named Tim. I never saw him again afterward. Andi, though, she was too perfect to know anything about the underbelly of society.

It felt like I was on a cloud above, looking down at my best friend as she moved. Even when the anger poured off her in waves, it didn't penetrate me. I was so high above that nothing mattered.

"We're taking a shower." She said nothing else of the gun as she stuffed everything into the big bag she had draped over her shoulder when she had come in.

I didn't want anything to do with the shower. I wanted everything to end. Showering was least on my priority lists. However, the strength to fight for the gun back wasn't there. No fight was.

The thump of Andi's bag hitting the floor had my eyes moving to her angry ones. She started tearing off her clothes, shoes, and panties before coming toward me naked. I did nothing. She then undressed me and hauled me into the shower, coming in with me.

Tears spilled over my face as I shook my head. "Just let me be done with this, Andi," I whispered.

She turned me around, the spray of the shower hitting my back as she held me up. "Listen to me," she growled, her words echoing through the tight space. "This shit ends right here and right now. I tried to let you work through it. I tried to be patient. I tried to let you do your thing." The water pelted my back, but it was like I couldn't feel a thing. "This?" She gave me a shake. "You trying to kill yourself? No. I'm fucking done!"

While she washed me quickly, I felt so damn defeated and worn I didn't put up a fight. Nor did I help her when she dressed me, nor did I when she made me get into the car. It was like I was floating over my body. I could see everything that was happening, but I was too out of it to care.

When Andi pulled up to Zachariah Hospital … That was the moment I snapped together, reality slapping me across the face in a powerful blow.

She wasn't! She couldn't! She was my best friend! She wouldn't do this to me!

"What are you doing?" I asked her through a very scratchy throat.

With her voice lowered, sounding resigned and sad, she said, "Helping you."

"By doing …?" I asked just as she threw the car into park and two very large men dressed all in white came up to my door. "You didn't!" I gasped, feeling my heart break all over again.

She turned fully toward me. "You need this. I don't know how to help you, and you're scaring the shit out of me, Reign. Then today…" She shook her head, closing her eyes, pain etched on her face. "I know I take the risk of you hating me because of this, and as much as that kills me, I have to. *I can't lose you.*" When she opened her eyes again, tears were streaming down her face.

Somehow, I snapped to alert enough to defend myself. It was pure instinct taking over as the panic set in. "I can't go in there, Andi," I told her bluntly, having her words cut me, not wanting to go. "I can fix myself. I promise. You know I can't be in there." I gave her a pleading look.

"I…" She started, but I dug deeper.

"You know my mom used to bring me to the doctors all the time when my daddy beat the hell out of me. I've been poked and prodded, asked all kinds of questions that I couldn't answer. They stuck needles in me and scared the ever-loving shit out of me. You can't leave me here."

Being in hospitals all the time was the reason I was taken away from my biological mother when I was six. I didn't understand it at the time. Hell, I still didn't understand why she let him beat on me all the time and never stopped him. I looked it up on the internet once and read about something called Munchausen syndrome and wondered if that was what my mother had, because why else would she take me to the doctor after my father hurt me? Didn't she fear she would get in trouble?

"I know," she whispered. "I love you. You are the best friend a woman could ask for."

I looked at her, wide-eyed. She was going to do it. I wasn't going to change her mind. I *had* to change her mind, though.

Before I could speak, she continued, "Nothing I do is helping. You have to go in there so you can get better."

"No," I answered instantly. "I'm better." I perked up as I felt the guys outside my door jiggling the handle. "I promise, Andi. I'll be fine," I tried. I was frantic, grasping at straws, hoping she would buy it. I scrounged around for anything to make her change her mind. "Child Protective Services brought me here when a foster brother of mine decided to cut me in my sleep," I blurted, trying anything I could come up with so she wouldn't let them take me.

Andi's eyes clouded as more pain filled them. I thought I had hit the nail on the head, but…

"I can't. This isn't going to work. You need this. It's for your own good."

I exploded, the anger bursting out uncontrollably when I realized I wasn't going to change her mind. I completely lost it.

"You fucking bitch! I can't believe you are doing this to me!" I clenched my hands into fists and pounded them into the dashboard hard. The doors to the car unlocked, and my head swung frantically to where the guys were coming at me. "You're a fucking bitch! I hate you! I'm gonna die hating you! Remember that!" I yelled as the two guys each grabbed one of my arms and hauled me out of the car. I kept yelling at Andi, spewing nasty thing after nasty thing, riding on panic. Everything inside me was on edge.

I looked back to Andi, seeing her tears coating her face along with agony.

"You can die hating me, but I can rest knowing I tried and loved you through this," she said.

I was too pissed to care.

I fought. I did. The first needle they tried to stick me with fell to the floor because I kicked so much. The guys had ahold of my arms pretty tightly, so the only things I had were my legs. The second needle didn't miss, and I screamed at the sharp pain just before I passed out.

***

Slowly blinking my eyes, I felt as if there were sand in them. I reached up to rub them, only to find my arms and ankles were attached to the bed. My mouth was dry from the sterile air of the room as I inhaled deeply, smelling disinfectant and that distinct smell of hospital. The beeping machines did nothing to calm the panic as it hit me head-on. I thrashed back and forth on the scratchy sheet, wailing, my arms and legs wanting to be free.

It wasn't long before a woman wearing kitten-covered scrubs appeared by the door with a small smile on her face. I didn't know what the hell there was to smile about.

"You're awake," she said in some damn, sing-song, happy voice.

Puke.

"Get these off." I raised my arms as far as the white straps would allow, which wasn't far, flailing them for emphasis.

She stepped into the room. "Sorry, Reign. I can't do that."

"Yes, you can," I told her sternly.

"Nope." She began checking all of the machines around me. That was when I noticed my hand had IVs plugged into it.

"What are you putting in me?"

She tapped the tube coming down from a large bag with her index finger, turning toward me. Her eyes were a chocolate brown that was so warm it could melt ice. Too bad it had no chance of working on me whatsoever.

"Fluids. You are severely dehydrated, not to mention very malnourished, young lady. Until we get you back where you should be, you'll remain hooked up."

"That doesn't mean you can't take the straps off!" I barked.

She smiled knowingly. "I'm not stupid. I've been doing this for more than twenty years, young lady."

I strained my head and torso, trying to get up from the bed. "You bitch! Let me up!"

"Now, Ms. Owens, if you don't lie down, I'll have to sedate you."

"Fuck you!" I snapped, not giving a shit if she sedated me or not. My blood thumped through my veins as I let the anger out.

"No, thanks." She reached into her pocket. "Maybe, next time you wake up, you'll be a bit calmer."

I snarled at her as she injected something into my IV. Then everything went black.

This routine went on for what felt like days. I had no idea how long. I hadn't been keeping track of days since I found out Drew was alive. However, it felt like I was in and out for a lifetime.

The one good thing about it was I liked being out. When I was out, I couldn't think. I couldn't let my mind race about Drew or Andi. I could simply sleep, something I had never done in my life. All the pain just melted away. I looked forward to the syringe. It was becoming my escape.

That was when the nurse stopped putting me under as much. It was like she had a nurse radar and could tell I was enjoying myself, and she wanted to stop it like the evil witch she was. One thing in my life that I actually enjoyed and she had to be a bitch and take it away.

No amount of name calling or threats did it after that. Nothing. It was like she totally tuned everything I said out. I could call her a fat bitch who needed to get laid, and she would just laugh at me. Yes, fucking laugh! Her comment was "Honey, you have no idea."

One good thing was I couldn't have any visitors, so I knew that traitorous Andi wouldn't be showing up any time soon. I couldn't bear to look at her. She had done this to me. *She* had put me in here.

One morning, the nurse came in, all happy and smiling like sunshine.

"What?" I groaned, seeing the light shining in from my lone window. I had been tied up a really long time, and the only reason my muscles didn't ache was because, while I slept or was sedated, Nurse Hatchet, or whatever her name was, said she stretched them. Otherwise, I would be in a lot of pain. At least she did one nice thing. Then again, it was her job, so she didn't do it to be kind.

"You have an appointment this morning," she said, moving the now unused machines out of her way to get to the other side of the bed.

The doctor came in and said I was physically fine, so I got the tubes out. When I didn't want to eat, Nurse Hatchet told me if I didn't, she was going to plug me up again. Therefore, I ate a little to keep her off my back.

"With…?" I asked.

"Dr. McMann."

I raised my brow. "Like the wrestler guy?"

She chuckled. "Nope, as in the psychiatrist."

My heart fell. I didn't want to see a shrink. I didn't need to know the thousands of ways I was fucked in the head. I especially didn't need someone to tell me those thousands of ways. I knew what they were. That was why I wanted away from this life. I also didn't need someone trying to pump drugs in me at every turn. No, thank you.

"No," I said as adamantly as I could.

"You don't have a choice."

"No. I'll pitch a fit until you have no choice but to put me under." I tried conniving, knowing she wouldn't give in. If she didn't give in when I called her a come guzzling, road whore and instead, laughed at my creativity, then she wasn't budging at that point.

She shook her head. "Young lady, don't you know that, if you're going to do something like that, it's best *not* to tell anyone so they can't do anything to stop it? Look, I'm gonna be straight with ya, because if I was in here, I'd want someone to be straight with me."

I was in shock at her tone. This wasn't ray of morning sunshine nurse. No, this was dead serious, about to tell me like it was nurse. The change in her face was a bit disturbing. How she could switch so fast was a bit alarming.

"You want out of here?" She looked at me expectantly, so I nodded my head. "The only way to do that is to talk to the people here and get yourself together. They aren't going to release you until you do."

"Why not? I'm an adult. I should be able to sign myself out." I didn't know the exact law, but I thought I had the right to refuse any medical treatment.

"True, but you've been determined to be a threat to yourself and others."

I stilled. *Others?*

"What?"

"Yep, and the only way to get out of here is to follow what we tell you and do what we tell you." She lifted her brows.

"I don't get how I'm a danger to others," I told her.

"Holding a gun on your friend."

A red haze went over my eyes, and strength I thought I had lost long ago came with it. Anger bubbled in my veins, setting my skin on fire.

"She told you that?" *That lying little bitch!*

Nurse Hatchet pulled up the lone chair in the room that had yet to be used during my stay. She grabbed my hand, and I instantly pulled away, though I was stopped by the white straps. She didn't stop and grabbed my hand, anyway. My skin felt superhot from her touch. I wanted to shake it off, shake *her* off.

"None of that matters."

"The hell it doesn't." My hands began shaking with the anger floating around me.

She squeezed my hand hard, either to settle me or comfort me. I didn't know which and didn't give a shit.

"You think I don't know that girl lied to get you in here? I know it and you know it. Her reasons for doing it are her own. Bottom line, at this point, it doesn't matter. Your behavior over the time you've been here has proven to the doctors that you *need* to be here. You can't blame your friend for that."

The hell I couldn't. She was the reason I was here. Regardless, I listened to what nurse Hatchet said and kept my mouth shut, even if I was thinking, *I hate you.*

"You did try to take your life, Reign. Let's not forget that."

"You have no idea what I've gone through," I snapped back, again pulling at my hand yet getting nowhere.

"I know more than you think, young lady."

My head jerked.

"Right now, we need to get you ready, and be warned, if you take a swing at me, I do fight back." She winked at me, rose from the chair, and did what she wanted me to do.

***

Boring. Absolutely, positively boring. Wrestler McMann went through everything I had ever told Andi from a manila folder, which proved nothing except that he could read. Good for him.

I ached when he talked about Drew, felt strange when he talked about Andi, and didn't know what to make of any of it. He asked me questions, which I mostly answered with one word or a nod of the head. I didn't feel comfortable with him.

It wasn't his appearance, which let me tell you, was nothing to tell a best friend about if I had one. He was round, short, and had a patch of hair that he combed over, trying to make it look like he had hair on the top of his head. He also had thick glasses that made him look like a closed-off snob. Like I wanted to open up to someone like that. Uh, no, thank you.

He told me that I was a very negative person and needed to find some positives. The only one that I could come up with was that, since I was on such alert here, I didn't have time to fall down the dark hole that is my life. It was still there, waving like a pool of water under my feet, but my focus was on this place.

The first order of business here was to get out. If that meant I had to play this sick, little game, I would do it. I had played lots of games in my life. This one should be no different. Second, make it all end.

"That was a good session. I feel like you did great. We will do these twice a day for the next week."

The next fucking week? Was that how long they were planning on keeping me here?

***

Drew came into my room after school with a look of fierceness. I was in tears again. It wasn't the first time, and I was sure it wouldn't be the last.

The girls at school were horrible, teasing and tormenting me at every turn. Today in the girls' locker room, the ring leader of them all, Tonya, started in on my small boobs. She said no one, not even Drew, would want some flat-chested girl. The words kept coming out of her mouth over and over again. I couldn't escape them. I ran and hid in the girls' bathroom down the hall until the last bell rang.

Drew hadn't said a word to me as we walked home. He knew

something was wrong, but he let me deal. He also knew I would tell him in time.

Drew came right to me, and I didn't hesitate to throw my arms around him, burrowing my head in the only safe haven I had. As the tears fell, he didn't let me go.

Suddenly, Drew's body was limp in my arms, all of his weight pressing on me.

I moved my head back only to see blood coming from his eyes and mouth, pouring all over me.

I woke with a jolt, my arms unable to move, which only made me fight harder. The images of Drew burned my eyes. I wanted to get up. I wanted to check the locks, make sure no one could get in. However, I was stuck to this bed in this hospital. I couldn't move in this white, sterile place. I was trapped not only here, but in my head. I felt like a prisoner in both places.

I allowed the tears to fall, never succumbing to sleep.

That stupid, little, baldheaded prick was what I thought, but I didn't say it as I stared at my shrink. For days we had been at this, and the only good thing was Nurse Hatchet didn't make me wear the restraints on my arms. She put me in a room that had nothing sharp in it, but at least I wasn't confined. That shit made my head swim.

There was no defending myself if something were to happen. I would have been at their mercy and stuck. I avoided getting stuck at all costs. It was a little ironic here, though, because each time I got up to check to see if the door was locked, it was, but from the outside. It did little to help my anxiety. While it used to comfort me to check the doors, in here, it only added to my unease.

Today, this asshole decided to get into the nitty-gritty of my time at the Petersons'.

I tried hard to keep my answers simple. I tried hard not to let everything hang out.

He looked over at me from his desk. "Tell me how you feel."

I sat in a chair across from him as he played with the corner of his glasses. I thought for sure he would take them off at any moment and put one end in his mouth like those corny TV shows, but he didn't.

"I want to know what is going on in that head of yours. I want to know what it felt like when you saw Drew kiss the other woman or when the child ran up in his arms."

My insides turned to ice and my throat began to close, suffocating me. I had blocked as much of that moment out of my head as I could, just trying to get myself out of here and putting all my strength into that. I didn't want to think of it right then, but he didn't stop.

He just kept pushing.

"How did you feel when the three of them went into the house?"

Nope. I wasn't doing it. Instead, I gripped the chair, holding on for dear life, using it to keep me firmly planted in the room.

"How did seeing Drew take off with his *family* and leave you behind, yet again, feel?"

The way he said family hit me in the gut. The knife already lodged inside twisted its serrated blades, shredding me to the depths of my core. There was no going back from that one. Nope. Nothing.

My heart constricted at the thought of Drew playing with his son out on that big front lawn while his woman sat watching, smiles on all three of their faces. The deepest recesses of my soul came to the surface, and I couldn't push them back.

Tears streaked my cheeks as I closed my eyes and wrapped my arms around my body, trying to hold myself together. I had been focusing so hard on getting out of here that the vault I had all these emotions in was left unguarded and sprang open. The swirling tornado sucked me into its depths, and there was nothing I could do to stop it.

"This what you want, doc?" I pointed to the tears dripping down my face. "Because this is how I feel." I got up from the chair, needing space, and began pacing behind the chair. My thumb went to my mouth as I began chewing on it as I moved. "I'm alone. Desperately, unequivocally alone. I have no one in this world." I stopped momentarily and stared him in the eye. "Do you even know what that's like?" I didn't wait for him to answer as I turned away and continued answering for him. "Of course you don't with all those family pictures behind you. Did you ever think someone coming in to see you had no one, and I mean no one, on this planet to turn to? No. You probably grew up in a house where people actually gave a shit about you. You probably didn't have to scrounge for food or result to eating dog food because there was nothing left for you after your parents ate their dinner. You probably did shit like play games or whatever it is parents are supposed to do with their kids. Me? None of that. I didn't even know what a game was until my first foster home, and they looked at me like I was a freak when I didn't know what Go Fish was."

I sucked in deep breaths and carried on. "Nope. You didn't have to do any of that. You didn't have to spread your legs to keep the only person on the planet who gave a shit about you from having to go through the same pain. You haven't watched that same person die in front of you, the life fading from the eyes of the one you loved." By this point, my words were so jumbled with sobs I didn't know if he was understanding, but I really didn't care. It was coming out without any way to stop it.

"You didn't have to live on the streets, surviving by opening your legs again just to get food or protection. It was all I had to offer anyone." I swiped at my nose, wiping the snot-covered tears on my hospital-issued pants. "You didn't have to pick yourself up from that, get two jobs, work your ass off, get your own place—hell, even make a new friend. But I wasn't living.

"The only thing I was living in was fear: fear that my father would find me; fear that Mr. Peterson would find me; fear that my mother would find me and give me back to my father; hell, even fear that Mrs. Peterson would see me out and drag me back so she could get back the money I lost her when I left, since I wasn't her paycheck each month anymore."

The doctor had a brown, ratty couch in the corner of his office, and I needed more space. I sat with my back to him, resting on the arm of the couch. I curled myself into the smallest ball I could make myself, wishing I had one of those superpowers you see in the movies so I could just disappear. Forever. No such luck. A small ball was the best I could do.

"Then Andi wanted me to get closure. She's the one who started all of this. She wanted me to go to Drew's gravesite and tell him bye. I didn't want to. I *really* didn't want to. It would be telling him goodbye all over again, and I couldn't do it. But her words played in my head for weeks, only to find out he's alive, happy, a father, a husband or boyfriend."

I began rocking back and forth, unable to stop the tears or my words. "So how I feel is I'm in a big, black void of thick, sticky tar. I've always been in it, unable to get above the surface as it keeps pulling me in. But seeing Drew, knowing he's alive and didn't come to look for me, didn't bother to even think of me … I'm under it so far now I can't breathe. I'm ready to end all of this.

"I don't want to be in this world anymore. I don't want this pain and ache to take me over, and I don't need you or anyone else telling me how fucked in the head I am. I know it. I live it. And you need to know, doc, nothing you do is going to pull me out of it."

I sat there, rocking back and forth, wanting everything to stop, wanting it all to go away. It didn't. It just kept getting louder and louder in my head.

No one wants you. You think you can survive out there now? You have nothing. You are *nothing.*

"In other words, you've fallen about as far as a human being can go," he said, not moving from his desk.

His words echoed around me, colliding with the ones playing in my head.

I was in the pits of Hell. There was no light. No hope. I didn't even care. It all came to me in a rush. It didn't matter if I ever got out of this hospital. It was only postponing the inevitable. I would end it as soon as I stepped out of those doors. Keeping me here was just prolonging the hurt. It was its own kind of torture that I had no control over.

Nurse Hatchet said I could get out if I listened and did what they said, but did it really matter? None of it did. I was stuck in the tar of my life, and it wasn't ever going to loosen its hold and let me up for air.

The doc came over to the couch, and I jumped away from him, afraid he might touch me.

He halted, not coming too close. "Tomorrow, we begin to rebuild. For now, I'm going to call Nurse Bennett to come and get you."

If I had been thinking clearly at the time, I would have learned my nurse's real name instead of calling her Hatchet, but my emotions were all over the place, and everything in my head was a jumbled, scrambled mess, so it escaped me.

He left my side to punch some buttons on his phone while I just sat there, my forehead resting on my knees, allowing my tears to coat everything, drowning into nothingness.

***

That night, Nurse Hatchet granted me sedation, and I welcomed the blackness.

***

I haven't talked to Wrestler McMann for days. I sat in his office while he tried, but I ignored him. There was no point, no point in anything. The black film around me was too thick to see above.

The doctor prescribed me sleeping pills, but I refused to take them. If I did sleep, it was because I passed out from crying or staring into lost nothingness. In those instances, I only slept an hour here and there, never any more. I hated to admit it, but I missed not having Andi to call and talk to or come and lay with me. I missed her making me feel a tiny bit happy, even for brief moments in this pitiful existence.

That was purely selfish, and it was weird how I would hate her one moment then miss her so much the next. It was something else that I kept from Nurse Hatchet and the doc: the up and down waves that my mind was taking me on. I kept them to myself and let them eat at my soul.

Nurse Hatchet opened the door to my room, and my head swung to it. Rarely anyone came to my room, and when someone did, it was for one of three reasons: one, to bring me food; two, to give me meds, which I gave into; or three, to take me to the doctor. This helped me relax just a touch. I didn't have the constant worry for the first time in my life that the Petersons or my parents would barge in and take me away.

"Time for your session," she told me, walking in and clasping her hands in front of her. She never felt any fear, or she was at least damn good at not showing it if she did. "You need to tell him everything."

I sighed yet didn't answer. I wasn't going there. He had gotten enough out of me; he wasn't getting any more.

She reached for my hand and cupped it in her grip. I tried to get away but couldn't, which made the panic start to bubble.

"Let go," I croaked out, having it get caught in my throat.

She stroked the top of my hand. "Calm."

This was gentle, comforting in a way. I stayed tense, though didn't pull away.

I took some deep breaths before she began. "Child, you need to talk and get better. Living inside your head does no one any good."

I wanted to say, *Living at all isn't good for me*, but I kept my mouth shut.

"Doc can help if you let him. You can go out and become the woman you were intended to be."

I scoffed loudly and rolled my eyes. I wasn't intended to be anyone in this world. I wasn't intended to live a life that many only took for granted. No, the life I was intended to live was the one I wanted to escape.

"Young lady, don't you roll those eyes at me."

I halted because the way she said it wasn't bitchy or condescending like I had heard it a million times from my foster families. No, this was caring yet assertive.

Unease slithered along my skin. No one cared about me. It wasn't something anyone did. She couldn't, either. I wasn't worth her time.

"You are a bright woman and deserve to be happy."

I stared at her, finally finding words. "Happy? What is that?"

Nurse Hatchet straightened, her eyes widening at the first words I had spoken to her in several days.

"You see, Nurse Hatchet, women like me don't get to be happy. Women like me don't have hope or prayers, because that's all a bunch of bullshit that people throw at you to make you *feel* better. Women like me are nothing. We are vapor, a puff of smoke. We mean absolutely zero to this world. Women like me would have been better off never being born."

I sucked in a breath as a tear fell from Nurse Hatchet's eye, her lip trembling as another tear followed. Of all the shit I had said to her over the time I had been here, never once had I seen her cry. Ever. I banked on her never crying, counted on it, relied on it. She was fucking it up! She couldn't have feelings for this. No!

"Stop it!" I barked loudly, ripping myself away from her and pasting myself to the wall farthest from her.

While she looked down at her feet, I could tell she was taking deep breaths from the rise and fall of her chest.

"You don't get to feel sorry for me!" I screamed at her. She couldn't. If she did, she needed to go behind that mask and not let me see it. She was strong, assertive, and for some strange reason, I needed that.

She swiped her face with her hands, took a few more moments, and then turned to me. "Get your ass moving. You're gonna be late."

At that, I felt my spine lose a bit of its starch. There was my nurse. That was what I needed.

***

A knock came to the door, and I jolted as it slowly opened looking from the doctor to it. A man, tall since he had to duck to come through the doorway, entered, and I stilled. He was lean yet fit if his muscular arms were anything to go by. He had tattoos up one of his arms, the hair on his head was cut super short on the sides, and the top was barely there, as well. He had a nasty scar down his chin to his throat that had to have gotten there with some serious pain involved. However, it was his chocolate brown eyes that stared at me coldly, unyielding, that seized the air from my lungs.

I gripped the arms on my chair so tightly I knew there would be imprints on my hands when I released, but something had to ground me as the floor beneath me began to spin.

What was this man doing here? Why was he here?

A nurse, who wasn't Nurse Hatchet, stepped in behind the man, a bored look flitting across her face.

"What's this now?" the man's voice rumbled through the room. Something in it reverberated around the space, bouncing like a million of those balls that go a mile a minute. He was mad, angry … hell, pissed.

He kept opening and closing his hands, making them into tight fists then flexing his fingers. Each movement demonstrated the strength in his arms.

"Lynx," the doctor greeted like he had known him for years.

What kind of name was Lynx, and why in the hell was he greeting him?

The man said nothing, merely stared at me sitting in the chair, his eyes cold and hostile.

My first instinct was to run and hide, get as far away from this man as physically possible, but I stayed rooted to the spot.

Movement to my side made me jump and turn. The doctor pulled one of the chairs from the far wall over to the side of his desk. It was a good distance from me, but way too close. And I just knew who would be sitting in that chair before he spoke.

Wrestler McMann gestured to the chair. “Please have a seat.”

“What’s going on here?” I demanded in a panic, thinking of all the ways I could get the hell out of this room fast. I didn’t know what this man was capable of, but from the coldness in his eyes, I was sure it was anything. I wasn’t afraid of dying; it was all the other shit that came before it that I didn’t want to endure.

“What she said,” Lynx said to the doctor, stepping forward and crossing his arms over his chest, making him look really wide and even more intimidating.

The nurse shut the door, and stood with her back pressed into it. Everything in this scenario was wrong, and I didn’t like it one bit.

The doctor touched the side of his mouth with a finger. “It seems you two have a lot in common.”

I looked to the man standing beside me, seeing absolutely nothing that we could have in common.

He didn’t look at me, simply focused on the doctor. It gave me a moment to see his profile.

The scar looked worse close up, and the angle of his nose told me he had been in a fight … or twelve. Since he was still alive, he must have won.

"And that would be?" Lynx asked the question that almost slipped from my lips, but I was thankful I held it in.

"You both have PTSD."

The doctor went over post-traumatic stress disorder, over and over when he didn't have to. I was fucked in the head, not stupid. Basically, the shit of my life gave me stress that my brain couldn't handle, and my actions were a result of that. See? Simple explanation, not that long, drawn-out bullshit I heard him drone on about for days. He also went over depression and anxiety with me. I admitted they fit.

Even if Lynx had PTSD, there was no way in hell he had the same kind as me. From his demeanor, stance, and the fact that power radiated off him like sun waves beaming, no one messed with this man. No one. He couldn't possibly have anything in his head like I did.

"So?" Lynx asked while I sat there, dumbfounded, my brain needing to catch up and get its shit together. I had checked out for so long it was more difficult than I hoped.

Doc pointed to me. "So, we're all going to sit and try to have a conversation."

I said nothing.

"I think you two are a good fit."

"No," I whispered, pulling my legs into my body and wrapping my arms around them.

As my body began to tremble, I yelled at it to stop, but I had zero control over it.

Lynx could overpower me in a heartbeat. I had no weapon to protect me from what he could do to me. Mr. Baldman and Nurse Creep wouldn't be able to fend off this man. Andi took my gun, which would have been the only way I could survive anything with this man. No.

"No," I said a little louder. "I can't."

I felt Lynx's eyes on me, the impenetrable stare looking down on me like I was a freak. No. No. *No*!

Please make this stop. Please make this stop, I kept chanting over and over as the grip on my legs got tighter and tighter.

Boot steps began and stopped as a large, resounding sigh came from Lynx. I looked up through my eyelashes to see his gaze on me. He sat in the chair next to the desk, facing me, his arms still crossed, but now his long legs were, too, at the ankle.

"Shit, I ain't gonna hurt ya," he said as I looked at his face.

The coldness was still there, but there was something in his eyes that was a tad bit lighter. I didn't believe him, though. I definitely didn't trust him. No way. Not going to happen. Never.

I said nothing, just burrowed in a tighter ball.

"Lynx, this is Reign. Reign, Lynx," the doctor introduced.

I raised my head, not looking at the man in the chair, but something sparked in me that I needed to keep alert. I hadn't been alert in more days than I realized, yet something inside my head clicked, and I took in everything right down to the pencil the doctor had in his fingertips, wiggling back and forth, hitting the desk every so often. I also took in Lynx's breathing. It was calm and steady. No anger, just resolve. I still said nothing.

"Lynx, you start. Tell Reign about yourself." What he said surprised me. Why would this man want to tell a stranger anything about what was going on in his head? It wasn't like I went around shouting to the rooftops about all my issues to everyone. I kept that locked up tight, and I wanted to keep it that way.

"You've got to be shittin' me," Lynx responded, the pissed-off attitude not lessening a bit. "I'm not talking about shit in front of someone I don't fucking know. Are you out of your mind?"

A small part of me, back in the recesses behind all the pain, fear, and anger, wanted to actually chuckle. That realization slapped me in the face, and I locked it down, giving my head a slight shake.

Wrestler McMann answered, "I think it would be good for you to talk about your experiences with Reign."

"Don't tell me she's been to war, because I know you'll be flat-out lyin'."

War? Oh, shit, he was a guy from the military. There was no way his issues had anything to do with mine.

"If I told this scared, little rabbit all the shit I've seen, she'd be crying in her Wheaties," he mocked, causing a fire to blaze in my stomach, one I thought had burned out, never to be lit again. I didn't know where it came from, and I sure as hell didn't know why, but it was nice and toasty warm. And I clung to it.

I sucked in deeply, and my lip curled. How fucking dare he?

How. Dare. He?

"Fuck you, asshole," I clipped as Lynx turned to me in surprise. I didn't think that was possible, but whatever. The doc turned to me, too, but I didn't pay him any attention. "You have no fucking idea. Don't sit there on your holier than thou throne and do the I-can't-say-shit-because-of-her-feeble-mind bullshit. You can stick that up your ass right now."

Lynx's eye twitched. It was the first bit of actual exprcssion I had seen, but as soon as it was there, it left.

"All right, little girl," he started condescendingly, only spiking the heat inside me. "Where do you want me to start? Where everyone in my battalion was killed in an ambush but me, or when I held my best friend's body in my arms with his head hanging on by only his spine?"

The thought sickened me, but it wasn't like I hadn't seen or been dealt with my own kind of hell.

I sat up and felt the blood pump in my veins for the first moment in a really long time. I let the warmth flow through my body, waking me up from a really long sleep.

I fired back, "How about watching a woman get gang raped by four guys who used broken bottles on every hole in her body then beat her within an inch of her life before leaving her for dead? Or how about the little twelve-year-old boy who was selling dope and came up short to his supplier? I watched him get a bullet to the brain. Or what about the guy who didn't pay the trick he was using? The pimp strung him up by his dick and balls to a tree, fucked him in the ass with a broomstick, beat him with the stick, and then left him there. Don't know if he lived or died." I shrugged. "So don't try to be big, macho, I've-been-through-hell man to me. That shit doesn't work. I've seen things that would make *you* wince." The entire time I stared at him, not flinching once, only seeing the slight tick in his jaw that gave any indication that he was listening to me. He stayed silent through it all.

"Seems we didn't even touch the surface during our discussions, Reign," the doc said. He wasn't wrong. He didn't need to know *everything* I had seen or done on the streets. That shit was buried. At least, I had thought it was until stupid military man had to open his big, fat mouth.

"Were you that woman?" Lynx asked.

My brows pulled together in confusion. He thought I was talking about me?

I answered flatly, "No."

I did open the door to this, so I had to suck some of it up and go with it.

His eyes bore into me like he was trying to read if I was telling the truth or lying. I really didn't give a damn if he believed me or not.

I turned back to the doc. "Can I leave now?" I wanted the safety of my small room. It wasn't much, but it was better than being here.

"We have thirty more minutes, Reign," he so kindly reminded me.

Even though I felt anger at that, it was good to feel something other than sad and alone. It might not have been the best emotion, but it was something.

"I don't want to talk to him anymore."

"*Him* is right fucking here. You can address me."

I glared as he spoke. It was so damn strange that one minute, I feared him, yet now I just wanted to brush him off like a tick.

"Whatever," I bit off, crossed my arms over my chest, and looked up at the ceiling, not that whatever was up there would help me. My hell just kept getting better and better.

"Lynx," the doc prompted.

"Fucking hell." He sighed and rubbed his hands over his bald head. "I get out of here soon, anyway."

I perked up at this new information. I needed that: to get out so I could be done with all of this. I couldn't go through another dog and pony show like this again.

"Army out of high school. Did damn well. Went to war, saw fucked up shit, and now I'm home."

Well, at least he wasn't in the sharing mood, either, since I really didn't give a shit.

"There's a lot more to it than that, Lynx," the doc chastised.

He shrugged. "That's the fucking gist of it. Not really much more."

Wrestler McMann pressed, "What about now? Why are you here?"

Why did I suddenly want and feel the need to know? Why did I care? I wished my head would stop with all the ups and downs; it was making everything ten times worse.

"Because I've been on edge since I became a civilian again. Loud noises, cars backfiring, fucking fireworks—all of it fucks with my head and puts me back into fighting mode. Got into a lot of fights and been arrested a couple of times. Came home the other night to my girl in bed with another guy. I beat the shit out of him, got my gun out, and shot a few rounds just to scare the fucker. I never got the diagnosis of PTSD off me, so that's what they say I have again, and I was put in here for seven days. I'm on day four, so I'm out soon."

Well, that sucked for him, but he seemed to be handling everything just fine. He probably had a mom and dad to go home to. Sure, he had gotten the shit end with the chick, but he would find someone else. I still didn't see how this could help me. If anything, it just drove the wedge between me and the rest of the world deeper.

Doc's eyes didn't leave Lynx. "You want to tell her anything else?"

"I didn't want to tell her anything in the first place. Why the fuck I wanna tell her more?"

"Fair enough. Reign," Dr. McMann called out.

I didn't move my head, just my eyes to him.

"You want to say anything?"

I looked at the clock. "Time's up."

He checked his watch, disappointment flittering across his face. He must have had high hopes.

"We meet again tomorrow in the morning and the afternoon."

I gripped the chair. "I'm not talking. Get it through that fucking head of yours. If you and Rambo wanna talk, fine, but leave me out of it." I rose from the chair and turned to the nurse by the door. "Take me to my room," I demanded.

She looked behind me and must have gotten the okay sign because she escorted me back to my room.

***

I lay in bed, Drew's dead eyes staring back at me. Then, in a flash, his happy ones came along with visions of his wife and kid. Every memory I had of Drew got tangled with the new ones tainting my old ones. I wished I could get the old back, but for a woman like me, wishes never came true.

Chapter Five

"I'd like to talk about a few things you shared yesterday," Dr. McMann spoke from his cushy, brown chair behind his desk.

Lynx sat in the same chair as yesterday. He had on black scrubs, while I had on blue.

When we got into the room, the doctor told us that we would have a double session today. I didn't care. When I opened my eyes this morning, all I could see was Drew happily holding his kid. I didn't have the strength to argue. I just wanted this over with, this entire thing over with.

I answered, "What?"

His eyes widened before he looked down briefly then back at

me. “You talked about watching a rape. Did that happen to you?”

It took me two seconds to know where he was going. He couldn’t come flat-out and tell Lynx what was going on with me because of doctor/patient crap, but if I talked about it in the sessions, he could bring it up and *pry,* which was what he was doing.

I said nothing, and neither did Lynx.

“How’d you feel watching that woman get hurt?”

When images from that night invaded me, I tried to blink them back, but it was no use. The woman’s screams as they tore her from the inside out, the moment when her cries for help stopped along with my heartbeat, wondering if she was dead—I was going to have to relive this shit, and it killed me.

My heart raced, and I could feel my body starting to burn from the panic.

“Do you get off on this shit?” I asked the doctor, focusing directly on him and ignoring Lynx.

“I don’t know what you’re talking about, Reign,” he responded.

“Get off on it. Enjoy hearing about others’ pain and hurt. Bringing up shit that needs to stay buried. You get off on it, don’t you?” Yep, I flipped from sadness to the spark I needed. It was better to deflect any hurt I felt with anger. Anger was always easier.

He set his hands calmly on the desk. “No, Reign. I’m here to help you.”

I let out a *humph* sound. “Bullshit.”

“Reign, I don’t enjoy for one moment hearing about you being hurt or seeing someone hurt. It’s my job to help you work through all of this."

I had heard enough. "Whatever."

"I'd like you to answer the question."

Lynx stayed quiet through the whole exchange.

Enough was enough.

"I'm done," I told him with finality, crossing my arms over my chest.

"You know you'll get out of here a lot quicker if you just talk and get it over with," Lynx said calmly. "Or do you want to be stuck in this place?"

My eyes focused on him. While handsome in the don't-fuck-with-me way, he was seriously an ass.

He shrugged. "I don't give a shit if you stay in here or don't. All I know is that I have shit to do when I get out of here."

"And what would that be, Lynx?" the doctor asked.

Lynx smiled in a sinful and devilish way, like he knew exactly what he was going to do and how to do it. I couldn't help my curiosity of wanting to know what it was.

"Now, doc, I may have shit floating around in my head, but I'm not fucking stupid."

I had to agree with him on that one. He might have issues—didn't we all?—but he was smart. He seemed to know this system much better than I did. Was it wrong that I wanted to pick his brain and find the key to getting the hell out of here?

"I'd like to know," I said quietly, but Lynx shook his head.

His gaze didn't leave me. "No fucking way. Doc may be here to 'help' us, but don't mistake that for him not burning your ass if you say something he thinks needs to involve authorities."

I figured that, but I couldn't help it. I really wanted to know, almost to a point that I would like to get him alone to find out. It kept spinning in my head the entire time I was there. Something in me needed to know, needed to get it. I didn't know why at the time, but it was strong and pulsing, pulling me hard.

Five minutes before the session was over, the doc asked me, "Reign, want to tell us why you're in here?"

I was tired from all the talking back and forth between Lynx and the doctor. I was tired of thinking. I was just plain, old tired.

"Because the guy I thought was dead for the past five years is alive and happy with a woman and a kid." My words came out before I filtered them. I had been cruising on autopilot for the past hour or so, and my damn mouth got away from me.

Anger pulsed in the room like a thick shroud.

"You're in here over a guy?" Lynx clipped at me. For the first time in that hour, the fog began to drift away. "You have got to be fucking shitting me. All that shit you'd *seen.*" He said the word like he didn't believe me, causing the fire to come back into my veins. "All that and what put you over the fucking edge was a guy? You've got to be shittin' me." He rubbed both hands over his bald head in a manly act of frustration.

"Fuck off! No one asked you for your insightful comments," I clipped, turning back to the doctor. "I have nothing in common with this man. I don't want to have sessions with him anymore."

“That isn’t your choice.” His calmness pissed me off more.

“Why the fuck won’t you just let me out of this damn nightmare so I can end it all!” I screamed aloud, standing from my chair and planting my hands on the doctor’s desk. “We are wasting all this fucking time on nothing!” I shrieked. “Do you think any of this is going to change what I’m going to do? Let me the fuck out of here!” I yelled loudly, so loudly the door opened and a big, beefy man came through, closed it, and then stood with his arms crossed over his chest. Great.

“Calm down,” the doctor told me.

“Fuck calm,” I bit back as I felt Lynx’s eyes on me while I glared at the doctor. “Let. Me. The. Fuck. Out. Of. Here,” I snarled.

“Reign, I can’t do that when you are telling me, as soon as I do, you are taking your life. It isn’t possible.”

I growled, seriously growled at the man.

“You do realize that all you have to do is tell him you don’t feel that way anymore.”

My head snapped to Lynx, his words penetrating. An escape.

“Lynx, don’t,” the doctor warned, but Lynx didn’t listen.

“They have to keep you for five days to make sure what you said is true, that you are not a danger, but then they have to let you go.”

My mind began filling in the blanks of what Lynx was saying yet wasn’t really saying. If I said those words, I would have to prove to all of them in the next five days that I was normal, whatever in the hell that was. After that, I could get out of here and see freedom again. Fuck yes.

As my mind processed this for long moments, the air in the room had a slight chill to it.

"I don't feel that way anymore," I told the doctor, looking at Lynx.

"I don't believe that for a second," the doctor stated, scowling at Lynx.

I didn't understand why he was so pissed at him. The doctor was the one who forced us together.

"I'm afraid I can't—" he continued, but was cut off.

"I'm a witness, and so is he." Lynx nodded his head to big, brute man at the door. "Legally, you have to." He never lost eye contact with me.

The doctor threw his pencil on the desk and ran his fingers through his not-so-there hair, clearly pissed off.

I turned to Lynx who, for some reason, had a small smirk on his face, like he was happy to piss the guy off.

The doctor huffed, "Fine. You have to prove it to me, though."

I had no idea how I was going to do that, but I would give it a shot. It was my only way out.

"The session just got extended."

Lynx groaned, and I sat back in my chair.

"Tell us about your childhood," the doc ordered, down to business now.

A tight knot formed in the pit of my stomach. I couldn't do this. Could I? I had to, so I guess I could.

I tucked my feet under my ass and my lips began. "My parents hated me from the moment I was born and let me know it at every turn. I was taken away from them because, apparently, I needed my arms and legs broken at the same time for the authorities to step in. I went into foster care. It was its own kind of hell." I blabbed on for what felt like forever, telling them everything that happened to me during those years. Bottom line, it was shit and hurt like hell to dredge up, but I did it.

"You're probably thinking, *why didn't she tell anyone*, right?" I didn't wait for either of their responses, just kept going. "I did: my court-appointed liaison through the foster system. I learned quickly that telling her anything was a horrible idea. Not only did she tell my foster parents what I said, she gave *suggestions* of my punishments for talking. I never spoke of it again."

I looked up at the ceiling at one point and could see a small speck of light flashing above me. I didn't want to think that it was hope, but I wanted out of here, and if talking was what I had to do, so be it.

The past assaulted me as a recording of my life played before me. The feeling of being nothing, no one to anyone, kicked me in the gut, but I didn't have a choice. I needed to get out.

"That's when I met Drew," I continued.

The doctor cut in, "And that is the perfect place to stop."

I closed my lips. I was on such a roll the time had fizzled before my eyes. I didn't want to admit it to myself, but something inside me felt a little lighter getting it out, even if it was in front of two strangers.

“Why did your parents hate you so much?” Lynx asked, pulling me out of my thoughts.

I stared at him, thinking, trying to remember. For some reason, it didn’t stick out in my head. I had never really thought of it.

“I don’t know,” I answered honestly.

“You never went and found out?” he asked, carrying on.

“No. Why in the hell would I want to hunt down two people who already hated me, who hurt me? No, thank you.”

“Your perception of things may be skewed.” He placed his elbows on his knees and leaned forward, eyeing me with an intensity that filled the room. “Because knowledge is power.”

“That’s all we have time for,” the doctor said abruptly, standing from his seat.

That night, those four little words rolled, trotted, and burned into my brain. *Because knowledge is power.* Power was something I had never had in my life.

***

The door opened, and Nurse Hatchet came in with a bright smile on her face, reminding me instantly of Andi. I wanted to be mad at her and I was, but I also missed her … desperately.

“Seems you’re on the fast track to getting out of here.”

I felt myself smile inside at that small thought. I could get out. There was an end to this. I just needed to tell the doctor what he wanted, and I could be done with all of this.

I shrugged.

She sat on the bed next to me, not saying anything for a long time. Finally, I broke the silence.

"What?" I prompted.

"I tried to take my own life when I was sixteen."

I sat perfectly still. This was not what I had expected to come out of her mouth. At. All.

"I had wonderful parents." My gut twisted as she continued on. "But they were killed by a drunk driver. I was in the car with them and the only one who survived." Her voice broke as she continued. "I saw them: their bodies, the blood. I still see it at night when I close my eyes." She shook her head. "The driver of the other car lived, actually walked out of her car while I was on a stretcher."

I really didn't know how to feel about that situation. I had enough pain of my own without trying to process someone else's. As she spoke, though, the words penetrated somewhere deep. Thoughts of Drew or even Andi in the same situation collided, and I felt it. I felt the pain for them, for Nurse Hatchet. I had been too caught up in my own head to see it, so it hit me with the force of a wrecking ball.

"I hated that woman. I had to sit in court and watch her cry because of how sorry she was, because she was stupid enough to get behind the wheel of a car that night. I had to listen to her sob that her life would never be the same and that she lived with it every day. I even had to listen to her beg the judge for leniency because she didn't want to go to jail." Tears rolled down her eyes, and for some strange reason, I wanted to reach out and wrap my arms around her, but I refrained. Instead, I listened.

"The judge determined that it was her first offence and granted it to her. She was charged with vehicular homicide and got five years in prison. The kicker? She was out in twenty-seven months and two days for good behavior."

Damn.

I scooted a little closer to her and tentatively placed my hand on hers. It was like she knew it was all I could give her, and she gave me a soft smile in thanks without a word about it.

"I was down a rabbit hole, as I called it. I had to move in with my grandparents, go to a new school, plus deal with everything else. I didn't fit in, and I had so much weighing me down I felt like I was rooted in cement."

I could totally relate to what she was saying. I never fit in at any school. I never had the right clothes, hair, makeup, nothing.

"Anyway, one night, I'd had enough, so I downed a bottle of my grandfather's heart medication. I had no idea what it would do to me; I was just hoping everything in my head would stop." I understood that. "It did until I was brought back. I spent two years in a place like this. Because I was a minor, I had no say so."

She turned to me. "Reign, being in that place was horrible, having to relive things over and over and over again every day. I hated it. I hated my grandparents for putting me there. I hated the world. I hated me. I mean, why did I have to live while my family died? I get it," she said, putting her other hand on top of mine.

I started, breathed deeply, and left my hand where it was.

"I learned something during my time there. I learned I had

control of what I did with my life. I had none when it came to the woman who destroyed my life. I had none when it came to my parents being alive, but I could control what I did with me. That was the point in my life when I picked myself up from the ground and began to take control of my life."

I said nothing. I couldn't. I was stunned, shocked, and just in awe of everything she had said.

"Enough of that. Let's go to your appointment."

Nurse Hatchet felt it. She felt the darkness. She understood it, lived it, and she was there right then, helping me. She broke through it to become … happy. She tried to end it, just like me, to end the pain, but look at her. She was helping others, and I never would have guessed she had lived that past.

Something twitched in my soul, but I was too afraid to put a name to it. Afraid of that "H" word that meant there was a way to get through it, to see the light, just like Nurse Hatchet had done. Was it possible?

The walk down to Dr. McMann's office was spent with thoughts of Nurse Hatchet and the words *power* and *control* banging around like drums. I wanted them both. I needed them both. I had never had either, at least not fully. Even living and working, I never felt like I was in control of anything. I always felt that everything could blow up at any minute, and I would be dragged back into physical hell.

Lynx sat in his chair, his tattooed arms crossed over his wide chest, legs outstretched, looking like he owned the space. Dr. McMann sat behind his desk as usual, and I took my seat as Nurse

Hatchet left me.

Power and control. Power and control.

The doctor inspected me like looking at me would show him the window to my soul. "How are you today, Reign?"

"Fine." I used the universal language of women. Fine meant so many things it needed to have three pages in the dictionary.

He turned to Lynx, "You?"

"Great." His voice was utterly sarcastic, and that little spot inside me wanted to smile again.

Before the doctor asked any more questions, I turned to Lynx. "Knowledge is power. How would knowing why my parents treated me the way they did give me that?"

Lynx smirked, tipping up the side of his mouth that had the scar. For the first time since Drew, my stomach did a small spasm, although I ignored it.

"That was what started you on this path in life. Why wouldn't you want to know?" he retorted.

"I'd never really put any thought into it. I took it at face value."

He and I carried on this conversation like the doctor wasn't in the room, watching the back and forth. I really didn't care. All that mattered was getting the information from Lynx, finding out what to do with these small tingles of feelings that were beginning to invade me and how to use them.

He pulled his bottom lip between his teeth then popped it out. "That's what you need to realize. Everything is deeper than face value. You have to get the whole story."

I pulled my legs up underneath my butt, giving Lynx my full attention. "But why does it matter now?"

He leaned forward, yet I didn't feel threatened by it as I normally would have. If anything, I had to stop my body from moving closer to hear what he was going to say.

"Because you never know what you might uncover," he said mysteriously. I didn't really know how to take that. "Getting back your power will pull you up to the light."

My breath caught as my eyes widened. The light? Did I want the light? I thought back to Andi and how her light made me feel when the warmth of it wrapped around me.

I sat there for a long time, just processing what he had said. Then it hit me.

"You've been inside one of these places before," I stated as I began to figure out my new therapy partner.

"This is my fourth time, and I'm sure it won't be my last." He leaned back, lacing his fingers together and putting them behind his head. "Most of this shit"—he nodded to the room and I guessed he was talking about being here—"is common sense. It's just we get in our heads from time to time and have a hard time getting out."

"Is that how you got so smart?" I teased, my breath catching.

Did I just tease this man? Holy shit, I did. What in the hell was wrong with me? Where in the hell did this easy camaraderie between Lynx and me come from?

I realized in that moment how I had totally lost control; the roller-coaster emotions were taking me for the ride of my life, going up and down, killing me slowly. I felt like I was unraveling.

When his smirk came back out like he knew exactly what was running through my head, I didn't like that at all. He needed to stay far out of there if we were going to make it through this session.

"Babe, you have no idea."

Babe? I did not know why his calling me that clicked in my brain, but it did. I liked it. Holy hell, how could I like that?

"All right. Let's get down to it," the doctor interrupted. "Tell us about Drew."

The one name snapped me out of my thoughts of power and control, the hard rock of my life falling heavily in my gut.

Drew. My Drew. *Reign, you want out of here ... talk.*

"I met Drew when I was fourteen when we were placed in the same foster home. I didn't talk for the first two months there. I wanted to be invisible, but Drew pushed. We connected on several levels, but mainly because we were both alone in this world. We had no one, and eventually, all we had was each other." As I spoke, neither man in the room said anything, as if they wanted to hear what I had to say, and once I got going, I didn't want to stop. It was nice reliving the old me and Drew, remembering the happier times. It had been a long time since I had allowed those thoughts to come through instead of the final ones I had.

"I ran away that night." I told them after reliving *again* that fateful night. "I hated living on the streets, but it was better than where I was. At least, out there, I could choose whom I slept with and what I got for it in return." I surprised the hell out of myself by refusing to dwell and continuing. "Anyway, I saw some crazy shit out there, but I survived."

"You sure did," the doctor said. "I know there is more to your time on the streets, but I'd like to get to the point where you learned Drew was alive."

"My best friend Andi wanted me to have closure with Drew and suggested I go to his grave."

Lynx said nothing, only uncrossing and crossing his arms or legs every once in a while as I dredged up all those feelings again and felt the hollow get deeper in my soul. It was pulling me back under, and I couldn't stop it as I spoke. The dreams I had when I was young with Drew vanished in a puff of smoke.

Lynx leaned forward, putting his elbows on his knees. "Why don't you just talk to him?"

"Pardon?"

He shrugged. "You know, talk to the guy. Even if he has a woman and kid, you could still talk to him, get your closure another way."

Talk to him, another thing I either hadn't thought of or was pushing from my head. I wasn't sure which.

"I can't," I told him.

His brow furrowed as he challenged, "Why not?"

"Do you think I want to hear about his happy life? His wife, kid, and how he's got this perfect life going on? Do you think that will help me in any way?"

He shrugged. "You never know."

"I think," the doctor started, snapping my attention to him, "that before you talk with Drew, you need to find you—the woman you are inside. You may be surprised." His cryptic words freaked me out.

"I have no idea who I am, doc, and I'm not sure I'll ever find out," I said honestly. I hadn't ever known.

"That is why you need knowledge. It'll give you power. The power will give you strength. In that strength, you can find you," Lynx said.

I gaped at him in shock. Who the hell was this guy, and what planet had he beamed down from?

"How? Where do you propose I start on this information quest, oh knowledgeable one?" I asked.

He let out a surprised chuckle then covered it up. "Your mother, of course."

I wanted to take what he had said as a smart-ass 'duh,' but it wasn't that. He was being totally serious. Deep down, I could feel that he really wanted to help me, which was bizarre.

"You're in luck. I'm a wiz at finding out information."

I raised my brow in question, and he gave me a one-armed shrug.

"I wasn't just killing guys in the Army. I picked up a few things."

Surely, I had heard him wrong. "You're telling me you'd help me?"

"As long as you don't bitch too much," he quipped, but I knew he was teasing me because his eyes were light-hearted.

I didn't know what to make of it, but I knew that a favor always granted a favor, at least in my world.

"What do I have to do in return?" I demanded.

"Not a damn thing."

Chapter Six

I sat, my eyes glued to Lynx. “Answer me this.”

It was his turn to talk today, and I wanted to listen. I wanted to know more of why he was here. More to the point, I wanted to know why the hell he had been in here four times. Once would be enough for anyone.

“Why four times?”

He quirked his brow. “In here?”

I nodded as he sat back in his chair, relaxed as can be.

Last night, while I lay in my room, I replayed what I could remember of my time with my mother and father, which let’s be straight, wasn’t much. I remembered my mother’s gangly brown hair and eyes that were always cold. I remembered my father striking me on several occasions; that all kind of blended together. But something that got me, that stuck out in my head, was the sadness behind my mother's cold eyes. I didn't dare think it was sadness for me, but I remembered it being there.

I asked for a paper and pencil yet got a paper and crayon, instead. Whatever. It worked. I wrote down everything that popped into my head, even the smallest thing regardless whether I could remember if it was an actual memory or something I had made up in my head over the years. I would have to sort that out later.

I wouldn't say I felt better falling asleep, but I did feel different and couldn't put my finger on it.

As much as I wanted to ask Lynx what he thought about it, when we first got in here, the doctor started pulling Lynx into a conversation, and my curiosity had been piqued, so I had my own questions for him.

"The first time was about three months after I got back. My folks are good people, but they didn't know how to 'fix' me. I couldn't sleep for shit, didn't get why I couldn't carry my gun on me at all times, shit like that. It's so fucking hard to be on your guard and alert twenty-four hours a day for fear that someone is going to come up and attack you and your brothers. Then to come here where it's not like that is a mind fuck in and of itself. Anyway, my folks checked me in, thinking I could get help for it." He shrugged noncommittally. "I did some time and got myself out."

I knew he didn't seem like the type of man without parents waiting for him, although I had started to wonder about his family.

I cut in. "Do you have brothers and sisters?"

"One younger sister. She's cool."

I refused to pay mind to the dull ache that formed in my gut, but it seized me anyway.

"So, you have people who actually give a shit about you, and you want to spend your time here?"

Lynx turned his full attention to me like he knew I was having a hard time with this concept, like he knew I was suffering an inner turmoil. I didn't know what to make of that.

"You can have good people around you, but that doesn't fix what's going on in your head. Yeah, I have a mom, dad, and sister, but you can be in a room of people and still feel absolutely alone." He paused, thinking, then let out a deep sigh. "I got put in here the second time because an asshole broke into my parents' home. I was staying with them, but was out with friends. The asshole beat the shit out of them, and unlucky for him, I showed up before he left. I assessed the situation, and let's just say the motherfucker won't ever walk again. It's what landed me in here again."

"Why would that put you in here?"

"Because I fucked the guy up pretty good. He was the enemy, and with my military training, I did quite a bit of damage. I had flashes of a different time in my life as I was laying him out. I got a bit lost in my head. I was deemed a danger to others." Through his eyes, I could see the flashes of anger for the man who had hurt his parents, but I could totally relate to the *danger to others* part.

The words fell from my lips. "But he beat up your parents."

"Doesn't matter. Once I had him knocked out and subdued, I was told I should have stopped, but I didn't. I couldn't make myself. That got me six months and four days in here."

"I just don't get that." I didn't. I didn't understand how Lynx could get in trouble for protecting his family. Even if the guy was messed up, that was on the other guy for breaking into the place. "What about him? What'd he get?"

"Fucker spent a lot of time in a state health facility, so by the time he was well enough to move out, he only had six months left to serve."

"The way of the world," I grumbled. Didn't I know it.

"But not my way." The depths of Lynx's eyes sparkled with menace.

In that moment, I wanted to ask him if he had made right by his parents, but I also knew him well enough to know he wouldn't say a word, so I kept my mouth shut. Maybe I didn't need to know that answer.

"Okay, so with those two and the reason you're in this time, I know about three times; what's the fourth?" I switched up.

"That was my own damn fault." The room was hit with a heavy wave. The more it permeated, the more I could tell it was anger. "Had a friend who wanted to go to the fireworks for the Fourth of July. Something told me I shouldn't have gone, but I didn't listen. The first one went off, and I ended up taking a ride to the police station, which led me back in here."

"The sound of the fireworks does that to you?"

He met my gaze. "Reminds me of bombs, gun shots, you name it. It puts me back in a place that I had to fight to get out of. I'm not talking about fighting to get out of my head; I mean physically fighting because I'm under attack. You don't forget that shit. In order to survive, you have to rely on your instincts. Some sounds or situations trigger those. Then it's like trying to tame a lion. It doesn't happen overnight; it takes time and a fuck load of awareness."

"I've only seen them once," I said quietly.

"What?" Lynx asked.

"Fireworks. In twenty-one years, I've seen them once. My foster parent at the time kept saying how beautiful they were, but I kept seeing them as little explosions in the sky. I was waiting for one of them to fall in my lap and burn me. I was so terrified of it that I would panic at just the thought of going to see them or watching them on television. With my luck in life not being so great, I just knew I would be the one who got hurt if I went." I immediately felt like an ass for putting that out there. Here Lynx was, telling about himself and what happened to him, and I was acting like a shit. Embarrassment flooded me, and my body began to get hot. "Sorry, Lynx, I didn't mean to—"

He stopped me by holding his hand palm up. "Babe, it's fine. I'd much rather listen to your shit than talk about mine."

I thought that was nice, but still. "No, I mean—"

"Reign." My name on his tongue was the most melodic sound I had ever heard. It was low, authoritative, but still gentle. I hadn't had much gentle in my life, and it made me pause. "I mean it. If you've got something to say, say it. If it brings up something for you, let it. Why do you think doc put us together?"

My head swooped toward the desk. I had totally forgotten he was sitting there. Hell, he wasn't even watching us. He was writing something down. Thinking about it, he was probably writing down what we said.

"Babe?" he called, and I instantly turned to him like my body just knew he was talking to me. "You're good?"

I just nodded yet kept quiet as he continued.

"So, each time they put me in here, I learned something. I never went to college, but I have always been a fast learner. My dad told me that street smarts were a hell of a lot better than book smarts. He'd say, with me knowing both, I was a deadly combination." His thumb and pointer finger began tracing his bottom lip, and then his tongue came out to lick it.

Holy shit. Why were parts of my anatomy that I had locked up starting to give a slight tingle? I shook my head and closed my eyes, but he was too deep in thought to notice.

"He had no idea how right he'd be."

"All right, Lynx. It's Reign's turn."

My eyes shot to Wrestler McMann as I took in his words. I didn't know why I was surprised that he switched it up on me, but I was.

"I want to talk about Andi," he said.

The blood in my veins turned cold. While I missed her, I still blamed her for putting me in here. She was the one who had said "get your closure," and when I did, bam, it blew up in my face.

"I'd rather not."

"Andi, is that a chick or a dude?" Lynx asked.

I didn't hesitate to answer him. "Chick."

"I know you are very angry with her; we need to discuss this," Wrestler McMann proclaimed, and I felt the sudden urge to claw his eyes out. "She is the one you held the gun on. I need to make certain she is safe."

The red film that covered my eyes couldn't be stopped, so I didn't even try. I clenched my hands into fists and tried to breathe, but that didn't work, either.

"I did *not* hold a gun to her. I'd never harm her in any way, shape, or form. The bitch lied to get me in here, and you all bought it." I shifted my feet and put my hands on my knees. They kept bouncing, driving me nuts. "She didn't know how to 'deal' with me, so she made it up."

"She just cares about ya," Lynx said.

I stilled. How could he be taking her side in this? He was supposed to be on mine. He was supposed to understand that form of betrayal couldn't be fixed. He had to know that it was fucked up that she lied. He had to.

"What?" I clipped out harshly at him.

"Put your daggers down."

I glared at him, but it did nothing. He kept going.

"You were going to off yourself, and she couldn't stop you any other way. I don't know the chick, but if you're her friend, then I see it. She gives a shit."

I sat back, some of the anger leaving me. *She gave a shit.* Such simple words, but they were ones that I gripped on to hard.

"Look, if she didn't care, she would have left the room and let you do what you had to do. But she didn't. She took action and did what she knew. You don't think she had a hard time coming to that conclusion? That driving you here didn't gut her? I bet it did and that she's spent this entire time you've been in here beating herself up for it."

"But she's the reason I'm here," I defended.

"The only other option she had was to watch you put a round in your head. Turn that around and put Andi in your place."

The thought shocked me to my core, and my toes curled as the air sailed from my lugs in a burst.

"Exactly," he said. "Don't tell me that she was doing it to be a bitch. She just didn't want to see someone she cares about on the ground in front of her, dead."

Somehow, the reverse scenario penetrated my thick skull. I could see it. Through the hurt and the anger I felt toward her, I could see where she had been coming from. I could see the gut-churning pain she must have felt from watching me go to pieces without being able to do a damn thing about it.

Imagining her sitting there with a gun in her hand was almost too much to take. She was sunshine, not dreary. As tears fell from my eyes, I didn't even take the time to bat them away.

"Babe, you have a somebody. You're not alone."

The dam burst open. I pulled my knees up to my body and rested my head on them, covering it with my arms. I wasn't sure if I was hiding or just trying to get small. All I felt was sadness. I did have someone who cared, someone other than Drew, and I was going to let her walk in on my dead body. What kind of person was I to do that to someone who cared about me? I fought the tears that craved to continue to fall as the hurt sliced me.

"But she deserves better than to put up with my shit," I mumbled into my knees.

"She's a big girl. If she didn't want to put up with your shit, she'd be gone."

I shook my head back and forth. He just didn't understand.

"Babe," he said, but I ignored him. Seconds ticked by before he said, "Reign."

This time, I jumped and shot my eyes his way.

"Better." He let out a heaved breath. "How many people have come and gone from your life?"

I should have thought about what he was thinking and where he was going, but I just answered, "More than I can count."

"She knew you had baggage because, babe, just from looking at you, I could tell."

I wanted to glare and give him a good *fuck you* yet didn't.

"Again, you need to talk to her and get this shit out. If you get this off your chest, it'll be better for the both of you."

Where in the hell did this man come from? Seriously.

I hated it, but he was right. Andi had proved she was my

somebody to me time and time again. She gave a shit, more than a shit. She treated me in a way I hadn't seen in my time on this planet. Sure, Drew had, but Andi was different. I didn't know how; I just knew it was.

I swiped my face with both my hands, feeling the wetness and wiping it on the green scrubs I wore today. The big, black hole that was always around me started to diminish just a bit. The cyclone moved down to a hurricane, and my heart squeezed.

I couldn't stay pissed at Andi. I just couldn't. No matter what happened to me in this life, I couldn't shit on her. She had never shit on me, never given up on me, and more importantly, she was my somebody.

"So what do you plan on doing?" the doctor asked.

I didn't know. I didn't know what the hell I was going to do with anything. I felt like I was in a sea of sharks: one wrong move and I would be eaten. But the weird thing was I didn't know if I wanted to be eaten alive yet. For the first instance in a really long time, the voices inside weren't as strong. The more they quieted, the more I wasn't sure that ending my life was the way to go.

"I don't know." My voice was quiet as I set my feet back on the floor and clasped my hands together in my lap. "I really don't know," I repeated with no less feeling.

"I actually believe you," the doctor said. "Time's up."

Chapter Seven

"Where's Lynx?" was the first question I asked as I stepped over the threshold into the doctor's office.

Normally, Lynx made it to the office before me, but it wasn't just that. It was the vibe in the room. The safety that surrounded this space like a shroud wasn't there. Poof. Vanished.

I had begun to feel remarkably comfortable in this room, but today, there wasn't any of that. I could almost taste the difference in the air yet couldn't put a name to it. The energy was off, putting me on edge to the point my palms began sweating and my heart rate picked up rapidly. Maybe I was making more of this than it was, right?

Wrestler McMann leaned against the front of his desk, his short, stubby legs crossed at the ankles and arms loosely at his sides. He didn't seem sure of himself or sure about me. Which? I couldn't tell. The unease chilled my body and my first instinct was to escape, but Nurse Hatchet was by the door, almost like a guard.

She didn't seem off the entire time we had walked here. She never gave any inkling to something being wrong, but as I looked at her, she had almost a fighter's stance, like she was waiting for me to come at her.

"What's going on?" I asked the two, looking between them. I wasn't sure who to focus on. At this point, both of them were making me nervous.

Wrestler McMann stepped forward and said, "Andi is here."

My knees nearly gave out. I didn't know how I kept them locked, but I somehow did. I wrapped my arms around my body as the coldness swept through. It did nothing to keep the heat inside me.

She was here. I had lost track of the days I had been locked up, but I knew it was a few weeks. It had to have been from all the talks with the doctor and the time before.

For most of those weeks, I had hated her, was so damn angry I couldn't see straight. Then, others, I missed her so much I ached down to my bones. Now, she was here.

I had just told Lynx and the doc about this yesterday. And now … BAM. He was either preparing me for it, or he had set this up. My guess was the latter.

"You need to face Andi," Wrestler McMann stated when I kept quiet. "You've made great progress, but your time is coming to an end here." Those words snapped my focus, because I needed out of here, like, yesterday. "But don't *act* like you think I want to see. That's why your nurse is here and will stay throughout the duration. We will make that determination."

A test, one I was more than likely going to fail. Perfect. My time here just kept getting better and better.

My head began to swim like water going fast into a drain, sucking down in a deep swirl. I closed my eyes, trying to stop myself from sinking, but I was still going. Around and around and around, I spun, trying to grasp anything to hold on to. Nothing was there. My breathing picked up, and I found it harder and harder to control.

Was I pissed? Did I miss her? Could I forgive her? What if she hated me for what I had said? What if she couldn't forgive me for what I was going to do when she was taking care of me?

A hand came to my shoulder, and I flinched away from it, flying across the room to the far wall and slapping my back to the hard surface. Wrestler McMann's special I-am-a-wonderful-doctor plaques shook from the impact, rattling in my ear.

Nurse Hatchet took a step closer to me, concern and comfort in her eyes that I had become accustomed to and liked, for that matter.

Thoughts of Andi spun out of control in the sea, and I started to panic—deep to my bones panic, like I wasn't in my body panic. Suddenly, I couldn't find air. I sucked in and out deeply but still couldn't find it.

Nurse Hatchet was right in my face, but she didn't touch me.

"Reign, breathe slowly, in and out," she kept saying over and over again, but it took a lot of times before I listened, started breathing, and brought myself somewhat under control.

It's Andi, a soft voice said in the back of my head. I knew it was right. This was Andi, my best friend. I thought back to what Lynx had said about her not really having a choice in what she had done, and the image of seeing her dead on the ground instead of me assaulted me.

I sank down to the floor and pulled my knees up into my body, finally getting my breathing under control. Nurse Hatchet sat next to me, mimicking my position.

"She misses you, too, ya know?"

It hurt to think I was the cause of her pain. I didn't want to be that. Even if she had betrayed me by putting me in this wretched place, I never wanted to be the source of pain to her; yet, I was.

As tears filled my eyes, it took everything I had to keep them in check.

"Do you want to get up before she comes in, or do you want to stay there?" Wrestler McMann asked.

I had half a mind to take off my rubber shoe and throw it at him. He wasn't going to give me an out on this. He was going to make me do this. He almost seemed gleeful that he had me. Unfortunately, like Lynx had said, we sometimes got into our own heads and the outside world's agenda didn't see ours. So the doctor's glee didn't register until much later.

I wanted to blame Andi for putting me in here. I wanted to yell and scream at her for doing this to me. It was like my mind wanted to take me there, but I fought it because what Andi had done was the only thing she could do given the situation, and she cared. When I needed to fall, Andi was there.

I didn't answer the doc. Instead, I rose from the floor, staying near the wall and using it as my anchor. The rushing water became swirling rapids so fast there was no slowing it. It was going to pull me under.

Nurse Hatchet started grunting from the floor. I noticed she was having trouble getting on one of her knees. Without thinking, I grabbed her arm and helped her up. At her slight touch, the rapids slowed just a bit.

It wasn't until moments later, when the door opened, I realized I was still holding on to my nurse; only, this time, I was clutching her hand like she was my life force. And she was. Any confidence I found in searching for answers and gaining my power vanished. I was back there, back in that dark pit.

As Andi entered the space, I sucked in a deep breath. Her face was void of the happy sunshine I had grown accustomed to. Now, her eyes were sunken in like she hadn't slept in a really long time. Her cheeks didn't have their normal natural glow, and her body was almost frail. This wasn't the Andi I had left in the car that day. No, this was a shell of her. Even her hair didn't catch the light like it used to.

My heart hurt with a pain that was harsher than a stab. It was worse. It was bleeding for Andi, just like all those years ago when it had bled for Drew. I had done this to her. I had made her feel this way. I had never wanted that for her.

Although I had wanted her to live her life without the weight of me dragging her down, I had done it anyway. I had sucked her down into my pit, which caused the ache inside me to grow.

I didn't make a play for her. No, I stayed rooted to the spot with my nurse, still clutching her hand with the force of a car clamp, using her as my brace. I didn't know what to expect, because I didn't know how to feel. I was pissed, hurt, scared, lost, and even a bit embarrassed. My blood was pumping through me so hard my heart was thumping in my ears like a loud band playing. I was sure the others in the room would be able to hear it.

Andi clasped her hands in front of her, her eyes locked on me. Tears filled them, and she didn't stop them from spilling over her cheeks. I could see the pain inside of her was deep to her core, almost totally extinguishing the light in her eyes that I had relied on so much for so long.

The realization hit me hard that I had taken for granted the sunshine she had given me for so long. She had given it to me freely, and I had sucked it up like a starving woman.

The hollow in my gut opened. I couldn't figure out if I had ever given anything back to her in all that time or if I had just taken.

I didn't think; I acted. I released Nurse Hatchet's hand and moved faster than I had moved in a long time. I didn't catch Andi's reaction before I engulfed her in my arms and rested my head on her shoulder.

She was statue still for only moments before her arms wrapped around me, and I lost it. Heavy sobs racked me, but these weren't ones I had shed these past few years. No, these were the earth shattering ones like the moment I thought I had lost Drew. These squeezed my insides and wrung them so tightly I was sure to combust.

Andi's arms constricted around me as her body began to shake from her own sobs, our bodies moving in tandem. That was when the weight of everything hit me hard, so hard my knees gave out. Andi wasn't prepared for it, so we both clattered to the floor in a heap without letting go of each other for a second.

We stayed in that exact spot for what felt like forever. Even after the sobs turned into horrible hiccups then into little whimpers, we remained clutched together. Even after the tears dried up, we didn't move. I simply held on to her, lost in the moment and not wanting to let her go ever.

"Ladies." The doctor's voice came from behind me, but we both ignored it, each of us gaining our breaths and trying to still our bodies.

I felt her warmth like a blanket. This was the first time I had felt warmth in so long, and I didn't want to let it go.

"Ladies." This time, the words were bolder and terser. I knew my time was up, but I still didn't want to release her.

"Reign."

I opened my eyes to see Nurse Hatchet bent down, her eyes shimmering and a small smile playing on her lips.

"We need to do this now," she told me.

Reluctantly, I released Andi. I smiled when she gave me another strong squeeze before letting me go fully.

When I looked at her, I couldn't stop a small smile from forming. She was a hot mess: snot down her face; eyes red, almost to the point of swollen; and tear stains all the way down her cheeks. However, it was her eyes that caught me. They were filled with something I couldn't put my finger on yet wanted to know.

Tissues were pushed in front of my face from Nurse Hatchet's waiting hand, and I snatched them just as Andi did. I was covered with the same as Andi and had to wipe myself clean. The nurse then handed us the garbage can and we disposed of the tissues, neither of us saying anything.

I was scared down to my toes that she would hate me, that the things I had said to her couldn't be unsaid. I was terrified what we had built—the friendship, sisterhood—was lost. I couldn't handle another blow, especially that one.

"I'm sorry," I whispered, which caused tears to well back into Andi's eyes. "I…" I trailed off, not knowing what to say.

My whole intention on opening my figurative doors was to get the hell out of here so I could end the voices, end the hurt, but I couldn't tell her that, and I didn't know if that was the truth anymore, not after the talks with Lynx, Nurse Hatchet—hell, even opening up to the doctor. I didn't know anymore if that was what my plan needed to be. I also didn't know how to pull myself out of it, how to stop it without going through with it. Subsequently, I wouldn't lie to her.

“I’m a mess,” I told her.

She sat in the chair that Lynx normally sat in; except, this time, the two chairs were facing each other in front of the doctor’s desk. The only place we could look was at each other, and as painful as it was to see her so hurt, I didn’t take my eyes away from her because I had caused that. I had made her hurt. I deserved to see that.

“Reign, I didn’t know what else to do.” She shook her head, a tear rolling down her now pale cheek. “When you…”

“I know. It’s—”

“Stop,” the doctor said, interrupting me.

I turned to glare at him. Wasn’t this what he wanted? For us to talk this shit out? Why was he interrupting?

“Reign, you need to let her talk. Let her tell you what she needs to say. She deserves that much.”

That took the wind out of my sails. The little prick was right; I did owe her that and so much more.

I said nothing, only nodded and turned back to Andi.

“Go ahead,” the doctor prompted Andi while Nurse Hatchet took another chair off to the side by the wall. I guessed all was calm and we didn’t need reinforcements so much anymore.

“When I told you to find Drew’s grave”—my heart sank at her opening—“I didn’t know that you would find this. If I had known, I’d have never said it. I swear.”

I made a noise to start talking, but the doctor cleared his throat in a small reprimand. It cost me to keep my lips zipped, but I did it. I only nodded at Andi for her to go on.

"I never thought he would be alive. I only thought that you could say good-bye to him, give yourself some closure so you could live your life instead of being locked up so tight."

She twisted her fingers this way and that, obviously nervous, and if I wasn't mistaken, scared. "When you came home and cried and cried and cried, I didn't know what to do. I called my parents, asking them, and they didn't really know how to help, either. The only thing they told me was, if I was that scared, then I should take you to the hospital. I did the best I could without going there because I knew you hated them."

And she had. I knew she had, but at the time, I was so lost that I couldn't put those pieces together. After all the shit she had done for me, she should get a fucking medal.

Her tears began to flow more quickly. "When I walked in and saw you holding the gun … I knew I couldn't help. I knew you were so sad, so lost, and I didn't have the power or the strength to get you back. I wasn't going to see you dead on the floor." Her tears became heavier.

I wanted to go to her and give her comfort, but I didn't feel like I should.

"I know you hate me, but the fact you're sitting across from me, breathing, is why I did it. But I don't want you to hate me." She sobbed, covering her face with her hands.

Fuck it.

I got up, knelt before her, and put my hands on her knees. She removed her hands to stare down at me. The grief and pain etched in every line of her face were like daggers piercing me slowly in and out.

"I was pissed," I whispered, and she nodded. "I said some things I shouldn't, and I'm sorry." I grabbed her hands and clutched them between mine. "I hated that you put me in here, but in a twisted way, I get it." And I really did. Lynx was right. "I still hate it here," I said softly. "But I'm getting out soon."

Hope sprang in Andi's eyes.

"You *might* be getting out," the doctor corrected.

I rolled my eyes to the ceiling. He was *so* not helping right now. Wasn't it his job to help people, not hinder them?

I ignored him. "I am. I'm doing better." Was that a lie even though I had said I wouldn't lie to her? Was I doing better?

Thoughts drifted to Lynx and his whole "finding my power and strength" business then to my mother and asking her why she hated me so much. It was becoming a bit irritating that he was right so damn much. I wanted those answers. I wanted to know why I had turned out the way I had. What actions had led to me being in a place like this? It was almost like I had gained a purpose in this life to find out why it was so shitty. Strange.

But I wasn't quite ready to end it all anymore. I *wanted* my knowledge. I *needed* my strength, and I *craved* my power. Therefore, in a way, I was a small, tiny bit better. In turn, I hadn't lied to her, and that felt good.

"You are?" she asked hesitantly.

I nodded. "You did what you had to do. I didn't like it … I *don't* like it, but—big but here, Andi—I get it. You doing this helped."

Then she smiled, and when she did, it was like the sunshine filled the room.

And I embraced it.

Chapter Eight

I sat there, tuning out Lynx talking to the doctor about some football team.

After Andi's visit the day before, I had spent the rest of the day in my room, thinking. The doctor and Nurse Hatchet had given me the breathing room I needed to process everything. It wasn't pleasant.

Andi's visit had been more difficult than I had ever expected. I was so tired of crying and letting the pain of everything crush me. Even though it was still there, I didn't feel like I was sinking as badly as before. Yes, it sucked, but the dark void wasn't encompassing me like normal. It was there—don't get me wrong. I didn't think I would ever get rid of it, yet the light … I could see a speck of it, and that minute bit seemed to calm me.

"Reign," the doctor called, snapping me back to him and Lynx.

"Yeah." My voice came out croaky, so I coughed a little to loosen it and repeated, "Yeah," a little more strongly this time.

"Want to tell Lynx about yesterday?"

No, I didn't. It wasn't that I didn't want him to know. I didn't want to rehash it. I thought Andi and I had left it in as good of a spot as we could. Therefore, regurgitating it wasn't on the top of my list. However, I wanted out, so I pushed through.

"There was a lot of crying and female bonding, nothing exciting."

"Female bonding?" Lynx asked, his eyes lit with amusement. It was that small flicker that caused my lips to move.

"I hurt her, and you were right." I waited for him to have some snappy comment or give me some sort of shit for it, but after long moments with nothing, I continued. "I can't fault her for doing something that she thought in her soul she had to do." I sat quietly, my stomach churning with some of the thoughts from yesterday. "I was a shit," I said more quietly than the rest. "She packed all my belongings when I got evicted while I was in here then put everything in her spare room at her apartment." I felt my lip tip up at what she had done for me. "She didn't have to do that. She could have walked away and wiped her hands of me, but she didn't." I turned to Lynx. "She told me, when I get out, I'm coming to stay with her so she can watch me like a hawk."

It was Lynx's turn to tip his lips, and what gorgeous, bowed lips they were. I looked away, wanting to kick myself for the thought.

"See? You've got someone."

I nodded because the jackass was right again.

I did. She gave a shit. She cared, and I couldn't help this overwhelming urge to not let her down. I couldn't give up on her, because she hadn't given up on me for a moment.

"So what are you going to do when you get out?" he asked.

I blinked a few times at him, not knowing how to answer the question. I had been busy digging myself out and hadn't really gone there yet. I hadn't known there would be an "after here." I had thought for so long I would end everything as soon as I stepped outside the doors, but now I couldn't do that to Andi.

The pain in her face yesterday was too much. I knew that if I followed through with it, I would hurt to her to a point that she couldn't bounce back like I had initially thought. How could I do that to her? I couldn't. I needed to find a way to find me and pull myself together.

I didn't want to say it out loud because I just knew Lynx would smirk or smile, but I had to.

"You're right. I need to find out why I am the way I am. I need your help." I let out a breath that came from the depths of my lugs. I felt like a balloon that had fizzed out, and as if on cue, Lynx's grin almost extended into a smile, like he was happy.

The doctor spoke up. "While I like the path you're on, Reign, I think you should tread with caution. Things you could find out about your childhood may send you back into the place you found yourself in before you came here. If that happens, I fear what choices you could make."

I didn't acknowledge the doctor's words; instead, I instinctively looked at Lynx. "You think it's a bad idea?" I would never know why I valued him over a professional. Then again, he'd been right so many times before, and my gut told me he wouldn't steer me wrong.

"I see what the doc's saying. You might find out shit that will hurt; I'm sure of it. However, I'll be there. Andi will be there. You'll figure it out."

I didn't know what to say. I was caught on the part where he had said he would be there, like he wouldn't just be finding me information, but he would be there with me every step of the way.

I tried to process it in the moment yet came up short. As a result, I focused on Andi, instead. She would be there for me if I needed her. I knew that down to my soul.

Maybe, if I found all this out, I could find me.

"Then there's Drew," the doctor said, making my stomach plummet to my toes. That so called confidence I had thought I was gaining melted into a pool around my feet, swirling and disappearing into nothingness.

Drew. What in the hell would I do about that part of my life?

"You have two options," Lynx said, rattling me. How was he in my head? "One, you never contact him again and let him live his life. Or two, you contact him and talk to him."

How could I never talk to him, never see him, knowing he's

alive and living? Then, on the other hand, what would I say to him? *Oh, hi, remember me, the girl you watched fucking her foster father before she watched you die?* Neither were on my list.

"I'm not sure I can do either of those."

"You don't have to decide right now. You have time."

Again, this was true because it was my choice. I had the control of both of these options. I liked that. I liked it a lot.

"I do," I whispered.

***

I didn't want to go to therapy today. It wasn't because I didn't want to talk. No, it was because it was my last session with Lynx. While I didn't think he'd renege on helping once I stepped outside these doors, there was no guarantee. There never was in life. However, if I wanted to figure myself out, I had to push forward.

As I sat in my chair, neither Lynx nor I spoke. I didn't even look at him. I couldn't force myself to do it. I had this disappointing feeling he would give up on me like so many others in my life, and I didn't want him to be that person. I didn't want to have any hope he could be different, but the burn in my heart was what agonized me the most, and I didn't know why. I couldn't put words to it.

"So, Lynx, do you think you have yourself under control?" Wrestler McMann asked him, but I still didn't look his way, choosing to chew on my thumbnail, instead.

"I'm good," he replied, not giving the doctor an inch.

"Not good enough. What are you going to do to tamp your anger? We've talked about several techniques; which do you think would work best?"

I looked up at Lynx through my lashes, not wanting to make eye contact yet unable to help myself as I listened to him speak.

"I'll stop and think before I react." He paused. "Oh, and keep taking those little pills every day."

My head snapped up at that, and our eyes connected, his registering a little shock.

"Pills?"

The nurse had tried to get me to take pills, but I flat-out refused. I had always had an aversion to them. I'm not sure when in my life that had started exactly.

"Yep, I get to feeling pretty good and think I don't need to take them anymore, because hell, I'm good." He shook his head. "I need the fuckers. Hate takin' them, but they help." He shrugged as if it weren't a big deal at all.

"I don't want any pills," I told him. I didn't even want sleeping pills. Nothing.

"This is something that we need to discuss," the doctor threw in, causing both Lynx and my eyes to come back to him. He sat at his desk, fingers laced together and eyes boring into mine. "I highly advise you begin the medication regimen that I've laid out for you, too."

I shook my head as Lynx spoke up. "Why don't you want the pills? Don't want people to think you're crazy?" He said this comment like it was perfectly natural for someone to think this.

"I don't have any people to worry about thinking I'm…" I

trailed off, not really wanting to say the word.

Lynx caught on. "So *you* don't want to think you're crazy."

"I'm not crazy," I barked a bit more harshly than anticipated.

I closed my eyes and sat back in my chair, tipping my head up to the ceiling. Flashes passed across my eyelids as my breathing became labored, and the tight noose around my neck started choking the air from my lungs.

She's a bit nuts. She has quite a few screws loose. Crazy...

"Reign!" Lynx's harsh voice snapped me from my thoughts as I gasped for breath, clutching the chair for dear life. "Tell me," he demanded, something he had never done before with me. I wasn't scared, but I also didn't waver.

"Being called crazy, having screws loose. My court liaison would tell my foster parents this when I was placed with them." I sucked in deeply as my father flitted into my head. "My father would tell me I was just as wacko as my mother." I shook my head. "But I'm not crazy. I ... I don't know what I am, but crazy isn't it."

"I can see how that word bothers you, Reign," the doctor said as my eyes stayed glued to Lynx, his look on me intense. "It is perfectly normal for you to feel this way."

I gulped, turning to the doctor. Was it really normal that I felt this way?

"It is?"

He gave me a soft, reassuring smile. "Of course. The word crazy means mentally deranged. Most of the time, people in the world use the word in a joking, light-hearted manner to tease someone who doesn't take the meaning of the word seriously. Others use it as a derogatory comment to put someone down. You see the word as the latter."

I nodded. I knew something was messed up in my head—it didn't take a rocket scientist to know that—yet I didn't want to be crazy. I didn't want to be associated with that word. It bothered me down to my bones, and it wasn't what others thought, because I only had Andi who gave a damn. It was inside of me. I wanted better than that.

The doctor continued, "From a medical standpoint, depression is a chemical imbalance in the brain. The medicine helps regulate what the brain isn't producing on its own."

An imbalance. That word didn't seem nearly as bad as someone calling me crazy.

"Taking the meds will help," Lynx added when I didn't respond to the doctor, too lost in my thoughts.

I placed my thumb in my mouth and began chewing on the nail again. This had always been a way to calm myself since I was a kid, and it had never gone away.

"It helps keep the calm, the peace," Lynx said.

My head swam with the word peace. That was what I needed in order to calm the waters inside me.

"So, if I take them, my thoughts will calm?" I asked.

Lynx nodded. "Yep. They won't go totally away, but the meds will help."

"But you said you stopped taking yours," I argued.

"Yep, I did. I also told you why. There comes a point when taking them makes you feel carefree, like everything is finally right … or close to it. Then, you think, *I don't need this shit anymore.* I thought it, stopped taking them, and I honestly can't say if it would have helped being on them when I caught that lying bitch. I don't know if I would have done anything differently, because I can't see myself doing so; but that was an extreme situation. Everyday situations, like the asshole who cuts me off with his car, when I normally would fly off the handle, I don't. I'm able to tap it down for the most part."

A chilling form of relief came over me. I was glad that Lynx had found help in the meds, but how did I know that I would, too?

"You don't know until you try, and chances are, it will take a while to find the right combination of medicine for you," the doctor threw in. "The chemicals in our brains all fire differently. What will work for you won't work for someone else. That's why we wanted you to start them when you got in here so we could get the right dosage, but you refused."

I did. The thought of already being attuned to what I needed made me ache now, though. If I had started the medicine, maybe things would be different. *I* would be different.

"There is nothing wrong with taking medicine. Ya gotta do what ya gotta do," Lynx stated, sitting back in his chair and crossing his ankles, his arms locked across his chest like he owned the place. "Reign, you've gotta take care of you. No more of this going to kill yourself bullshit. They're offering you help. You need to take that shit and run with it because trust me, you don't want to have to come back here." His smirk made my insides relax a bit.

The bottom pit of the void I was in started to swirl, but I sucked in deeply and began to climb up.

"Okay, I'll try."

***

The rest of the session, Wrestler McMann talked to Lynx about keeping an even head and going over all the different techniques to sooth himself when triggered.

I didn't say much. I was still processing my agreement to take meds. I couldn't believe I had or even wanted to. I had been so set on ending everything after getting out, but now I didn't want to hurt Andi. If I was really serious, I wasn't sure I wanted it for myself anymore, either.

I wasn't anything to sneeze at, and I really had nothing to show for in my life except the fact of being alive, but what if I could be more? What if I could do something to make life better for me instead of living in the same circle over and over again, replaying my past like a broken record? What if I could throw the record in the trash and have a life? What if …?

I was told once by a foster father that the "what if" game was stupid because you couldn't change the past. "What if" didn't matter; it was what you did now. Mr. Johnsboid was the only foster father who actually gave me anything I could take with me in life, and those words now meant more to me than I had thought at the time.

I had to move forward, but how did I do that when Drew was out there, alive? That was a huge hurdle I didn't know how to overcome, but at least I was now thinking about how to do so. Although it was a tiny step, it was something.

"Time's up," the doctor said, causing all thoughts to slip away.

This was it. Lynx was leaving, and I had this small ball inside of me where my hope started to burn just a bit—the hope that he would follow through on what he had said and help me outside of here.

I knew I shouldn't have any of the H-word. It had never helped and had always let me down. I thought Lynx was different, though. I wanted to believe he was.

"I'm out of here." Lynx's grin widened into a full-fledged smile, and I sucked in a breath. It was beautiful, totally transforming his rock hard, stern face into something women would swoon over. And I hated to admit it, but I was included in that. *Holy shit.*

My stomach had these little flutters, and my throat felt like it was going to close up.

When Lynx rose from the chair and moved toward me, I had to bend my neck way back to see him.

"Up," he demanded sternly but not harshly.

I complied, taking a step back to give myself some space between us.

Funny how when I first saw him, I wanted to run and hide. I didn't want to be in the same room with him for fear he would hurt me. Now, sadness was racking me down to my core that this could be the last time I would ever see this man who, in his own way, had helped me so much.

He took a step closer, and my breathing became labored. He was too close, but something inside me wouldn't allow me to move back any farther. I wasn't sure how or when this had happened, when I had become so trusting of this man that I was able to stand my ground and not move into my own personal space when he was so close. I wondered if that meant I was getting a little better, but I didn't want to have the H-word. Therefore, I stared into his eyes, transfixed, instead.

"I'll come to you when you get out," he said.

I had tonight and tomorrow night in here, which felt like an eternity. It was a lifetime before I would find out if Lynx was the guy I thought he was or a disappointment like all the rest.

"I didn't tell you where I'm going to live."

He gave me a half-grin and raised his hand toward me. I flinched out of habit, but I didn't move as his hand came up and cupped the side of my cheek. His warmth caused my pulse to spike so hard I heard the thunder of my heart in my ears and breaths were becoming hard to find. I was letting this man touch me, and all I was doing was clenching and unclenching my hands, not saying anything. On top of that, I actually liked the feeling of his hand on me.

"Reign," he whispered until my focus was back on him. "I'll find you. We'll get this worked out together."

My chest squeezed unnaturally. I didn't know how, but I leaned into his hand, taking the warmth he was giving me. If this was the last time I would see him, I was going to enjoy this sliver of feeling.

"Bye, Lynx," I whispered softly.

I had been let down more times than not in my life, and he didn't know for sure what would be waiting for him outside these doors. Hell, his woman could come crawling back, and then I would just be a small blip on his radar of that one-time-when-I-was-in-the-hospital. I wanted to hold on to his words, keep them, and lock them away someplace, so I did.

His thumb lifted my chin, making sure he had my full attention. His eyes glistened as he spoke. "Not bye, Reign." He studied me closely. "You think I'm full of shit." I didn't think those exact words, but how the hell did this man know what was floating in my brain? "I see I have a lot of work ahead of me." His intensity bore into mine. "I love a good challenge." His hand slipped behind my neck, and before I could do anything, he face-planted me into his chest.

I froze, unable to move, my body feeling as stiff as a board, my arms straight at my sides. Lynx's arms wrapped around my back, and I did nothing, including breathe. When I did start to breathe again, I sucked in deeply, and damn did he smell good, but I didn't melt into him. No, I couldn't. I had only had this with Andi; that was it. No one else.

I full-out gasped when he kissed the top of my head, his arms giving me one last squeeze before releasing me. I took a hasty step back, unsure what to think or do. I was out of sorts in more ways than one because not only had I let this man touch me, but I had liked it. I might not have shown him I had, but terrifyingly, I really had.

"I see we need to work on that, too." He chuckled with all the patience of a saint. He and Andi would get along well.

"Why?" I whispered.

"Pardon?"

"Why? Why waste your time helping me? Why be this way with me?" I was terrified of the answer. No one in my life, besides Andi, took time to help me. Everyone let me down.

"I'll answer that when we're out of here."

"Time to go," his nurse said, entering the room, and Lynx started walking toward her. I couldn't blame him. If they said those words to me, I would hightail it the hell out of here, too.

He did turn around to me, though, and said, "A couple of days." He winked before the door shut behind him.

For the first time, I cried that night for a man who wasn't Drew.

Chapter Nine

The morning session didn't go well. All I could do was stare at the empty chair that Lynx had occupied. I didn't feel like talking; however, I didn't feel like I was drowning, either. It was strange.

Nurse Hatchet had given me two pills last night and then two this morning. She had told me what they were, but hell if I could remember. Before I took them, I thought of Lynx's words then downed them in one gulp. I felt no different, and when I told that to Nurse Hatchet, she said, "Honey, it'll take about a week for it to build up in your system."

Great.

I had to spend tonight here, and the small light at the end of the tunnel was closer because, tomorrow, granted Wrestler McMann said so, I could leave this fine establishment. I would be out. I was actually nervous about leaving. I didn't think I would be or could be, yet I was.

I had a home to go to thanks to Andi, but I had no job and no money.

"Reign," the doctor called out then slammed something hard on the desk, my attention quickly going to him. "That's better. I'm tired of hearing myself talk."

I doubted that, but whatever. I had come down for my last session about twenty minutes ago. I wanted it over and done with. The sooner, the better, but that didn't mean I wanted to chitchat.

"Plans," he continued. "We need to talk plans for when you get out of here."

I didn't say anything, so he continued, "What are you specifically going to do?"

I again stared. I went from wanting to end everything to now making plans for days with unexpected outcomes. I didn't have a plan. I was only surviving at the moment, another thing I didn't think I had wanted to do.

"Reign, you have to have a goal, a plan for when you walk out those doors and back into the day-to-day world."

Panic crept up my spine and twisted around my neck. I had gotten used to not having visitors to my room; therefore, it was a safe place. Now, I wouldn't have that. Anyone could come anywhere I was, and there would be no stopping it or them.

I tried to stay in the moment. The panic, the emotions, the thoughts, they crept in. Then, like a whirlpool in the ocean, they spun together in my mind. Too many swirling feelings hit me hard in the gut, knocking the wind out of my sails.

Here I had thought I had grown quite a bit, but maybe not as much as I had believed.

“Reign,” he called again as I blew out deeply.

“I don’t know,” I finally answered, getting my breathing and thoughts under control. “I know I’m going to live with Andi. I don’t know how it’s going to be or where I’ll sleep, but I know she’ll help me. I need to find a job and make money. Other than that, I don’t know.” I knew I kept repeating the same words, but they were the truest words I could speak.

I didn’t know. Even if I had twenty bucks right now, I wasn’t sure I could buy a clue. I had so many thoughts and emotions spinning around I didn’t know if there was room to add a clue.

“That’s a good start. What about what you have with Lynx?” Just his name put me on alert, even if I had no idea what was going on there. “He says he’s going to help you with your past. Tell me how you feel about this.”

I sat for long moments, not saying anything. I wasn’t sure if he wanted me to talk about Lynx or finding out about my past, but I guessed they were linked in some weird way I had never thought possible.

The storm was brewing inside me, but I closed my eyes and simply breathed, hoping I could put it at bay.

"I'm nervous to speak to my mother. She's hated me since I was born, so there shouldn't be any change. I don't want to see my father." I was adamant on that one. I wanted nothing to do with that man. "I'm still not sure how it will help me." I paused. "But if Lynx says it will…" I let my words drift out. I was going to say that H-word then thought better of it.

"What if Lynx doesn't follow through?" he asked.

My gut twisted as pain speared through it. I didn't want Lynx to be like everyone else. I wanted him to be the one who was different, who knew what they were doing. I wanted to have something to hold on to, even if it was by the tips of my fingernails. I wanted him to be that, but the little niggling of doubt was a lot to bear.

I only shrugged.

He continued, "Will you find her without him?"

That was the million-dollar question, and as I sat there in the silence, I decided, "Yes, I will."

"What are you going to do about Drew?" The doctor was good today, because this shot through my heart.

I shrugged again, not giving any more to him this time.

"No, young lady. As your doctor, I need you to have a plan in place for what you will do when you feel down. You get to choose whatever techniques we talked about, such as the deep breathing; counting to fifty when your anxiety builds up; doing some type of relaxation, like yoga, to keep yourself centered; or writing all of your feelings in a journal. Then when you close it, you find something positive to do. You have to learn to control where your mind goes and retrain your way of thinking so it's not negative. I can't let you out of here without it."

That perked my attention. I was so stepping out of those doors tomorrow, the unknown be dammed.

"But Drew is the catalyst which brought you to the point of needing to come here."

I bit my bottom lip and pulled my knees to my chest, wrapping my arms around them. "I'm not sure I can go and see him. I'm not sure I can stay away, either. I need to know me before I make that decision. I need to get back my control."

"Sounds like you're relying on Lynx for that."

I couldn't deny that I was. He seemed to have his shit together and knew what he was doing. At least his words proved that, but who knew for sure?

"When I put you two together, I never thought you two would come up with a plan to meet up after therapy." He sounded a little discouraging. That wouldn't stop me, though. If Lynx came, I was going for it. "Since it sounds inevitable, professionally, I need to say something." *Okay...* "Dependency. I've seen how you are with Lynx. You need to make sure you are doing this for you, not because of Lynx."

I stared at him, thinking, *I am doing this for myself; I just don't want to do it alone*. I didn't think I could. I didn't think that made me dependent on anyone. If anything, it was the support system Wrestler McMann had droned on about when I had kept telling him I had no one for that. Now, I did and was going to take it however it came. I couldn't say I wasn't nervous as hell about it, but if I could gain my power and control back, I was going for it.

I said nothing.

"I want you to be aware of it," he finished.

Nurse Hatchet took that moment to walk in the door. Ready to get the hell out of this room and not have to come back, I rose from the chair.

"Reign," the doctor said, and I reluctantly turned back to him, not wanting to hear any more or talk about my feelings again. None of it, but I wasn't going to screw up my shot of blowing this place. "I'm very proud of you, young lady."

That knife speared me. No one had ever been *proud* of me before … ever.

"You don't realize this, because you were dealt a hand in life that many never have to experience, but you are incredibly strong. You may not feel it, but you are. People don't get thrown blow after blow, only to still be standing upright. You have a future, and you need to grasp it."

I had no words for the man. However, inside, something began to grow, and it was warm and inviting.

I tipped up the corner of my mouth, giving him the closest thing to a smile I could, and then walked out the door.

That night was like no other. I actually felt a twinge of excitement, an unusual feeling for me. I grabbed on to it because it warmed me.

***

"Now, Reign," Nurse Hatchet started upon opening the door to my room.

I had been waiting on her for what felt like forever. She had brought me my breakfast and pills earlier. Although I had been too excited to eat, I had choked down some toast since she said the pills wouldn't feel well on an empty stomach.

She went over my pill schedule. Yes, I had a pill schedule: two in the morning and one at night. If I still wasn't feeling quite right, I had a second pill that I could take at night.

I still had mixed feelings about the pills, but I was going to try.

"Yeah?" I responded, more than ready to get the hell out of there. I hadn't slept at all last night, yet I wasn't tired in the least. No, I just wanted to step outside those walls.

Nurse Hatchet came up close. "Your life is worth too much for you to take it. You are someone. You are an intelligent woman who deserves to find happiness, wherever that comes from. You have choices, and *I* expect *you* to make the right ones. You only get one life. It's up to *you* to decide how to live it."

My eyes began to well up with tears I tried hard to hold back, but my throat was starting to tighten, and I knew it wouldn't be long. No one in my life had ever had enough concern to give me any sort of advice in this world. I'd had to learn everything the hard way. Never had anyone given me any direction. Consequently, her giving me that was one of the biggest gifts I had ever received.

She reached out and took my hands, and I forced myself not to pull back as she held tight. "Happiness isn't something you've had much of, but it's out there, and you need to find it, hold on to it, and embrace it. Don't turn or push it away."

The damn woman had me figured out. I couldn't hold back anymore as tears slid down my cheeks. I wouldn't miss this place one bit, but a small, tiny part of me would miss Nurse Hatchet, even if I still didn't know her real name.

I tried to speak yet choked on my words. Clearing my throat, I told her, "I'll try." It was all I could give her. I didn't know what life held for me beyond those doors, but I had a very strong urge not to let her down. There was this woman who took care of me because it was her job, and I was thinking about not disappointing her. Weird.

She gave me a soft squeeze then released my hands. "Let's get you out of here."

***

I felt the smile come across my face as Andi came barreling toward the door. She was waiting for me, and I really liked that. She didn't stop until her arms were wrapped around me. I sucked in deeply and reciprocated.

"Let's get you home."

Chapter Ten

Walking into Andi's apartment felt surreal. I had been here before many times, but this time, I was walking into it as my home, and that gave me a bit of unease. Her apartment was just like her with lots of yellows, oranges, and greens—happy colors, just like her. It was warm, inviting, and comforting. My boxes piled in the corner were a definite eye sore.

Andi led me to her spare room, and my heart sank. This woman took so much time putting together a space where I could feel comfortable. It looked almost exactly like my room before except with the boxes lining the walls. I didn't have much, but it was enough to make a mess.

She saw the emotion all over my face and left me alone to gather myself. I loved how she knew what I needed and allowed me to have it.

As I sat on the bed, I couldn't help chuckling at the irony of the situation. I had left one place where I spent most of my time sitting on a bed, only to return to another and do the same exact thing. So far, there wasn't much difference.

Andi didn't leave me to my thoughts long. "Come on. Help me cook."

I groaned. I was a terrible cook. The worst. I could burn water, no problem. Something in the oven would come out black. The only thing I could do was make a sandwich, which I used to live on. You can't burn those.

"I suck at cooking."

She just smiled at me like she was so excited I was there with her, and dammit, I was, too.

***

We sat, eating chicken and rice, which I did not touch in the cooking process, in the living room. The vibe between us was very off, but I should have expected it. Yes, we had left things on good terms, but that didn't mean everything between Andi and I was back to the way it was before. We needed to talk. Judging from the apprehension written all over Andi's face, though, she wasn't going to be the one to start the conversation. It was up to me.

I sighed, setting my fork down. "I'm sorry. I don't know what I can do to make it up to you or make things right between us."

She set down her plate immediately, relief washing over her features at my words. "I need to know you are really better."

"Huh?" Her words took me a bit off guard. I wasn't expecting them. I expected, "*It's all right*" or "*We'll work it out*." Not this.

"Better. Are you better?" She moved quickly over to the couch, sitting next to me where she grabbed my hand, and I breathed through it. "I need to know you aren't in that same place you were before. I need you to be better."

It was more of a plea than a question, but I answered, anyway.

"Better is relative." I shrugged then let it out. "The entire time I was in there, I wanted to get out so I could end all the pain. I was drowning, Andi, and I couldn't get up. I refused to take the medicine or talk to the doctors at first. I was in so much pain."

"Where did the pain go?"

That was a really good question. "I'm not sure. It's still there, but it's different now. I don't know how to explain it." I honestly didn't have a clue. It was still inside me because I felt it, but the sinking feeling I'd had didn't pull me as hard as before. All the swirling emotions were beginning to slow, but they hadn't found their resting place yet, and I didn't know how to express that to Andi.

"Do you want to kill yourself?"

I sucked in air, clenching my top lip in my teeth. That was the million-dollar question. Nevertheless, I had already decided the answer while I was inside.

"No." The word came out strong and sure, unlike how I felt

inside. "I talked about finding myself, the real me. I think I need to do that first."

The smile that crossed Andi's lips could have lit up a football field, and it gave me a small bit of confidence that I was doing the right thing.

***

Andi spent the previous night and all of that day not leaving my side. I knew she feared what I would do, but this keeping an eye on me like a hawk thing was a bit much. It did give us time to talk, though. I had talked more in the last few months than I had in my entire life. I had never been a talker; it's hard to be when you're told to be quiet all the time. You learned quickly to keep your mouth shut.

I was nervous, almost to the point of my hand being jittery. I had checked Andi's locks several times throughout the day, but she had never said a word. I had hoped that little quirk of mine would have disappeared while I was away, but that wasn't why I felt this way. It was because I had some decisions to make, and I was lying to myself. I was jittery because I had been out now for over twenty-four hours with no sign of Lynx.

It was asinine for me to think he would come right to me, but I had that H-word, and I could kick myself for it. Every second that ticked on the clock was a small bit of that H-word chipping away.

After the next full day of Andi's hovering, I was happy when she went to work. She didn't want to and was worried. However, I reassured her over and over and over that I would be all right. The truth was, I needed some time to myself. I needed to think, so that was what I was doing.

I needed a plan, one without Lynx in it. I didn't survive all that time out on the streets without being smart. He might show; he might not. Regardless, I needed to gear up for the latter because sitting around this apartment wasn't helping.

First things first, I called my old boss, Judi, at the bar. Luckily, she needed someone part-time starting in a week. The waitressing job didn't fare as well. It was a big no, but at least I had something.

I then grabbed Andi's laptop, firing it up. I typed in Rebecca Jameson into the search bar, hovering over the enter key for quite some time before eventually hitting it. Several things popped up, but it appeared there was a famous actress by the same name. Judging from the picture, the woman looked around my age. It was a dead end.

I typed in Robert Jameson. Surprised wasn't the word for it. Shocked, torn in a small way, happy. The first thing that popped up was an obituary. I was scared of the man. Terrified. I had never wanted to see him again, but I didn't expect to see this. I clicked on the link, opening up the document, and sucked in a breath. My body temperature spiked as my father stared back at me, his cold eyes still as hateful as I remembered.

I read though the words, not feeling an ounce of sadness. Should I? I couldn't, not after what he had done to me.

It said he had died of massive heart failure and was survived by Rebecca Jameson, no mention of me. Why would it? I was nonexistent to them. However, it didn't stop the small pang of hurt that aimed right at my chest, and I could feel the waters beneath my feet beginning to swirl.

I closed my eyes and took in some calming breaths. *I can do this. I can.* Opening them back up, my father's gaze cut through me like a knife. Yes, if it made me a bad person, then so be it, but I was glad he was gone. He was one less person I had to worry about coming to find me. He didn't need to matter anymore. Ever.

I wasn't going to tell Andi. If she even suggested I go to his gravesite, I would lose whatever I had in my brain holding it together.

Trey. I needed to get ahold of him to help me find my mother. I liked this. It gave me purpose, a goal. It made me feel like I was doing something worthwhile instead of just sitting on the couch and staring into space.

I didn't have my old phone; therefore, I didn't have Trey's number. I could go to the bar, but the only thing I could do there was wait for him. As a result, I did the next best thing: I called my boss who gave me his number.

When I dialed, it went to voicemail.

Two days later, when I hadn't heard back from him and still had no word from Lynx, I started to feel anxious. I could feel it climbing up my skin, cloaking me in heat, each inch it covered getting hotter and hotter. I couldn't control my breathing, and my hands began to shake.

I wanted to believe Lynx would come back, but each tick of the clock was a second lost.

Deep breath, Reign, I told myself, sucking in a breath as I sat on the toilet.

Andi was making dinner, and I didn't want her to see me like this. I didn't want to worry her, and I knew it would be exactly what she would do.

In. Out. In Out, I chanted as I inhaled and exhaled. *You're all right, Reign. You'll figure this out.*

I kept sucking in air. After several minutes that felt like hours, the heat began to recede. It didn't fully disappear, but at least my hands weren't shaking anymore.

I rose from the seat and looked in the mirror. My eyes looked scared. I closed them and reopened them, hoping they would change. When they didn't, it felt like a punch to the gut.

The plan, Reign. What's the plan? The plan … right.

I kept breathing and then began counting down from fifty. At number twenty-two, I felt the control slowly come back and grasped on to it with two hands.

Looking back in the mirror, I watched color come back to my face as my eyes began to look more relaxed. It was then that something weird happened.

I felt … pride. I was proud of myself for coming back and not getting sucked down into the dark tunnel. I had that control, and that was a great feeling.

I hadn't heard anything from Trey, but it didn't affect me as much as not hearing anything from Lynx. It had been five days since I had gotten out, and nothing. He had forgotten about me, not that it was a hard thing to do. My parents had done it easily enough, but I wanted him to be different.

Digging through my stack of stuff, I finally found what I had spent the last hour looking for: a blue and gold, large shoebox. Gripping it tightly, I pulled it from the larger one. I had almost forgotten I had it. It had been so long since I had looked at it.

This was the only thing I had that connected me to my past. This was it, and it was in this small, little box. It was sad my life was reduced to this container.

I opened the lid, sucking in a deep breath. Inside were documents of my early life, including my birth certificate, the report from when I was taken, and my first foster family's information.

Tears welled in my eyes before I pushed them back. I needed the address of my mother. It was a long shot, and I had no faith she would actually live there, but with my "help" not responding, I had to do something. I shuffled through the papers, finding the exact one I needed. As my eyes skimmed, I found the address. Gathering the rest of the papers up, I shoved them back in the box and then shoved the smaller box into the bigger one.

I grabbed Andi's laptop and plugged in the address. I didn't have a fancy phone that had GPS anymore. I was lucky enough Andi had gotten me a prepaid flip-phone for emergencies. I was so grateful for it. It was just the small bit of security I needed.

I wrote the directions diligently, noting it would only take a few hours. I knew it wasn't the smartest thing to go alone, but I had dropped Andi off at work today, so I had her car. Since she was getting a ride from a friend of hers, I didn't have to worry about that.

Would she like it that I went? No, but it was something I had to do. I wanted to know why. Why did she allow my father to hurt me? Why didn't she put me first? Was I nothing to her?

The motivation to find the answers was what pushed me. It was a drive, a purpose, a reason to keep going, to find out why I was the way I was. The sea beneath me was spinning, but I was treading water for the first time, strong enough not to get swept up in the current. *I could do this. I* had *to do this.*

I was a bitch because I only left Andi a note, knowing she would be livid with me. I should have called her at work and told her, yet I didn't know how she would react.

I grabbed my bag, throwing a few things in, instantly missing that I couldn't throw my gun inside for protection. Andi had said I wasn't ever getting it back, and "*It wasn't in the apartment, so don't even try to find it.*" I thought about what I could grab. The only feasible thing was a knife. It was stupid since I didn't have much control over it, but it was all I could get.

I didn't know what I would find or even if I would see my mother, but I needed something to keep me safe. I needed to feel some type of control. After all, knowledge was power, and she held the key.

I tossed the bag over my shoulder just as a loud banging noise came from the door. I jolted, looking to see if the locks were in place. They were. I breathed out on that one before slowly inching toward the door and looking through the peephole.

Everything stopped. For one moment in time, I felt time stand still. Lynx was outside the door. He was there. He had come … for me. *Holy Shit!* An unusual feeling came across me, although I feared trying to label it as joy or excitement. I hadn't felt either of those since my time with Drew, and that was the only time I had felt them. They were back. *He* was back.

My hands began to shake as the realization set in that Lynx

wasn't like the others. He didn't leave me behind to be forgotten forever. No, he had kept his word and come for me. It stabbed me that I had doubted him, but with my record, it wasn't good odds. He did, though. He had defied those odds and shot right through them.

My fingers continued to tremble as I unlocked the locks. I stared at the door handle for a beat, trying to gain my composure before opening it to him. A knock on the other side had me jumping and gasping. I flew into action, turning the handle and opening the door.

He wore jeans that looked faded beyond their years, black boots, and a black T-shirt. He looked utterly different than when he had worn the hospital scrubs, and I hesitated to say, undoubtedly attractive. He was taller than I remembered; I had to tip my head back to meet his. His face looked softer than before, though there was still an edge to it. His hair was cut to his scalp, but his eyes … His eyes called to me, sucking me in and making me breathless.

"Reign." He said my name in a low groan that sent shivers down my spine.

I had missed that sound. I was in such shock that he was actually standing before me that words lodged in my throat. All I could do was smile—yes, genuinely smile—at all that was Lynx.

I watched in avid fascination as his face contorted from his brows drawing together then relaxing, and then a grin tipped up his lip.

My smile faded when I realized what I was doing: flirting … with Lynx. I shook my head, trying to clear the fog out of my head. I couldn't flirt. I didn't flirt … ever. Even when attractive men had come into the bar, I never had. Why him? Why this man?

"Babe, I liked it better when you were smilin'. What took it off your face?"

I couldn't tell him that, for a brief moment, I had forgotten about all my problems and that everything in my world had focused on him. I didn't think of Drew or Andi, my life or job, nothing but him for that small blip of time. Him being this close to me covered me with a shroud of comfort that I had never had in my life. For the first time, I wanted to run into his arms and feel them wrap around me, surrounding me within his safety. No, I wouldn't tell him any of that.

I cleared my throat, giving my mind a second to come up with something to say. "I just wasn't expecting you," I said stupidly. I didn't say I was good at covering it up. If anything, I should have just kept my mouth shut instead of answering.

"I told you I'd come." His arrogance did not go unnoticed by me, but I would give him this one, only so I didn't have to tell him my real reasons.

I lifted my shoulder in a noncommittal shrug.

"You thought I wasn't coming," he said confidently.

I schooled my features, hoping like hell I didn't give the relief or happiness away, but I was pretty sure I did. How else would he have been able to call me on it?

"It doesn't matter."

He moved fast, stepping into my space, and I panicked, the anxiety hitting me hard. I went to take a step back, but his hand came out, landing on my hip. My blood began thundering through my veins rapidly. It took everything I had not to move away from his touch, but something in his eyes was telling me I needed to stay exactly where I was.

"First, I'd never hurt you, Reign." Even though I believed him, I was unnerved, so I just nodded my head. "Second, no lies. What you and I have together cannot have lies between us. Not small ones like 'I'm not tired' or ones like you telling me it doesn't matter. It fucking matters."

It did, more than I could ever express. Not to mention, it scared the ever loving shit out of me that it mattered so much, and there wasn't merely one reason. There were so many I was losing count. His showing up on the doorstep gave me a small bit of that H-word I knew I shouldn't have, but for the first time, I wanted to cling to it.

He was right, though. What we had wasn't built on lies. Sure, it had started in a hospital therapy room, but there were no secrets or lies. I had told him everything, and he had done the same. That couldn't change. Even more, I didn't want it to change. I wanted to trust him and have him trust me.

It was strange that I felt such a connection to this man, to want to have these things with another human being. For the longest time, I hadn't thought I deserved them. Now, I still wasn't sure I deserved them, but it felt good, and I couldn't back away from any of it.

I sucked in deeply, knowing the words I needed to speak. I didn't know if he realized how damn hard it was for me to admit, how letting him in was a huge step for me, one I really wanted. "It matters that you came. Thank you."

His face changed at my whispered words right before my eyes, the anger or frustration draining from him as the tension in his shoulders began to relax a little.

"Let's go in," he said, taking two wide steps inside, and since I was so close, I took them, as well, until he kicked the door shut with his boot.

I became hyper-aware of every single movement he made, from the way his arm swayed as he moved to the small tick in his neck. And as our eyes connected, I could see the fire blazing in his. I could only assume that for me to admit it mattered meant something to him, something big. It scared the ever-loving shit out me, but not in a fear for my life way; in a whole new way that was odd yet compelling.

We were close, not nose to nose, but closer than I had let any man get to me in a very long time. Nerves started sparking throughout my body, especially my heart, from the look he was giving me. He wanted to kiss me. I could see it as plain as day, but that couldn't happen. I had locked that part of me up years ago, and as much as I felt the zing of it through my bones, I couldn't reopen that. I wasn't ready.

I pulled out of his grasp, stepping back and breaking the connection. I needed air to breathe, and I was pretty sure there wasn't enough in the apartment for me.

Moving to the other side of the kitchen table, I put a huge amount of space between us and grasped the back of one of the chairs, needing something to steady me.

"Are you okay?" His voice was laced with concern, which only added to my confusion.

In truth, I had only been kissed by one man who meant something to me. I had never gone any further than that unless it was out of necessity. In a lot of ways, I was so new to any of this, especially the whirlwind of feelings that kept piling on top of the other.

I wasn't okay, not really. The scariest part of everything was that I thought I *wanted* to kiss him. I, Reign, wanted to kiss *him*. My hands began to tremble at the realization.

To most looking in, it wouldn't be a bad thing at all. He was a very good-looking man any woman would want, but I couldn't. I was too messed up, too broken, too used.

I felt myself sinking as I stared down at my hands gripping the top of the chair. It wasn't helping me stay grounded anymore. This flip-flop of emotions was wearing on me. I went from determined to excited to lustful to sadness. It was all too much. I had been taking the pills the doctor had prescribed, but they didn't seem to be doing any of their voodoo magic on this situation, or maybe they were and my reaction would be worse.

"Reign." My name being said from only feet away snapped me to attention, but I didn't have time to think. Lynx pulled me into his body, wrapping his arms tightly around me.

I froze, unable to move, my arms stiff at my sides. Then he began rubbing his hand up and down my back, and it felt good.

"You're okay. I've got you," he whispered in my ear.

Something inside my head clicked. For the first time, I felt those words to my soul. *I've got you.* He had said each of those words with such authority and conviction that I had no choice except to believe him. Each muscle in my body began to lose its tension.

Without thinking about it, I wrapped my arms around his torso. It was such a mundane thing for most people to do, but for me, it was big. It was a huge step I didn't think I would ever cross with a man. It was one leap I was scared shitless to take, but I needed it. I needed him. I missed him, and the fact that he had come back for me told me that I mattered to him.

This moment was enormous on so many levels, and the darkness around me didn't bog me down. If anything, the tides slowed as I melted into him.

I turned my head so my cheek rested on his rock hard chest as tears filled my eyes, silently spilling over my cheeks.

I didn't let go. I couldn't let go.

His touch was so reassuring. The light grazes of his fingertips up and down my spine and his other hand snaking up to lay against my neck were like he knew exactly what this moment meant for me and was helping me through it as best as he could. He didn't use words; it was his mere presence that caused my body to fully relax into him, something I had never done with anyone. I still didn't understand that, but I was going with it. After all, the moment was what mattered.

Although his shirt became soaked with my tears, I couldn't stop them. It was like they were cleansing me, freeing me in some way. We simply stood there for a long time while he let me get out what I needed to and absorbed everything I gave him. Selfishly, I let him. I needed it. I needed that safe place to let myself go.

Andi had been that person for so long, but realizing how much I relied on her had been an eye opener. I didn't want to shift from needing Andi to needing Lynx. I was aware of it, yet at the moment, I couldn't stop myself.

His strong hands came to my shoulders, and I gasped as he pushed me back so he could look at my tear-stained cheeks. They hadn't stopped flowing, and I was sure I looked a mess.

As his hands left my shoulders and came to cup my cheeks, my heart stopped along with my breathing. The touch was so gentle, so personal, so intimate, leaving me feeling so bare—bared to him, bared to myself—but I didn't pull away.

He swiped the tears with his thumbs as he said softly, "Babe, you get these tears because I get that you need them, but you've got this. You've got me."

More tears flowed. What he had said was so sweet it cracked my heart. He was doing something to me. It wasn't bad. No, it felt damn good and terrified me at the same time. I wanted whatever this was, but I was petrified of it at the same time.

The door to the apartment flew open, and quick as a flash, Lynx had me behind him. His arm was snaked around my back, pressing me to him, and my hands came up to his back, bracing for impact.

"Reign, I'm…" Andi's words were cut off as I peered my head

around Lynx's broad shoulders. "What's going on?" Her words were hesitant at she set her purse down on the chair, her eyes glued to Lynx.

I patted Lynx on the shoulder to tell him it was okay, but he didn't move his arm from me, holding me. The strange thing was I didn't feel trapped. No, I felt comforted.

"Andi, it's okay. This is Lynx."

Her eyes slowly came back to me, her brows drawn in a tight bundle. "Lynx?"

Had I not told her about Lynx? No, surely I had.

"I told you about him. I met him in the hospital."

Her face grew tight. "No, you did not, and you definitely didn't tell me that you two were this close." She waved her pointer finger up and down the length of Lynx's body, all attitude.

"I thought for sure I did." I hadn't? That didn't seem right. I thought for sure, during those conversations about my time there, I had told her about him. Hadn't I?

She jutted out her hip, placing her hand on it. *Oh, no. Here comes bitchy Andi.* I didn't get it much, but when she roared, watch out.

"No. I would have remembered."

I patted Lynx. "Let me go. I have to talk to her."

His hand flexed against my back, but he released me.

I moved quickly over to Andi. "I'm sorry I didn't tell you about him."

"So why is he here?" Anger laced her tone. I didn't get why she was so angry about the man, though. She hadn't even met him, and already, she seemed to dislike him.

"He's going to help me find some information about my past." My hand shook as I reached out and put it on Andi's shoulder, her hip jutting toned down instantly. "It's okay."

"You let him touch you," she whispered so softly I didn't think she meant for me to hear, but I did, and she was right. She also knew the significance of it, as well. From her wide-eyed expression, she was shocked, and I believed I saw a little hurt, as well.

"We'll talk about this later," I said, not wanting to get into it with Lynx right there. I couldn't explain things to myself, let alone explain to someone else. I definitely couldn't do it with an audience. I had taken steps, but they were baby steps, and that wasn't on the list.

"What's going on?" As she wrapped her arms around her body almost protectively, confusion of why she looked like that plagued me, but it was something I would have to figure out later.

"I found an address to my mother, and I'm going to go and check it out."

"You were going to go by yourself?" This question came from Lynx, who was still behind me.

Suddenly, I felt way too boxed in, too enclosed to the point of air being difficult to take in. I stepped out from between them so I could look at them both as I talked. That small bit of distance helped calm me slightly.

"Yes. I need to get control back in my life. I have questions that need to be answered." I eyed Lynx. "I thought a lot about what you said. I need the knowledge. I need to know the why. Why did she allow my father to hit me? Hurt me? Why didn't she protect me? Mothers are supposed to do that: protect their young. Why didn't she? What was wrong with me that she didn't?" As the questions came out, the hurt pierced through me like a knife starting to shred me. The darkness moved in, suffocating the room. I tried to breathe through it, but I was on a roll with the questions and couldn't stop. "Why didn't she want me? Why didn't she fight for me? Why didn't she love me or show any bit of love toward me? Why didn't she care about me?" Angry tears cascaded down my face. I knew I was ranting, but I didn't care.

One thing I had learned from the doctor was talking about it and letting it out helped. Having the only two people I trusted in the world to do it with was even better.

"Babe," Lynx said, taking a step forward.

I stepped back and shook my head. "Don't. Give me a minute." He couldn't touch me right now; I was too raw. I needed air to breathe.

I moved to the kitchen, which wasn't far from the living/dining area, my thoughts going up and down slippery slopes. Why was everything I had to deal with such an issue? How come I couldn't be like the rest of the world and just deal?

I decided in that moment that I was going to be one of those people. I was going to be one of those who could handle it when things went badly. I was going to learn to cope and find answers because being this way wasn't working for me. How I was going to do that was up in the air, but having that thought in my head gave me the determination to figure it out.

"Reign?" Andi asked.

I wiped at my face before facing the two people who had decided I wasn't getting much space and followed me.

"Yes, I'm going to go and find my mother. I was going to go alone." My eyes focused on Lynx. "I didn't think you were going to come, so I was going to do it on my own. I'm pretty proud of myself for that." I focused on the two of them. "It's not going to be easy, but I'm doing it." I felt to my bones the confidence in my words, and I loved every second of it.

It made me feel just a tad bit stronger, something I craved.

Chapter Twelve

“I’m coming with you,” Lynx practically demanded, crossing his arms over his chest in challenge. Little did he know he wouldn’t have a fight over this. I was happy he wanted to come with me, that he gave a shit.

“Okay,” I replied.

A smile came across his face, lighting up the entire space. The warm feeling in my belly grew. I let it alone, though, because it felt good. These days, I was storing everything good as much as I could, never knowing when the dark hole would want to drag me down again.

"Are you sure this is a good idea after what happened last time?" Andi spoke up.

I had no doubt she thought that whatever I found would send me to the place where she had found me before. I had to admit I was scared of that, too, but I was in a different place.

"I need to do this, Andi. I didn't know what I was getting into last time, and I wasn't expecting it. With my mother, I don't have high expectations."

"But what if you can't take it?" The panic in Andi's voice rocked me to my core. I didn't want to upset her again. I didn't want her to worry. It was another reason I had wanted to get out of there before she got home: seeing the hurt sucked.

"I don't have any answers for what will happen. All I know is I have to do this. I have to find out why. Whatever happens or comes of that, I'll deal with it." How I would deal with it was the question of the hour. However, I would do my damnedest, especially since I didn't want to bring Andi down again. It was a whole new reason to fight my way out.

"Do you want him to go with you?" she mumbled, tipping her head in the direction of Lynx. It was cute and almost funny, but I didn't laugh.

"I know this is sudden and different, but yes, I want Lynx with me."

A look of defeat fluttered across her eyes, tugging at my heart. I didn't understand it. Was she upset that I wasn't taking her?

I stepped close to Andi, sucking in deeply before I wrapped my arms around her, pulling her to my body. She rested her head on my shoulder, reciprocating the hug.

"I worry about you," she said in my hair.

"I know. I'm going to be fine. I'm hoping"—damn, I said the H-word—"that this will make things better for me … Help me understand better."

"I know," she whispered back, retreating from my embrace. "Be careful," she said into my eyes then turned to Lynx. "If anything happens to her, I hold you responsible." Her tone totally changed when she addressed Lynx, making the hairs on the back of my head stand up in surprise.

"I'd never let anything happen to her," Lynx said.

***

After giving Lynx the address and climbing up in his monster of a truck—I kid you not, it was huge, like having to lift my knee so high it touched my chest just to get in huge—the ride to the address was quiet. I was pretty sure Lynx was trying to give me some space after what had happened with Andi, and I appreciated that. I liked how he knew when to give me time to process things.

The drive seemed to go on for hours. Lynx would stop, and we would use the restrooms, grab something to eat, and then head back out. It sucked, though, because Andi forced money into my pocket before I left. I felt like a heel having to use it and not having my own. The feeling burned me. Still, I knew that no matter what, I was paying her back every last cent. Lynx gave me space on that, too, not demanding he pay or making me feel any shittier than I already did.

"We're about an hour out," he said, still facing the windshield. He had a profile I was sure women would swoon over: a strong jaw and nose with bowed lips that looked so damn soft. Even the scar he had didn't take away from the beauty that was this man. I wanted to ask him how he got it yet refrained. It wasn't my place. If he wanted to tell me, he would.

"Okay," I replied.

"You ready to talk to me yet?" He glanced my way, his face a mix of concern and something else I couldn't put my finger on.

I huffed out, "What do you want to talk about?"

"Want to first explain to me what your relationship with Andi is?"

That question caught me off guard. We had talked about Andi before. He knew she was my best friend; therefore, I didn't know where he was going with this.

"Sorry?"

"Are you two dating? Have you been together?"

I gasped, my stomach doing a triple summersault at the thought of it. Why on earth would he think this?

Chills raced down my arms as the memories of earlier flitted in my head. Her look of disappointment, the shadow that had crossed over her eyes, the way she had snapped at Lynx…

Holy shit. He couldn't be right, could he?

Lynx ginned. "I can tell by your deer-in-the-headlights look that you didn't suspect a thing."

I had to shut my mouth because my jaw dropped open. I hadn't.

How could I have missed something like that? As soon as I thought it, I knew the answer. I was so caught up in my own head I didn't see what was right in front of me.

"Oh, shit," I said softly, covering my mouth with my hand. "I didn't…" I couldn't say anything more. This could change everything between me and Andi, and I couldn't lose her.

"I get that you didn't, but a blind man could tell she loves you."

Shit. Shit. Shit. She loves me? Like that? My head spun as this tumbled around in a kaleidoscope of colors so vivid they were almost blinding.

With a *thunk*, I rested my head against the headrest, fully taking all of it in. First, I had closed off that part of me for so long that, not until Lynx, had any rumblings or tingles come to me. Second, she was my best friend, and if this were true, she could get mad that I didn't reciprocate those feelings.

She was beautiful—don't get me wrong—but I had never once thought of her as anything more than a friend, a best friend whom I cared deeply for, who had been there for me, stuck by me like no one else had. She had never elicited those tingles or feelings inside of me. I almost felt guilty for not feeling the same way because I could hurt her badly. No, this couldn't be happening. It just couldn't.

"Babe, I didn't mean to dump this shit on you, but you two are gonna need to have a talk."

Talk … I didn't want to talk. No, I wanted to run. I didn't want to talk to her about her liking me then tell her no. She of all people knew I didn't have relationships, but seeing me with Lynx had to have hurt her, and I absolutely did not want to do that. I never wanted to cause her any pain, not like I had before. Regardless, I had a feeling this was going to go badly no matter what way I dished it out.

“Yeah,” I answered. He was right; we were going to have to talk. I so didn’t want to, but if that was how she really felt, then it would need to be addressed. Of course, I hadn’t the slightest inkling of how to do that.

I dug down deep inside myself. I needed to deal with my mother first. Then I would talk to Andi. I could only handle one thing at a time, and adding in Lynx’s closeness, I was already juggling two. Math was never my strong suit, but I was definitely one over my quota.

“How have you been doing?” Lynx asked, changing the subject, something I was grateful for. The tension was there, but this was a good reprieve.

“Good, I think. I got my job back at the bar part-time.”

“That’s great, babe,” he encouraged, and it felt good to have that, even with my chest heavy at the new revelation.

I kept going. “I’ve been searching for a steady job, but there aren’t that many out there for someone like me.”

“What do you mean by that?”

I shrugged, looking out the window. “All I’ve ever done is wait tables and bartend. There are only so many bars and restaurants around this place.”

“Maybe you need to do something else,” he suggested.

I wanted to chuckle yet held it in.

"Right. Like what? There isn't much for a high school drop-out to get." I had always had a complex that I hadn't finished school. I had hated it when I was there since the kids were downright cruel, but looking back, I wished I had that small, little piece of paper, just to show I had accomplished something in life. As it stood right then, I had nothing, which didn't sit right with me.

"Anything you set your mind to. What did you enjoy growing up?" His question made my throat constrict.

"I didn't have things I enjoyed growing up. I didn't have toys or crayons or any of that kid shit." I thought back, not one thing standing out. At Christmas, I would get second-hand clothes, never any toys or anything fun. Regardless, I was grateful for them. I needed them, but it would have been nice to have something.

"Let's think about the last few years. What's something you enjoyed?" This question wasn't any better. It was really sad and made me realize just how far I had fallen into myself. It was time to climb up.

"All I've done is work since getting my own place."

"Do you watch TV?"

"Of course." Everyone did that. It was nothing special.

"What do you like to watch?"

He was going to laugh at me; I just knew it. I didn't want to tell him but did, anyway.

"Don't laugh," I told him, a small smirk playing on my lips. He said nothing, so I continued, "I watch home improvement shows, ones where they take old houses and fix them up." I turned to look at him, recognizing a small smile gracing his lips, but he didn't laugh. "But I can tell you I know shit about fixing anything and have never built anything in my life."

"You never know." He winked, and my heart did a flip at the silent gesture. I wanted to yell at it and tell it to stop, but it wouldn't do a damn bit of good. "Maybe we can find a birdhouse or something," he joked.

I felt the smile spread across my lips and looked down, instantly embarrassed.

"You know you have every right to smile, babe," Lynx said with conviction, but I hadn't reached that point yet, the one where I thought I deserved anything. Deserving anything wasn't on my mind while I dealt with the bumpy road I was on. Therefore, I said nothing, just stared out the window, watching the trees fly by.

"Reign," he said, and I turned to him, giving him my full attention. "I mean it. Everyone deserves to be happy, and sometimes, it happens when we least expect it." Those words hung in the cab until we pulled up to a small box house.

"This is it," Lynx said as I took in my surroundings.

Around the home's exterior were bushes that looked so overgrown they should have been pulled out by their roots and replaced. The brick and mortar looked decent, but the broken down car and camper off in the driveway looked like they could use a lot of work. The house didn't look horrible at all.

I wasn't sure what I was expecting, but this seemed almost

normal, whatever in the hell that meant.

“Let’s park around the block, and then we’ll go up.”

Puzzlement filled me. “Why?”

“Trust me?” he asked.

I froze. I hadn’t expected him to ask me something like that so bluntly. Trust had always been something I didn’t give. It made me vulnerable. Giving someone your trust meant they could hurt you in ways you never dreamed, and it wouldn’t be a physical pain. No, it would be the emotional backlash that killed.

Then again, on the flip side, I did trust him. It was in my gut, and I had to follow it.

“Yes,” I answered.

He grinned like my answer was the perfect one before he pulled onto a side street and parked the truck.

My heart began to thump in my chest so hard I swore if you looked at my flesh, you could have seen it. My skin got clammy just as my hands began to sweat. Air didn’t want to go into my lungs, and I had to pull hard for it. The blackness was threatening me. It was right on the cusp, and if I didn’t hold on with two hands to something, anything, I was going under.

When a hand on my knee caught my attention, I turned to Lynx.

“Calm,” he said soothingly. “You’re just fine.” His eyes told me it was going to be okay as he gave my leg a soft squeeze that I didn’t pull away from.

I just wished I could get my body to listen. It was strung so tightly I didn’t know what would loosen it. I breathed in and out, hoping it would work.

"She hates me, Lynx. Why am I even here?" I pled with a crack in my voice. I was struggling. I was digging down deep for some sort of strength to get me through this, and it was only coming in small amounts. It wasn't fast enough as the darkness began to threaten.

"You tell me," he responded, not answering my question, obviously trying to get me to talk so I would calm down.

I drew in a deep breath, letting the air fill my lungs, my hands calming from the shaking before I answered, "To get answers about why she allowed my father to hurt me."

He didn't give me an inch as he prompted, "And …?"

"To find out why she didn't fight for me when they took me away." I felt kind of proud of myself for getting it out. It was small, but it was the little bit of confidence I needed. It didn't stop the nerves or the panic attack that was right there, but it helped relieve it a bit.

His knowing eyes bore into mine. "Right. You deserve to know. Knowledge is power."

"I remember," I whispered softly, recalling every little thing Lynx had ever said to me. He didn't need to know I remembered all the details, even how he was sitting in the room when he had said them. Lynx was right, and that was why I was here: to get that knowledge.

"You always start what you finish. Always follow through once you've made your decision. Right or wrong, you deal with that after, but never back down." His words seemed to have come from experience, and I had none, so I was taking his.

I nodded in confirmation.

"Let's go." He nodded back.

I couldn't make my hand reach for the door handle. It wouldn't move to grab it as frustration built alongside my nerves. The panic began to move around me in swirls as I fought to gain control.

I closed my eyes. *You can do this. You have to do this.* I chanted those phrases in my head over and over as my door swung open.

Lynx was standing there. He didn't extend his hand; somehow, he knew I needed a minute to gather myself.

Digging down deep, I could feel my body changing. My shoulders rose, my spine stiffened with resolve, and my hands stopped shaking. *Yes, I can.*

Once I rose from the seat, Lynx held his hand out to me, which I took willingly. One, it was like he was my helping hand, so I clutched it, and two, because the damn truck was so big I was sure to fall out of it without any help.

The door slammed shut and bleeps came from the locks. Lynx turned to me.

"You deserve answers. I'm so damn proud of you for taking this step."

My insides warmed. His compliment hit me on so many different levels I didn't have time to count them all. However, I felt it down to my bones, and I liked it.

"Let's do this." The authority in his voice was comforting. I focused on that, or tried to, the entire walk to the driveway.

Upon hitting the space where the camper rested, I froze, my feet unable to move. It was like they were stuck in thick cement.

"Reign?" Lynx's voice seemed far away as I stared at the brick home. Thoughts scurried through my head like little mice on their way to find food. There were so many questions, so many what ifs.

I didn't remember this place. Had I lived here with them? And what if I had been a better little girl? Would my father not have hurt me? Would my mother have treated me better?

I was getting slammed from all directions by them, my head beginning to spin. The dark pit below me began to open, sucking me in. My only thought was, *If I let it take me, then I wouldn't have to deal with this.*

"Reign!"

The voice was loud, and I turned to the source: Lynx.

"Babe, you've got this. Answers, remember?" That voice… I was coming to find that I could listen to it all day and never get bored with it. It was deep and powerful.

Slowly, things came into focus as the vast darkness threatened to take me away. *No, Reign, pull your shit together,* a small voice in my head rang out, and I listened to it. I forced the thoughts inside of me to calm. I was in control of this, not them. They did not have power over me. I had the power, and I was going to take it.

I looked Lynx dead in the eye with every bit of strength I had. "Let's do this."

He gave me one of those rare smiles, and I felt my knees

weaken, but I desperately tried to brush it off.

Walking to the door, the doorbell stared back at me like a wicked snake. If I were to touch it, it would be dead set on biting me. Lynx didn't touch it, either; he waited. He was there, beside me, but he wasn't going to do the job. I had to.

Snake be damned, I pushed the bell. We heard it blare and then movement behind the door.

My pulse spiked as a cold sweat beaded all over me. This was it. I was going to see my mother again. Then it hit me that she probably didn't even live here. She had probably moved a long time ago, and I was getting myself all on edge for nothing. Of course, I wasn't sure if that was wishful thinking or avoidance talking.

Locks on the other side turned and then the knob of the door. When it opened, I fully stopped breathing.

The woman was about five-feet-five, my height, with long, dark brown hair, like mine and emerald green eyes, again, like mine. What was different were the lines marring her face. They weren't laugh lines around the eyes; no, these were like I had seen time and time again. These lines were from stress, hard work, and if I wasn't mistaken, lots and lots of drugs.

"What?" she barked, her brow raised at us.

It took me a moment before I asked the question I already knew the answer to. "Are you Rebecca Jameson?"

She held a cigarette and waved it around as she talked. "Who wants to know?"

"I'm Reign."

She stared at me blankly, nothing registering in that head of hers.

That was the moment the fire began to burn in my belly, but not from nerves. No, it was from anger. She didn't remember me? I had the same first name that was on my birth certificate, which she had to have given me.

I gave her a little help. "Your daughter."

She burst out laughing, the air getting trapped in her throat as she began to crouch.

There I was, serious as a heart attack, and she was laughing … at me.

I didn't move.

"My daughter is dead," she said between coughing and laughing.

What was wrong with this woman? I wasn't dead. I looked just like her, only younger.

"I can assure you that I'm not dead." I placed my hands in the front pockets of my jeans, the urge to reach out and strangle the woman burning brightly. I fed off that anger, allowing it to help keep me together.

Rebecca took some heaving breaths, a smile still plastered on her face as she said, "She died when she was six." Which was the time I had been taken away from them.

I had questions, and I was going to ask them.

"If she died, why are you laughing about it?"

I felt Lynx's heat at my back. It was all the encouragement I needed as the flames scorched higher inside me.

She chuckled. “Because she was a pain in my ass.”

My heart felt the hit on that one, but I kept charging along.

“I’m laughing because, even after she was gone, Robert left me. I should have known he wouldn’t be man enough to raise someone else’s kid.”

The bricks above me started to tumble down, each hitting me on the head as everything I thought I knew was blown out of the water in an explosion so big it shook me to my foundation. I tried to hold on as it quaked.

“Someone else’s kid?”

She took a puff on her cigarette and blew the smoke out the door and into Lynx and my face. “I hooked up with my boss a couple of times. Robert couldn’t have any kids, so he knew I fooled around. Damn, he hated that little girl.” Every word that came out of her mouth came with nonchalance, like I had meant nothing to either of them.

The air around me began to press in, but I did my best to force it back.

“Yeah, I looked.” She looked me up and down. It was like her clouded brain had cleared and thoughts started firing. Her eyes widened, and she crossed her arms over her stomach. “It’s you.” This time, there was no laughter, only disbelief. She had to be shitting me if she thought I had bought that whole I-thought-you-were-dead spiel.

“I told you who I was; you refused to see it,” I said with

confidence I didn't have on the inside, but there was no way this woman was seeing any of that. "Who is my father?"

"Didn't think I'd ever see you again." She paused, and for a brief moment, my heart latched on to the words, hoping she would turn around and be happy to see me. Then she had to go and ruin it. "Damn. I could have lived my whole life without it. And you fucking look just like me. Fucking hell." The disappointment in her words was more than evident, and I tried to keep my anger from taking back over.

At least I knew now why my "parents" hated me so much. My mother was a cheat, resulting in me, pissing her husband off; something so fucking simple that had absolutely nothing to do with me. It was all on them. This was their burden, not mine. Yes, they had treated me like shit, and my life was hell, but what if I would have stayed with them like I had thought so many times before? I had thought if I would have been better, we could have been a family. I realized in that moment there was never going to be a family here. I was the product of an affair and had to live the consequences of it.

The earth below me started tipping, but it wasn't pulling me under. No, it was righting itself.

Sure, I had a lot of shit to deal with, but this part was clearer. The more I thought about it, the anger and hate for this woman swirled around me. She was never my mother, only an incubator, and by the looks of her, there was no telling what I'd had in my system when I was born.

"Who is my father?" My words came out monotone, but there was a tinge of demand there.

"You think I'm gonna tell you that? He doesn't even know you exist." Another blow, but I took it and still stood tall. "No matter. By the look of ya, he wouldn't want you, anyway." That one hit hard.

"Considering I look like you, and he fucked you, I'm sure he'd see me." Even though my comment was immature, it still felt good to say since it was true.

Lynx's hand came to my hip, giving me a slight squeeze that I didn't shy away from. I needed to know he was there, that he had my back. I was the one doing this, but he was there to support me if I needed it, and although I did, I wasn't going to let this woman see that.

"I'm not telling you nothing, and I don't want to see your face here ever again," she snarled.

"You don't have to worry about that." But I was going to find out who my father was in one way or another.

Knowledge is power.

Chapter Thirteen

"Where are we?" I asked as Lynx pulled the truck into a large lot. Off to the side was a lit up park. We were the only vehicle around, which made my stomach do a flip. "What are you doing?" I tried not to panic, but today had been too much. After the discussion with the incubator, I needed time to process, something Lynx had given me as he was driving, but apparently, he was done waiting.

"You've had a shitty day. Let's do something fun."

Fun? What the hell was that? I didn't do fun. I never had the money for it. I worked, paid my bills, and lived in my apartment. I did the occasional going to grab a bite to eat with Andi, but I didn't do fun.

"What?"

"Something fun for us to do. You may not want to, but you need it, and what I have in mind will help."

He was right. I didn't want it. I wanted to go back home and figure out who my father was. There had to be something that would tell me. The determination to find out burned red hot, and I was anxious to try to figure out who he was.

"I need to get back."

"No, you need to have fun and let all that shit go for a while. You said you trusted me. Has that changed?"

"Of course not," I answered.

"Then let's live."

***

I looked around the vast, open space. Fields lined the area with a baseball field in the center that had a large track circling it. "What are we doing here?"

Lynx reached into the back of his truck, pulling out a pair of tennis shoes then handing them to me. "Put these on."

I didn't take them, just raised my brow. "Why?"

He chuckled. "So much for the trust." He wiggled them in his hands. "I'm going to show you how I deal when I have a shitty day."

My curiosity was piqued. I really wanted to know. Any coping mechanism was like gold. Therefore, I grabbed the shoes, took my boots off, and put them on. They were quite big, but I made due by tying them extra tightly. Lynx kept his boots on as he led me to the large track. He didn't touch me, but he walked right beside me, close enough that I felt the brush of his arm every once in a while.

At the field, he bent down on one knee and made sure his laces were tied then rose. "Laps. We run laps."

I stared at him. He was joking, right? My jobs required me to be on my feet, but running wasn't on my list of things I did.

He smiled, reading the look on my face. "Yes, we run. It'll help you clear your head and get rid of all the shit by pounding it step by step into the track."

Lynx picked up one foot, pulling it to his ass, stretching his muscles. I stared in awe at his fluid movements. Each one was so precise and with reason. Each of his flexes made parts of my body come alive that I hadn't noticed since I had Drew in my life.

"You gonna stretch?" he asked, and I snapped my eyes away from his flexing, following his lead. My muscles were tight and not used to this, but surprisingly felt pretty good.

"Come on," he said, taking off in a jog.

I couldn't stop staring at the fluidity of his movements, like years and years of practice had been put into each. Of their own accord, my feet took off, catching up to Lynx.

We fell into step with each other, my breaths trying to keep up. On the second time around, Lynx spoke.

"I do this to clear the shit out of my head. When I run, I don't have to think about anything but my feet hitting each step. Any emotion I have racing through me, I push into the steps I take." He paused, and I thought about his words. Then I thought about my mother and her hurtful ones.

I sent them down to my feet and hit the pavement a bit harder than I had previously. It felt good, almost relieving.

"When I have visions of my brothers"—my stomach dropped for him—"I go to a track like this and run. I could run for fifteen minutes or hours. It all depends on what mood I'm in."

I was happy he had an outlet he could use to cope.

As each step I took hit the ground, I allowed the emotions of the day to fall with them, the tension slowly leaving my body along with my energy. Each step was putting distance between me and the buildup of pressure inside myself. Each time my knees came up and feet went down, I could work through the thoughts in my head as my body worked through the motions. Motions and emotions all worked together for a common goal: to keep moving, keep going.

"Catch me," he called out as he darted forward.

He thought I could catch him?

"Come on!" he called back when I didn't move. "Show me what you're made of."

I took off, pushing my used body hard. I gained feet on him, reaching out my hand and feeling the urge to tag him. With one more push, my fingertips grazed his shirt. *I did it!* I stopped, doubling over at the waist with heaving breaths.

Lynx's hand came to my back, and I stilled. Taking some more breaths, I let it go.

"You okay, babe?" he asked with laughter in his voice.

"I got you." I rose to see his smiling face, pride coming off me.

His hand came around my side, resting on my hip, the tingles hitting me hard with the slight touch. I wondered why he wasn't heaving like me. His touch wasn't helping.

He took a step closer, and I sucked in deeply. "You did," he said in his deep, baritone voice. He reached for my hand and placed a soft kiss on the top of it. Every bit of breath was knocked out of me because it was so tender, gentle. In that moment, I wanted to kiss him, but I was scared shitless of it.

He surprised me by saying, "Come on." Then he held my hand, tugging me back to the truck. He let go only long enough to grab a blanket from the back before he was leading me to a wide open area. I felt nervous, but at the same time, I didn't. Everything with Lynx came so naturally.

He laid out the blanket then motioned for me to sit. "Let's take a break."

Knowing I could use one of those after that run, I sat and Lynx followed, giving me some room, though not much. His shoulder and leg grazed mine from time to time, and instead of getting nervous about it, I began to like it. The warmth of him helped break the ice inside of me, and I cherished the heat.

I lay down, looking up at the sky beginning to fade into darkness, the glow of the sun peeking over the trees. My breathing calmed, and was it weird that I felt safe and comfortable?

I broke the silence of the night as Lynx lay down next to me. "So tell me; why Lynx? Is it your real name? Because I've never met someone with that unique one." In all the time we had spent together, we had focused a lot more on me than him, and I needed to know more.

He reached over and grabbed my hand, but I didn't fight it. I liked the touch too much.

"Last name. Brody Lynx. In the service, I went by Lynx and it stuck."

"I like it."

His hand gave mine a soft squeeze.

"What about your parents? Are you close?" He had said in the hospital that he had crippled a man for his parents. I had inferred that to mean he was close with them, and I was hoping I was right.

"They passed." His eyes held a vacant, glassy look. I instantly wanted to take that expression off his face, but he continued, "My mom had a heart attack, and my father couldn't handle her not here anymore and ended up getting sick with sepsis. He passed in the hospital."

"Oh, Lynx." I laid my head on his shoulder, trying to give him some sort of comfort.

"Shit happens, babe. You deal."

I nodded then asked, "Do you see your sister a lot?" I remembered him telling me about her back in the hospital. It was only a brief mention, but those were the things that stuck out in my head.

"A few times a month. She's married and has a kid, so I see her when I can."

I continued staring into the sky. "Are you close?"

"We don't call each other every day or anything like that, but

I'd say we are."

I really liked that he had someone he could turn to.

I had a question that I wanted to ask, but I was nervous to. After long moments had passed, I just said, "Can I ask you something?" Stupid, so damn stupid. I was already asking him things. Why would this be different?

He gave my hand a small squeeze. "You already are, babe. Ask me anything."

I sucked in deeply. "What took you so long to come to me?" I didn't want to sound needy or whiny; I genuinely wanted to know. I had lain in bed so many nights, wondering where he was and hoping he wouldn't let me down.

It was his turn to suck in deeply. "I had an episode."

My head snapped to him as he continued to look up.

"I was at the grocery store, walking down the aisle. All of a sudden, a loud pop came from above me. I didn't recognize until later that a bulb had gotten too hot and shattered. I was too busy pushing my way out of the store. Bottom line is, I wanted to get myself together before I saw you."

While it was unbelievably sweet he would think of me in that way, I felt a little sad about it also. I wanted him to have come to me. I could have helped him. I didn't know what I would have done, but I would have figured it out. Wouldn't I?

"Sorry, Lynx," I whispered as he turned his head to me with a soft smile.

"I was going to come to you as soon as you got out, but then that happened, and I didn't want you to see me like that."

My gut twisted, and I rolled to my side, fully facing him. "You've seen me a lot worse, Lynx."

He let out a gush of breath. "I know, babe. I know."

"It doesn't go away, does it?"

"No, babe. You just learn what works for you to combat it."

I tried not to let it get me down, but it saddened me that I would be living with this the rest of my life: learning myself and what I needed to do to keep myself in check. The medicine helped, but would I be on it for the rest of my life? I didn't know that answer.

"Running helped," I said honestly.

His fingers intertwined with mine. "Good." He lifted my hand to his lips and gave me a soft kiss.

***

"Your mother is a real shit."

My mood was tarnished as Lynx spoke. We had been driving for a while, and I had been riding a high from the time we had together. Sure, most people wouldn't categorize what we had done as fun, but they weren't Lynx and me. He had taken us somewhere where there wasn't a lot of people so both of our triggers would hopefully not come into play. We had laid together for hours, talking, and I had loved every second of it.

"Yeah," I answered, not wanting to talk about this. I didn't want to bring it all back up after I had stomped it into the pavement. "I prefer to call her an incubator."

He laughed deeply. I liked that I could make him lose himself and bring him some type of joy.

"Okay, we'll call her that. What's going on in that head of yours?"

So many damn things I felt like I was in a rubber ball being bounced around all over the place.

"It's on them, not me. I didn't do anything but exist. The way they treated me is on them. I can't feel like I wasn't good enough anymore, because no matter what I could have done, I had a huge black X on me from the moment I was conceived." I paused, not knowing if I should say the rest, but then went with it. "I wonder if I was better off in the foster homes than at home with them. He hated me so much. He would have made it a painful death, and no child should have to go through that." *Not even me,* I thought yet didn't say.

"You're right. All that shit *is* on them. They are sorry excuses for humans. I don't do the 'what if' game, though. It's a game you'll never win, you'll never see or know the response to. Therefore, it's pointless."

Damn if he didn't make a shit-ton of sense.

"I saw the way you looked when she told you about your biological father. What's your plan?"

I liked that he had said *my plan.* It was. It wasn't Lynx's or Andi's. No, it was mine to learn and discover.

"I'm going to find out who he is."

"Good girl. I'm proud of you."

I felt like I had just scored the winning touchdown in a football game, and part of me wanted to do one of those stupid, little dances the players did when they scored. He was proud … of me. *I* was proud of me.

I was working on finding a way to hold on to the light and not drown in the dark. I still couldn't say what the future held or even if someone like me would have a future, but I was learning to hold on to the moment.

"I don't know how I'm going to do it, but—"

"That's easy, babe. Go back and look at her employment history. There's a paper trail somewhere. You find out where she worked then start digging into who her boss was."

"You make it sound so simple," I grumbled.

"Babe, it's easier than you think."

And I believed him. The panic didn't come, surprising me. I had thought for sure searching for an unknown man and springing it on him that I was his kid would start it up, but it didn't, and I liked that, too.

***

"We're close to home."

I wanted to be relieved, but I was scared as hell to face Andi. If she really felt that way about me, it was something that needed to be discussed. However, with everything I had learned today, I didn't know if I could take more.

The day had been an emotional rollercoaster. First, Lynx had showed up then seeing my incubator and the shit she spewed, and finally, the park where Lynx and I had fun. I had to admit that going from low to high had taught me that with the bad, there was good out there. It had made everything balance out in a way I hadn't experienced before. Everything had always been weighted down on my shoulders, pushing me farther down. Unfortunately, the weight was still there. It just didn't seem as heavy for the first time, but I was afraid seeing Andi and talking about what needed to be discussed would tip that scale again.

"You wanna go and get something to eat, or you want me to take you to Andi's?" Lynx asked.

I turned to look at him. "Dinner."

It was selfish of me—I knew it—but it wasn't because Andi was probably waiting for me. No, it was the mere fact that I didn't want this night to end. I didn't want to say good-bye to him.

The corner of his lip tipped up. "Dinner, it is."

I had never traveled much out of my surrounding area, so when Lynx pulled up to a tan, brick building with windows on every side of it and lights flashing, I was excited. Yes, I was excited about going to dinner. Something so mundane that most people do regularly and didn't think twice about. For me, on the other hand, it was new, an adventure.

There I was, a twenty-one-year-old woman, and going out to dinner was exciting. I didn't let the thought seep in, though, because I was letting in the good, instead. I didn't want to ruin the moment. I couldn't.

The sign flashed Sully's, and underneath it was a billboard listing some Italian dishes. Since I didn't cook much, I only had spaghetti when Andi made it and brought it over or when I worked late at the diner and grabbed something to eat in the back before heading home. It dawned on me how closed off my life was, something I was going to change.

Lynx parked the truck and came over to my door, helping me out of his monstrosity.

"You know, if you downgraded just a bit, I could actually get in and out of your truck without so much effort," I teased, not shying away from him. No, I liked it. I also liked the glint in his eye from amusement directed at me.

He leaned in close, and I didn't move. "Babe, then I wouldn't be able to help you in and out of it," he flirted back.

Holy crap. I wasn't overcome with panic or the need to get away from him. No, I was … comfortable, something I had never truly been.

"I love it when you smile," Lynx said, reaching for my hand then lifting it to his mouth and giving it a soft kiss. My belly fluttered as the fire in his eyes burned brightly. "Come on; let's get you fed."

The inside of the restaurant was quaint. It almost looked like the diner I used to work in, and that made me relax even more. Lynx sat across from me in the booth, the waitress came, and we ordered.

There was something niggling me in the back of my head, so I had to ask Lynx, "What do you do for a living?"

"A little bit of everything." His vagueness wasn't going to happen. I lifted my brow for him to continue. "I told you I'm good at finding information. People come to me to find what they want to know, and I get it for them." He shrugged.

"So, like a PI or something?"

He chuckled. "No, babe. More like an independent contractor." He held out his hand across the table, and I didn't hesitate to put mine in his. "Sometimes, I do good things, sometimes, not so good." His hands tightened around mine. "Many people know my skills and pay top dollar to get them. I'm no saint, babe. But I'm not involved after I give my clients what they need. I don't touch whatever it is they do with the information."

"So if a pimp is looking for his cash, you go and find it?" I really only had my experiences to relate to, so I was going with it.

This time, I got a full-out laugh. It was a beautiful sight to see so close and an even better feeling that I had made him do it, despite not knowing what the hell he was laughing at.

"No, babe. You need to think higher: government officials, CEOs of fortune five hundred companies, real estate moguls, investors. They pay a lot for me to do what I do. I don't deal with common thugs."

Wow. He must really be good at what he does to get that high up on the financial food chain, which meant Lynx had money. Hopefully, he didn't think—

"No, I don't think you're after my money," he stated bluntly.

"How do you do that?" I said in a huff as he squeezed my hand again.

"It's written all over your face. You tell me so much just by a look."

I did?

"Yep, you do," he answered with a grin.

"You should have become one of those psychiatrists they made us talk to."

His lip curled in disgust. "Fuck no. I've got enough of my own shit."

"You could have used your talents for good and not evil," I joked. Damn, it felt so nice to do that: to let that part of me go and not close it up so tightly it suffocated, to really feel alive.

"I do both, babe. It's the way of the world."

I knew he spoke the truth. I had seen enough evil to know there were so many different types of it: different levels, different degrees.

When I got home, Andi was already asleep, and for the first time, I smiled while falling asleep myself.

Chapter Fourteen

I woke to the shower running. I couldn't believe I had slept the whole night through without waking up even once. In the hospital and even here, I couldn't get through the entire night. By some miracle that night, I had. I didn't know if I had Lynx to thank for that or the overwhelming feeling that there was some good out there.

I tossed the covers off and went in to the kitchen to make some coffee. Andi was always good at setting the thing up, so all I had to do was push a button, and it would start brewing. She knew me so well, probably better than I knew myself at times.

I sat at the small table, holding my cup of Joe in my hands, feeling the warmth hit me all the way down to my toes. Then I took my meds just as Andi came out, wearing jeans and a T-shirt, her blonde hair damp from the shower.

I had an instant tightening of my nerves. I had almost forgotten about needing to talk with her, but judging from her not so perky face, it needed to be done. Andi didn't do un-perky. No, she was always happy no matter what. Seeing her like this … I needed to make that go away.

"Come and sit," I told her after she had gotten her coffee.

She sat across from me, her eyes focused on her mug.

"Is there something you want to say to me?" I asked, trying to get the ball rolling. After all, it wasn't going away, so I needed to face it head-on, even if it scared the living shit out of me.

Her pained eyes caught mine. "I just …" a tear streaked down her face, cutting my heart to shreds. "I thought that you and I had something." Her words were soft and hushed, like she wanted me to hear them yet also didn't.

"I didn't know, Andi," I responded, her eyes coming to mine. "I've been locked in myself for so long it was all I could think of. I didn't see it." I sucked in a huge breath and gathered whatever strength I could muster. "You're my best friend in this world. I'm so sorry, but I don't have those feelings for you."

Another tear streamed down her cheek. "I get that now. I can't say it doesn't hurt, but it's on me. I made us out to be something we weren't. I'm sorry about that."

"I didn't even know you liked women," I confessed.

She shook her head. "It only started in the last few months before you went to see Drew. I should have never told you to go and find him." The dam broke.

I moved to her, wrapping her in my arms as she cried, the pain so evident it hurt me.

"I'm sorry. So, so sorry," she cried.

I brushed her hair as I held on tightly. "I hate to say it, Andi, but you did the right thing. Yes, I know Drew's alive, and I haven't forgotten about him, but he's happy with a family. I can't do anything about that. I would never want to hurt him like that."

She pulled away, her brow quirked. "Even though he hurt you for all those years?"

My mind wandered to the moment I had seen Drew again, and my heart cracked. It had hurt, and it still did. However, after seeing a small glimpse of happiness, I knew it was out there. I just had to find it.

"Even after all those years. I can't keep living back there. That's what's bringing me down. I need to live."

She pulled away from me. "Lynx," she whispered.

"It's not just him. It's that he taught me it's okay to be happy, to have fun."

"You like him."

It was hard to admit, but I had to. She was my best friend.

"Yeah, I kinda do."

She wiped the tears from her eyes, her smile coming back to her face. "Good. You deserve good."

I really believed I did, another first for me.

***

After a week back on the job, I quickly realized my feet were more acclimated to resting instead of being on them for ten hours straight. My boss had decided she needed me back full-time, and since I needed the money, I had quickly accepted.

The vibe in the bar hadn't changed, but I had. When I looked out amongst all the people, I didn't see the despair anymore. No, I focused on the laughter, instead. That alone put me in a better mood.

I hadn't found anything on my father via the web, but Lynx had told me to give him some time to come up with something.

Life was life, and I felt as if I were living it instead of just existing for once. It wasn't as though I were traveling the world or any grand gestures like that. No, it was more that I got out of the house.

Even after my conversation with Andi, she didn't change around me. She was bright and happy, taking me to some of her favorite places, and I had fun. Yes, fun. We laughed, smiled. It was like the me I was supposed to be had come out, and I didn't try to hide her.

The walls around me didn't feel as constrictive as before. I felt like I could breathe and live for the first time. The medicine had to be working. I had a follow up with Wrestler McMann in a few weeks. I thought he would be proud of how far I had come.

"Hey, babe." The words caught my attention.

I watched as Lynx slid onto a barstool, feeling almost giddy inside that he was there.

Lynx had picked me up the night before from my shift. He had taken me to get something to eat while we talked, and then he had taken me home. He had been doing that sporadically throughout the week, and I had to admit I enjoyed it when he did. While I was new at the whole guy thing, I thought things were going fairly well.

"Hey, yourself." I smiled welcomingly. "What can I get ya?"

"Bud. Bottle."

I made quick work of getting the beer, setting it in front of him.

"You're off at eight, right?"

"Yep." It was the first night I was off at a decent hour. Other people might not think it was decent, but when you normally worked until two a.m., eight was early.

"Good. We've got plans."

My smile widened as I leaned against the bar. "What's that?"

"It's a surprise," he replied before tipping his beer up and taking long, hard swallows.

I watched in avid fascination as his Adam's apple bobbed up and down. My tongue darted across my lip, instantly feeling dry.

"Babe, that's not a good idea."

My eyes snapped to his heated ones. "What?" I asked dazedly.

"Licking your lips. I'm a man, babe, and there's only so much I can take." It came out as a warning, but inside it made me burn, like sex hot.

A switch inside of me clicked, tingles spreading throughout my body and dampness growing between my thighs. *Oh. Shit.*

I turned away, embarrassed. "Sorry," I muttered. "I'll be back."

I needed a little bit of distance from him. In the time we had spent together, he had been so damn patient with me, holding my hand, for goodness' sakes, and kissing it. He had never once taken it beyond that, knowing he had to be slow with me. There were small touches, even a slight hug, but nothing more.

Was it wrong of me to want something more? To want more of his touch on my body?

I picked up a wet rag and began wiping down the bar as a waitress came up, giving me their orders. I filled them quickly, handing them back out. I didn't look down at Lynx for fear he would see into my thoughts.

The only touch from a man I had experienced that wasn't forceful, beyond my control, or for survival was from Drew. When he had kissed me, it had been thrilling and exciting, but we had never taken it a step further than that.

The punch to the gut hit at the thought of him, but like so many times before, I dug down deep, trying to shake it off.

The other men I'd been with…

I shook my head, not wanting to think of those others, not wanting to acknowledge some of the things I had done. I was ashamed of it, dirty for it.

Sex had always been a tool for me on the streets, something I could use to get what I wanted. It was all I had to give, and there were plenty of men willing to take it.

I had seen movies and the way the guys would be so tender with their women. I had never had that. I never believed I even wanted that, because I buried myself so deep I never thought of it at all. All sex reminded me of was hurt and pain.

I didn't want to associate Lynx with that. I didn't think I was capable of giving that part of me to a man. A man like Lynx—one that was so self-assured, handsome, and fun to be around—wasn't going to sit around and wait for the day when I might be ready. No … No man would do that. I was going to have to let him go.

My chest tightened to the point of pain at the thought, and tears sprang behind my eyes. I wasn't good enough. I was broken beyond repair. I could never make a man like Lynx happy. Hell, I could never make any man happy, because I couldn't give him what he needed, what every man craved. No band-aid or medication would ever fix the part of me that was so hurt, so torn.

As tears streamed down my face, I batted them away, turning away from all the customers. *Pull yourself together!* Work was not the place to do this.

The blackness I had kept at bay for the past week came back with a vengeance, swirling so rapidly it almost knocked me to my knees. I clutched the small desk that held the register, trying to get some grasp on myself, trying to stop myself from falling under, trying to gain some sort of control.

Large hands came to my arms, and I jumped, turning around fast. Lynx was there, his face set in hard lines.

"Come on." He grabbed my hand, pulling me away from the bar and down the hall toward the bathroom. I didn't resist, only followed. "Here." He pointed to the women's room.

I shook my head, pointing to the door on the opposite side. "Break room."

He wasted no time getting us into the small room and flipping on the light. He pushed the lock on the door, but I felt no panic from that. No, the panic was from me. My short comings, everything I was lacking as a woman hit me like a wrecking ball, crashing down the structure I had started to build within me.

I scurried around, trying to pick the pieces up to snap them back in place, but they were in a piled, jumbled mess, only making me feel more lost.

"Talk to me," he demanded.

I shook my head, not wanting to tell him, still wrapping my head around the turmoil inside as my world began to tip.

"Yes, we talk. That's what we do, Reign. You can do this." His words came out encouraging and light instead of demanding, which I felt some sort of relief from. It was nice to have someone in my life who understood what was happening to me.

Then I blurted, "Why are you with me?"

It was the million-dollar question, one that had plagued me since he had showed up on my doorstep. I was a mess and had more issues than a person could count, so why would this big, strong man want anything to do with me? After all, judging by the looks the other women gave him, he could have his pick, and none of them would have so much weight on their shoulders.

"Because I want to be," he answered quickly, his hands coming to my arms then sliding down to my hands and intertwining our fingers. It felt good, comfortable, and safe, which made this so much harder, but there was no way I was letting go.

"Why?" I challenged, clutching him for dear life, wanting to know, not wanting to know, scared of the answers.

"Because you're Reign."

My brows drew together. "What?"

"The moment you sat in a ball like a scared little rabbit, I knew. When you smarted off to me, telling me about the life you'd lived, I knew. When you opened up at the hospital, I knew. And when you talked to me, ignoring the others in the room, eyes solely focused on me, I knew. When I saw you again after all those days, I knew. When you allowed me to support you when we went to your mom's, I knew. And I definitely knew when we were lying there, talking like we'd been doing it for years."

"Knew what?" I asked softly, my nerves bouncing all over the place. It wasn't the blackness that was starting to envelop me by that point. No, it was something else that I didn't have a name for.

When he raised our laced fingers, pulling them between our bodies, I had to take a step closer to balance myself.

"I knew there was a spark in there. I knew, whatever man was lucky enough to ignite it, he would be in for the most special gift you could give: you."

Tears fell from my eyes in a steady rhythm. That had to be the sweetest, kindest thing anyone had ever said to me. I believed he meant every word of it, too.

I didn't want to ruin the moment, but I had to ask, "What if I can't give you what you need?"

He smiled. "You can. You do. You just don't know it yet." His eyes flared as he pulled me even closer to him, his head dropping down before he brushed his lips against mine. It was almost an illusion. The only way I knew it had actually happened was from the tingles on my lips. "When you're ready, we take this further."

I was beginning to feel like the lucky one in all of this as he brushed his lips against mine again. It felt so good, so damn good I wondered what it would be like to have more.

Damn, I hated that my emotions bounced all over the place. I was hoping the medicine would even out my ups and downs, but it was still early and the doctor had said it could take a month to six weeks before it showed any improvement.

"Plans just changed for the night," he said, not releasing his grasp on my hands that felt warm in his.

"To what?"

"It's still a surprise." He reached down and kissed my forehead.

The giddy and excited feelings came back, which I liked much better than the others, as the blackness was kept at bay, even if it was only for a little while.

Chapter Fifteen

"Where are we?" I looked around the wide open space. Trees lined the road we traveled down, opening up to a clearing with even more trees and bushes along the space. In the middle was a cabin. It was rustic and looked like it was built by hand, like one of those I had seen on the DIY shows I liked. It was lit up with lots of light casting a glow around the entire space, showcasing a beautiful deck that, from what I could see, looked as if it went around the entire home. Plants hung from the rafters of the porch, and old rocking chairs were a focal point along with a small table. It was nice. Secluded, but nice.

"My place."

My breath caught in my throat as my nerves came on high alert, sending every one of them into electric overstimulation. I pulled my hands together in hopes of stopping the shaking, but it did nothing except pull attention to them as Lynx set his hand on mine.

"Babe, look at me." His voice was calm and gentle, and my eyes went to his. "As soon as I unlock the door, I'm giving you my truck keys. At any time, if you feel you need to go, you go. But I ask that you talk to me before you take off."

I let out the huge breath I hadn't realized I was holding and nodded.

"That's my girl. You have nothing to fear from me."

My words came out whispered, "I know." I really did.

He gave my hands a squeeze, parked the truck, and hopped out.

I reached for the handle, willing my hands to quit shaking. I wasn't scared; I was nervous. Not that I believed he would hurt me, but that he would kiss me. I felt like such a child. What woman at twenty-one would be nervous about a hot guy kissing them? I shouldn't have all these newbie jitters, but I did, and they scared the ever-loving shit out of me.

My door swung open, and Lynx held out his hand to me, something he had been doing much more of lately. Not only that, but simply holding my hand all the time, which I liked, too.

I took it, and he helped me out of his monstrosity of a vehicle. He held my hand, leading me up to the front door.

I was so on edge that, when a large, black animal started running toward us, I screamed and clutched Lynx for dear life.

"What is it?" I yelled, burrowing myself into Lynx's back,

knowing that, whatever it was, he would protect me from it.

I heard a bark then Lynx's deep voice. "Pepper, sit. Stay," he commanded.

That was when it clicked. A dog. He had a dog.

I slowly peered around his shoulder.

"Babe, it's fine. Reign, meet Pepper. Pepper, this is Reign." He introduced us like Pepper was a person.

I cautiously stepped out from behind Lynx, noting a striking, black dog sitting on his bottom, his front legs tall and straight. Its tongue was out, panting. He didn't look mean, but more excited to have humans around.

"Do you like dogs?" Lynx asked when I didn't say anything after the intro.

I paused. "It's not that I don't like them." I sucked in deeply. This would be more of letting Lynx in. "When I was out on the streets, there were many dogs fighting for the same scraps of food I needed. Some were mean and won out because I couldn't afford to get bitten and sent to the hospital. There was one dog, a bull dog, I later learned. He became my buddy." Thoughts of Bullet spun in my head. I hadn't thought of him in a really long time. It was strange how something so simple could be scrounged up.

I continued, "Bullet was his name. The other dogs would pick on him because he wasn't as big as them. I took him in and kept him with me. I did the best I could, but Bullet was sick, and I had no way of helping him. He ended up dying."

Lynx's arm came around my shoulders, and he pulled me to

him. It took a moment for me to relax, but I was getting so used to his touches it didn't take nearly as long as before.

"Oh, babe. Sorry about that. I've had several dogs and gone through several of them dying. I get it."

He whistled and Pepper came closer, but before he got too close, Lynx yelled, "Sit. Stay."

Pepper listened.

"Pepper here is a black lab. *She* gets very excited when new people come around. Since I know you have a slight fear about it, we'll take this nice and slow," he said just before he put his hand up to the dog's nose. "I want you to do the same so she can sniff you, know you're good people."

Tentatively, I did. It tickled when her cold nose touched my palm, and I smiled. "Hi, Pepper," I called out just as she stuck out her tongue, giving my hand a lick. "All righty then." I chuckled, wiping the dog drool on my jeans. "That's kinda gross."

Lynx smiled at me, even giving me a soft chuckle. "Seeing you smile is like watching the world light up. You have no idea the power you have in that one little act."

My insides flipped, warming uncontrollably. With his arm still around me, he leaned down and kissed my temple. I took it, but deep down, I wanted more.

"Come on. Let me make ya somethin' to eat." He gave a soft squeeze, called Pepper, and just like he had told me he would, he handed me the keys after unlocking the door. I set them by my purse. I didn't think I would need them.

Pepper stayed close. Every time she tried to jump up on me, Lynx would be right there, blocking her, to the point he told her to go lie in her bed. With a sad whine, she did.

I felt bad. This was her house, not mine. She should be able to move around without having restrictions. Besides, she seemed like a good dog. She listened to Lynx every time he told her to do something. That gave me the confidence to do what I did next.

"Lynx?"

He turned from the stove where he was making spaghetti since I had liked it so much at the restaurant he had taken me to.

"May I call over Pepper?"

"You sure? She's gonna wanna jump on you."

I nodded. This was okay. I had nothing to fear.

"All right. If it's too much, you tell her to sit and stay, all right?"

"Yep." I moved to the dog. "Pepper, come here, girl," I told her.

She looked to Lynx, who must have given her a sign because she then came straight to me. It was weird, though. She didn't barrel down on me like I had thought she would. She came up slowly, excitedly yet still in control. It was like she knew I needed this to go smoothly and was helping me. How could dogs know that?

As she came up to my feet and rubbed her head against my leg, I ran my hands through her fur, loving the softness. That was the moment my heart warmed to the point of bursting. I knelt down as she moved closer to me, accepting me into her space. I had nowhere else to put my arms, so I wrapped them around her.

"I take it you like her?" Lynx asked, kneeling down as I pulled away from her.

Pepper got more rambunctious with Lynx there, so I rose, taking a step back.

"Yeah. She's a good dog."

"That she is. Come, sit." He motioned to the table, telling Pepper to go lie back down before he joined me where two plates of steaming hot pasta with meat sauce were waiting. It smelled so good, making my stomach rumble, and Lynx chuckled. My arm unconsciously reached out and nudged him.

Then I stilled. I didn't just do that, did I? I so did.

"I'm sorry," I whispered, wrapping my arms around my body, feeling like I had done something terribly wrong.

When his strong arms came around me and pulled me to him, I didn't retreat. I looked him dead in the eye.

"Babe, that's normal. You didn't hurt me at all. I rather liked it. I fucking love when that playful side comes out of you. You've shown me a time or two." He smiled and I was mesmerized by it. "Babe," he said, but I didn't listen to anything except my thundering heart that sounded as if it was ready to jump out and win a race or something.

I cupped the side of his face, knowing I was going to mess this up, but I was unable to stop myself. It was like his lips were magical, and I wanted to taste them.

"Let me?" I whispered, seeking his permission.

"Babe, I'm not stopping ya." His lips formed each word perfectly.

Unable to control the urges building inside me, I leaned in, feeling his breath on mine, hot and ready. I tried to remember how to do this then gave up and decided to just do it, and I did.

As our lips touched, a searing heat spiked with the contact. It was like something bigger was at play here, like the planets were aligning, making everything right in the world, even if for only this moment.

He didn't take over the kiss like I thought he would. He simply let me lead.

I didn't know what I was doing, but as our bodies pressed together and his arms tightened around me, I knew I was doing something right. I went with it, tilting my head and loving his warmth.

It wasn't enough, though. I needed more.

Tentatively, I licked his lips as I kissed him, wanting to really taste him. Lynx didn't hesitate on my offer. He thrust his tongue fully in my mouth, the unbelievable taste of him exploding. Only briefly did I wonder if I was doing it wrong, but his groans spurred me on, wanting to have more, needing to have more.

I wrapped my arms around his neck, pulling his head down harder to mine, taking, giving. It was utterly the most wonderful thing I had ever experienced.

My breaths turned into pants and my core started to burn. I lifted my leg, wrapping it around his hip and feeling his hard length through his jeans. Something inside me craved, needing more.

When he broke the kiss, I immediately felt stupid. What in the hell was wrong with me? How had I gone from not kissing this man to wanting to rub myself against him? Shit, I was a whore.

As he rested his forehead against mine, his breaths labored, I put my leg back down on the ground.

"Babe, I can feel your body tightening. You didn't do a damn thing wrong. Nothing." He gave my lips a soft peck. "Everything was fucking amazing. I knew that spark was in you. Fuck, I'm one lucky son of a bitch."

I shook my head. "I'm sorry … I—"

"No sorry. No going back, Reign. You did nothing wrong. It was fucking perfect. I am the one slowing things down. I don't want you jumping too soon, babe. You've told me your past, so you've gotta let me take care of you, make this good for you." He kissed me again. "Fuck, now I can't stop tasting you. You're so fucking beautiful."

"I shouldn't have…" Everything he was saying was wonderful, and parts of me were so excited he felt this way, but the other parts were telling me it was my fault, that what I was doing was wrong. That was why he didn't want to take it further. And how far did I want to take it? Now that the lust levels had gone down, did I want to take it to us being naked together? So many questions.

I was realizing quickly why Lynx had slowed us down. I got it.

"You should kiss me more. Abso-fucking-lutely." He kissed my lips all too quickly. "But let's eat, talk, and take this at our own pace. No one is setting rules for our lives. We do that. We decide when it's the right time."

I nodded, feeling so damn happy he'd had the strength to take a breather. This was more than some passion-filled moment. This would determine how things progressed with us from here on out, and I didn't want to screw that up.

"Let's eat," I said with a smile, the giddy feeling making the warmth fill me.

Was it joy I was feeling? Yes, I thought it was, and I let it. It was one of the best feelings I had ever had.

***

Dinner flew by in a flash. Lynx would ask me questions about my night at work, and I would ask about his night. We kept things light, without the heaviness of the moment we had shared falling down on us like a ton of bricks.

I didn't feel panic. The emotions I felt when I first got there didn't arise. I felt comfortable, like I was meant to be in that exact spot at that exact moment.

Lynx lead me over to his couch after dinner, putting some movie on then patting the cushion next to him. I sat, and then he pulled me up against his body. Damn, did it feel good: warm, hard, safe, comforting—all the things that I never thought I could have in my life. With Pepper at our feet, it felt … right.

As the movie went on, I didn't feel right. Not sick, but different. I looked up into Lynx's eyes.

"What's wrong, babe? Don't like the movie?" he asked as I stared at those lips.

I wasn't sure where my sudden boldness manifested from as I

fully turned into his arms.

"I need you to kiss me," I told him softly.

"You sure about that, babe? 'Cause if you are, I've got no problem with that."

"Yes," I whispered.

He reached around me, running his fingers through my hair as our lips connected. While he had let me lead before, this time, he took over. I felt the power of each touch down to my core. I felt Pepper move away yet was too caught up in Lynx.

Our tongues massaged each other's, each one trying to dive deeper. It was the hottest thing I had ever experienced, and I lost myself in it, only allowing myself to feel, not think.

Somehow, I ended up straddling his legs, my core rubbing against his hard shaft. My hips moved of their own accord, brushing up and down his length, hitting a place on my body that I had never allowed myself to experience.

He groaned in my mouth as we continued locking lips, dueling it out for supremacy. I found that I really loved kissing this man.

I rocked my hips back and forth as he broke away from the kiss, his words coming out breathless. "Babe, I want you to rub me until you come. I want to see it."

I had no time to say anything before his tongue dove back into my mouth. I kissed him back with all the passion that coursed through my veins. I did as he had said and rocked my hips, loving the friction between our jeans and bodies.

When I had said I had closed that part of me off, I hadn't been exaggerating. I had never had an orgasm before. Not self-induced, not when I was with anyone, ever. I had never allowed myself to feel any of that. I had faked it with a couple of men who got pissed I wasn't going to, but that was the extent of it. Therefore, this building in my body was like a slowly churning tornado, building speed with each swivel of my hips.

I hit just the right spot, and my body set off like a rocket as explosions went through every nerve and piece of flesh on my body. I screamed out, not able to hold it in as it crashed over me again and again.

"Fuck," Lynx groaned out, his hands on my hips, moving me so I could feel the aftershocks with each tilt of my hips.

My eyes shot open to his, immediately thinking I had done something wrong. However, his eyes were lidded, a sense of serenity, more than normal, washing over his features.

"What's wrong?" I asked in a bit of a panic.

"Babe, calm down. Watching you come was the fucking hottest thing I've ever seen in my life. I came in my fucking jeans from watching you."

I felt the heat hit my cheeks.

"That's pretty fucking beautiful, too." He laughed. "You know, I haven't come in my jeans since I was thirteen." He meant it as a joke, and to him, it was, but to me, it brought me back to my time as a thirteen-year-old. I didn't have the same kind of memories he had, and I felt the dark cloud begin to encompass me.

"Babe. Don't. Here and now," he said, snapping my focus back on him. "I loved every second of that. We only think about what is happening right here and now."

I nodded. He was right; none of that other stuff mattered.

"Not a word about me coming in my jeans."

That made me chuckle.

"Why's that?"

He lifted his brow. "The fact that I couldn't hold it in because you looked so damn hot … Never mind, tell whoever the fuck you want. I don't give a shit." He pulled me down to him and kissed me softly and tenderly. "Now you're gonna have to let me up so I can go clean myself up."

I moved and smiled to myself as he left the room. I focused on the now, and it was fantastic.

Chapter Sixteen

It was going to be a bad day. I knew it as soon as my eyes fluttered open and the day's sunlight came in through the curtains. I also knew it because of two things: one, I got up twice in the middle of the night and checked the locks on Andi's doors, something I hadn't done in a long time, and two, I dreamed of Drew.

The past four days since Lynx had brought me over for dinner had been wonderful. With each day that passed, he would either meet me before work or after. There hadn't been a day that he had neglected to show me in some way that the kiss and other stuff we had done wasn't wrong.

I had thought it at first. I had believed I was completely wrong for wanting something that felt so good, but over the days that had been relieved … until today.

I rolled over in bed and pulled the blankets over my head. I didn't hear Andi and was thankful for it. The light that I had found over the course of my time out of the hospital seemed to have vanished, nowhere to be found. The only thing around me was a cloak of winding darkness and for no other reason except a dream.

It was irrational, but I wasn't thinking; I was only feeling. And that was what was pulling me down.

In the dream, Drew had come to me. He hadn't for a very long time, and I had thought that part of my head was straightening out, but I was wrong.

If anything, it was building to the point of combustion.

"I can't believe you let him touch you." Drew's angry voice vibrated as spittle left his lips, and his body pulsed with his rage. "You let him kiss you, Reign!" he screamed, and I jumped back from him.

He gripped my arm so forcefully it hurt, and something I had never felt with Drew came over me: fear.

I had never seen him this enraged before.

"I'm sorry," I whispered, feeling I needed to say something yet not knowing what to say, the confusion of the moment spinning my head. How could Drew be here and be angry with me?

"You should be sorry." He shook me, causing my neck to snap painfully.

I cried out in pain, and Drew let me go instantly.

"I'm so sorry, Reign." He ran his hands through his hair and

paced back and forth across the floor.

I moved as far away from him as I could, afraid that he could act like that and, more, wondering how he even knew.

Guilt filled me like water in a vase, each of the curves bursting to their limits until it overflowed.

I had let Lynx touch me, and I had liked it more than I had ever thought I would. I was having real feelings for him and liked being with him, his touch, his lips.

Still, how could I just forget about Drew? How could I let all those feelings I had held for him dissipate with Lynx's touch? What kind of person did that make me?

"And you gave him your orgasms ... something you never gave me. How could you?" Drew rambled as he continued walking.

I felt the urge to comfort him, console him. "I'm—"

"A whore. You're nothing but a whore!"

It was the same last line each time that woke me from sleep. I had been doing so much better, being able to sleep for pretty long periods of time. Even when I had woken, I hadn't needed to check the locks or get Andi. I had been able to handle everything on my own. But this … This was something I didn't know how to take.

Drew thought I was a whore for giving myself to Lynx, and the guilt from that ate at me. If I had been thinking rationally, I would have known it was a dream, and Drew was happy with his family, but I wasn't rational, and I didn't want to move from the bed. It was weird. I felt like I was mourning something yet having a hard time figuring out what it was.

I did nothing except lay there with the blankets over my head, letting my mind go to places I had thought I had overcome. I let it go back to the place where I had seen Drew and his family, how I had felt. I let all of it overcome me.

***

"Reign?" Andi called from the side of the bed as it depressed from her.

I didn't want to talk, and I hadn't looked at the clock to know how long I had been lying there, but I had to pee quite badly, so I figured it had been a while.

"Yeah," I answered quietly.

"What's wrong?"

I didn't have the answer. The darkness had taken over, and my thoughts were all over the place, so I shrugged.

"You're scaring me, Reign."

The pang in my chest hit hard. I tried to pull myself up, tried to be able to answer her in a way she would understand, but I knew nothing I said would make it okay for her. She wouldn't get it.

"Leave me be," I moaned, pulling the covers more tightly against me and letting the warmth fill my coldness.

"Tell me what the hell is going on!" Andi yelled, causing me to jump, but I still didn't tell her. No one got it.

Then it hit me.

"Lynx," I murmured.

Andi stilled. "What?"

"Call him please." I said no more, just burrowed into the covers.

I felt her leave the bed then the room. I didn't know if she would do as I had asked. I only let the darkness take me in.

***

The covers were pulled from my body, the coldness jolting me. I must have just dozed off, but I didn't remember falling asleep.

A warm body hit my back as the covers came back over me. I froze and sucked in deeply when a strong hand came to my belly. Then the smell of Lynx invaded me, and my entire body relaxed as I let his warmth invade me.

We lay like that for long moments before he spoke.

"Babe, what's going on?"

He would get it. I knew he would understand if I told him.

"Drew came to me in my dreams. He called me a whore for being with you."

His grip on me tightened.

"He said I shouldn't be giving myself to you, that…" I stumbled a bit. "That I shouldn't give you my orgasms." I shook my head from side to side. "He hates me." My words were grumbled into my blankets. I wasn't even sure if he heard them all, because he said nothing, just started rubbing circles on my hand with his thumb.

I continued, "I had to check the locks, Lynx. I hadn't done it since I first got out of the hospital."

"Where are you now?" he asked softly.

"In the dark." It wasn't pitch black like it had been before, but the light that had been cast over me wasn't shining brightly.

"I feel guilty," I mumbled, needing to say it, but scared to, as well.

His lips came to my ear. "Babe, you need to pull deeper, find the woman I found, and let her help you up. I'm here, and I'll stay here until you get there. Then we'll talk."

He was right. I wasn't in a place to be rational or listen, so I didn't. I lay there in his arms for a really long time until the urge to pee hit me so hard I needed to get up.

Lynx's slow intakes of breath told me he was sleeping. I tried to get up softly, pulling away from him, but his grip tightened.

"Where are you going?"

"Bathroom."

He let me go. I did my business and came back to find him fully awake, lying with his back to the headboard, his hands behind his head.

I ran my fingers through my hair and sat on the end of the bed. I dropped my head in my hands and began breathing slow breaths as the panic hit my chest like a sledgehammer. All the while, Lynx said nothing.

Deep breath, one ... I inhaled. *Deep breath, two.*

As I continued counting to myself, the overriding anxiety and fear began to fade, leaving me behind. When I lifted my head, Lynx had his arms out to me. I wasted no time climbing into his arms as he held me tight. This time, his warmth penetrated me down to my soul, and I sucked up every drop of it.

"You ready to talk?" he whispered.

I wasn't, but I would for him.

"What we have is beautiful, so beautiful. I didn't think I'd ever have it, Lynx. I don't know why I'm dreaming of Drew or why he's saying those things to me. I don't know why I felt so guilty." I tipped my head up, looking into his eyes. "I don't regret anything, Lynx. Nothing."

His lips brushed mine, and I instantly lifted my hand to his scarred cheek, kissing him more deeply, not wanting him to think I believed any of what we had done was a mistake. It was just all so much.

"Babe, you have unfinished business with Drew. I thought it would have happened a lot sooner, but you're stronger than you give yourself credit for." When he gave me a soft peck and pushed my head to his chest, I nestled there comfortably. "You need to go and talk to him."

I jolted, trying to lift up, but he held me to him.

"Settle," he ordered, and I tried to relax, but it was difficult. "Babe, you need to talk to Drew. Work this out. You're never going to be fully yourself until you do."

"I don't know if I can."

"Wasn't it you who was going to see her mother, come hell or high water? Was it you who had the courage and strength to do that? The woman who wouldn't let anyone touch her"—he stroked my hair—"but allows me to do so freely?" He wrapped me securely to his body. "You're ready to do this."

"But I'm just finding out things about myself: that I like to go on long walks with Andi or that I like running with you. Won't going to see him take me back there? I can't go back there, Lynx." My body shook. I couldn't. The day was bad enough with feeling that cloak surround me. I didn't want to do anything to bring it back.

"If you want the darkness to fade, you must face the things that put you there. Drew is your catalyst. It's the one thing you must face."

I didn't want him to be right. I wanted to yell at him that he was wrong. Even though I had a good man at my back, I still didn't want to open the old wounds. I didn't want to have those attack me.

Why did my life have to be so messed up? Why couldn't I be normal and not so messed in the head? I shouldn't have to live my life like this.

"I'll tell you what. We keep living like we've been living, and after your appointment with Dr. McMann, you can decide what you want to do." He gave me an out, and I took it. I needed it. I needed to process it all, and he knew that.

I didn't know what would change from that point to this, but I was going to take him up on it because I didn't think I would ever be okay enough to see Drew again.

***

"Hang on!" Lynx called from behind me as I gripped the chains with all of my might.

The wind rushed through my hair and onto my face, sending exuberance through me as I climbed higher and higher. It was almost like an emotional high as I flew up into the air and back down. My lungs filled with the scent of the trees around us as Lynx pushed me from behind, as I let my legs and body soar, swinging.

I had done it at school a couple of times, but after getting picked on, I stayed as far away from the other kids as I could. This was different, though.

As I gripped the chains, they were hard and unforgiving, but the air around me was so freeing.

This … This was freeing.

I turned to see Lynx's large body behind me, his hands on his hips, and a smile across his face.

"Babe, we'll come here every day if you're gonna smile like that."

I didn't wipe it from my face. I felt it: pure utter happiness from a swing. I was a kid, so free and climbing up so high. My heart thumped in tune with the ups and downs of the swing, and I loved every second of it.

That entire week, I hadn't had another nightmare about Drew. I believed it was due to the strong man whose arms wrapped around me at night, but he said it was all me. It was a tossup, one I wouldn't know since there was no way I was giving up waking up next to him if I didn't have to.

We had been staying at his place, because I didn't want to hurt Andi in any way. I had hurt her enough when she had come in that day and seen Lynx with his arms around me tightly.

Every time I turned around, I kept doing hurting her, and I hated myself for it. Therefore, I had made myself a promise that I would do everything I could so she didn't hurt. I had early dinners with

Andi, and we talked on the phone regularly, but my nights were spent at Lynx's place. No way would I bring Lynx to Andi's to spend the night. It was disrespectful.

Also, I had come to really love Pepper. I asked Lynx why he had a dog, just out of curiosity. It surprised me when he told me the VA he went to had suggested it, saying dogs were great companionship. In turn, it would help him through his dark. Hearing that, I allowed Pepper to help me out, too. I really liked the pup.

I had thought long and hard over this time, as well, and knew a visit to Drew was in my future. I was tired of living in the shadows. I didn't want to feel the darkness overtake me again. I wanted to be happy, free like I felt today. I deserved a small sliver of it. I needed to grab life by the balls and take it, which was exactly what I was going to do.

No more running. No more hiding. I had wiped my incubator from my life and all her toxicity. Now I needed to get right with Drew. I needed to know that he was okay. I needed closure, just like Andi had tried to get me all those months ago. She had been right then. I hadn't seen it and reacted. It was time to be proactive, instead.

Knowledge is power. Lynx's words rang through my head. It was time to get the knowledge so I could move on.

Even as I flew through the air, letting the wind take my hair whichever direction it wanted, I felt the change in me. I had lived in the dark for so long, but I had a choice. I could either stay in the dark or make it so my life was filled with more moments like these. I chose to live.

If going to see Drew would help me to move to that, I would do it.

I hadn't told Lynx yet, but I planned on going there after my talk with Wrestler McMann the next day. I knew he would be by my side if I asked him. Nevertheless, I was going to do it on my own two feet. I was a woman now, not some scared child. I had choices now, and I was going to make the best ones for me. I was putting me first.

"You about ready?" Lynx moved to the side of the swing.

I gave him a pouty lip. "Already?" I mock whined, playing with him.

He smiled. "*Already?* We've been at this for over an hour."

We had? Damn. Time always flew by when I spent it with Lynx. It was so natural, easy, like I was meant to be with this man.

I slowed the swing and hopped off with a giggle, walking right into Lynx's arms. I stood up on my tiptoes and connected my lips to his. Each time I tasted him, he tasted better and better.

It only took seconds before the kiss turned scorching, and we had to pull away for fear we would blow up Lynx's backyard. Yes, he had a swing that hung from a tree in his backyard. It was beautiful out there, serene, relaxing. Some nights, we would eat dinner out on the deck before I went to work if I didn't meet Andi because she had a shift. Luckily, tonight was my night off.

The tips were helping me out tremendously, and with Andi not allowing me to pay for anything, I was saving every penny. Soon, I would be able to get my own place and my own car. That would be freedom, independence, and power coming back in my life full-fledged.

"Come on. I've got snacks set up and the movie queued up, ready to go." He wrapped his arm around my shoulder and led me up to the house.

It was amazing how comfortable I felt in this space and how wonderful I felt just being with Lynx.

The evening had been going so well, just like every other evening I had spent with Lynx. After the movie, we climbed into bed. I loved that he never pushed me when it came to being close, but tonight … Tonight, I was ready for more. I needed Lynx like I needed to breathe. I was ready to live.

I turned over, our faces inches apart when Lynx opened his eyes, questioning me. I answered his look by kissing him with every bit of emotion I felt yet didn't have the guts to say.

Our lips melded together in a dance so beautiful I almost didn't want to stop it, but I did.

I sat up and straddled him. Then, gripping the hem of my shirt, I lifted it from my body, exposing my breasts to him. I was nervous, so damn nervous I would mess this up or not do it right. However, I just went with my instinct and didn't second-guess myself a thousand times like I had done a few days prior. I had known it was coming, and I had tried to prepare myself. Regardless, nothing could prepare you for the way a guy looked at you like Lynx was looking at me. It was like I was the only woman he had ever wanted in his entire life, and I was beautiful to him.

Lynx coughed. “What’s going on, Reign?” he asked, his hands clenching on my thighs. He wanted to touch me, but he was holding himself back for me. I loved how he took care of me.

I spoke softly, “Touch me.”

He paused. “Reign, you’ve gotta tell me where this is going, babe.” He coughed again. “I’m doing my damnedest to hold back and not push, but this is like letting a lion out of its cage after being tempted.”

I liked that I tempted him, that I could feel his erection through his pajama pants. I did this to him. That in itself was a hefty thing. It was power, control.

I gripped his hands and brought them to my breasts. He didn’t move them, but the lust pouring from his eyes told me he liked where they were.

“I need to feel you, Lynx,” I told him, moving his hands for him, the warmth seeping into my body.

“Fuck, babe. Are you sure about this?”

I stilled my hands and leaned down to his lips. “I’ve never been surer about anything in my life.” Then I kissed him as his hands worked my breasts, sending pings throughout my body.

I pulled back briefly. “You need to be patient with me and let me be on top.” I needed that control, to not be pinned down. I knew it would help me to have that little bit of an escape if I needed it, which I hoped I wouldn’t. There was that damn H-word again. I was starting to feel it more and more as the days passed.

"Anything you need, Reign. Anything."

I kissed him, showing him how much those words meant to me. And they meant the world.

His skin twitched as I moved my hands down then pulled his shirt from his body. He was gorgeous. There was no denying it. From the muscles where they needed to be to the tattoos lining his arms, everything about him was beautiful.

I sat up and raked my small nails down his chest, watching each muscle twitch as they went down.

"That smile is about to undo me, babe."

Our eyes connected as I stood from the bed, pulling my pants down along with my underwear. He sucked in a breath so deeply I didn't think there would be any air left in the room for me.

"Damn."

I had shown my body before, of course, but never to a man who looked at me like Lynx did, not one who held my heart, which he probably didn't even know.

"Your turn," I told him.

He removed his clothes without taking his eyes off me. As the pajamas flew by me, I took in all that was Lynx while he lay there, letting me take my fill.

His legs were toned from all the running and his training. It was his penis that caught my attention, though. I had never paid much attention to them before, but the thickness and the way it jutted out to his bellybutton had me a little worried everything would work between us.

Instead of straddling him, I let my nerves win for the moment and lay next to him. “I don’t really know what to do,” I said then quickly added, “I mean, I know what to do, but I … don’t.” I sounded so stupid, so immature for my years. Lynx had to have had a lot of practice at this, while there I was, nervous to even touch him.

“Do you want me to guide you?” he asked, his hand brushing away the stray hair that fell to my eye.

“Yes.”

“I need your hand around me. I want you to feel me.”

I did as he had said, feeling the steeliness of him, yet the flesh was so soft. His hand gripped mine, squeezing him more tightly than I ever would have. I followed him.

“Just like that … up and down.” Then he groaned, “Okay, babe, gotta stop.”

I smiled at that, loving getting to him.

“I need to get you ready for me. You have two choices: either lay your pretty, little ass down on the bed, or you can bring that sexy, little pussy up to my lips.”

An excited, lustful thrill raced through me, and I went with my gut.

“Lips.”

“Get up here.”

Tentatively, I crawled up his chest. He positioned my knees on either side of his head, and I couldn’t help feeling a bit embarrassed. He didn’t see it that way, though.

“Fuck, I’ve wanted to taste you since I saw you.” His hot mouth attached to my flesh, and everything in my head left, my focus solely on the man between my legs.

He readied me, slipping his fingers in and out, and I was right there, ready to explode, but he then stopped.

I looked down at him with wide eyes. "What are ya doing? Don't stop!" I almost cried.

"Babe, trust me?"

"Of course I do."

"Then you come on my dick. I wasn't planning this, but I have condoms in the bathroom."

I smiled before removing myself from the bed and going to my small bag where I had packed foil packets.

"Had this planned out, did ya?" He gave that sexy, flirty smile that made my heart flutter.

"Something like that." I handed him the packet, and he placed the condom on his shaft. "I'm a little scared," I told him honestly. That was what we had between us: talking and honesty. I knew I would always give that to him.

"I know, my little rabbit. Take it nice and slow."

While he waited for me, I felt absolutely no pressure from him, but I did feel it from myself. I wanted to make this good, make this right—perfect for him and for me. I had never had a gentle touch in this way until Lynx, and I didn't want to mess that up.

Slowly, I straddled him again and sucked in deeply.

"Why don't you kiss me?" he suggested.

I dove on it. I didn't see it as an out; I saw it as a way to get myself right. It was the right choice as my body lit up.

Before I realized I was doing it, I was guiding him into my body. I ripped away from his lips as I sat on his hips, him fully inside of me. I stared into his eyes, hoping he would see everything I couldn't put into words. Then he rocked my world.

"You are the most beautiful thing on this planet. I'm so fucking happy I was in that hospital with you, so damn happy you snipped at me and made me want to know you. You, Reign, are my light. You make my world right. You are my everything."

A tear rolled down my cheek. My heart was so full I swore it would burst from my chest.

"I love you, Reign."

More tears fell as I let his words seep into my soul. He loved me. Me. Reign. Problems, issues, everything, this strong man *loved me.*

I wanted to say it back, but I couldn't form the words. They were lodged in my throat. All I could do was show him.

I moved up and down on him, our eyes never leaving one another's. The build came quickly. Still, I couldn't look away from Lynx, his hips moving with mine as we came together in a rush.

It was the single best experience of my entire life.

"Reign…" came out of Nurse Hatchet's mouth on a soft, happy sigh.

I turned to see the woman who had given so much of herself to me during my stay at the hospital.

I had taken most of what she had given me at the time for granted, telling myself it was her job. As I looked back, though, I realized she didn't have to tell me about her struggles or give me more than her job required. She had done it because she gave a shit. That was something I could never repay her for. That was something I would never forget and would carry with me forever.

Nurse Hatchet's smile filled the white space as she held her hands together in front of her. I knew she wanted to reach out and envelop me in a hug, but she held back. She knew me, knew my struggles. Regardless, this was my nurse, the one I had grown close to when I had told myself I wouldn't. Therefore, I stepped close, sucked in a deep breath, and wrapped my arms around the lady.

Her body stilled only momentarily before she reciprocated. In my ear, her raspy breath told me she was fighting back tears, so I didn't move. I didn't want to see her with tears for me. She was my strong, take-no-shit nurse, and that was who she would always be for me.

I waited until her breathing came back to normal before I slowly pulled away. She swiped at her face, clearing all the wetness, something I was grateful for.

"How are you?" she asked as she took a step back.

"I think I'm good," I told her honestly.

She burst out laughing. "You *think* you're good?"

I smiled back at her widening eyes, but she masked it quickly.

"Yes. I have really good days, and I've had some bad days, but I'm still here, so I think I'm learning how to cope with the bad."

"You have no idea how proud I am of you."

My breath lodged in my throat as my heart tightened as if strings were wrapped around it so strongly it would burst. She was proud … of me. Maybe she knew what those words meant to me, or maybe she didn't, but I was holding on to them for dear life. It felt so damn good to have someone feel that way about me, especially since I felt it, too. I felt the pride in making the choices I had since getting out. Her reiterating it only gave me more confidence that I was doing something right.

"Thank you," I said softly.

"You need to get to your appointment." She pointed to the white door I had walked in so many other times, but this time, I was a different person. I wasn't the same. I was still me, just different.

Nurse Hatchet knocked on the door for me before it opened, revealing Wrestler McMann standing there with his bald self.

"Reign, I'm so glad you came. Please come in."

I smiled one last time at my nurse then entered the space.

It seemed so much bigger than I remembered, despite it being the same pictures on the walls, same chairs, and couch. There was no chair next to his desk where Lynx would sit, but that was okay. I didn't feel that overwhelming panic I had when he hadn't been there before. I knew he had my back, but I also had two legs that I held myself up on.

He pointed to the chair I had sat in before, and I sat while he walked around the desk, sitting in his seat.

"Tell me how you've been," he opened with a huge smile on his face.

I felt the apprehension creep up, but I pushed it down. "Good. Learning."

"Wonderful. What have you learned?"

I breathed out. "That I'm not the scared child I was before. I have choices. Before, I didn't see it that way. I thought I was drowning in a world that I didn't want to be part of. I didn't see my choices. I thought my life was all laid out, and I just existed."

"And now?" he prompted.

"Oh, now ...?" I stopped, thinking about what to say. "There's fun out there, and I'd like to explore it."

"Have you been taking your medicine every day?"

"Yes." I had, like clockwork. I had even set an alarm on my phone to remind me.

"I can tell by your words that you've seen a difference?" It wasn't a statement; it was more of a question.

"I don't really know if it's the medicine or that I'm getting out there and trying new things. But Lynx told me that even though I'm feeling good, I need to keep taking it."

He leaned back in his chair. "Ah, Lynx. I was wondering if you were going to mention him."

A blush crept up my cheeks, but I didn't say anything.

"He came and found you," he surmised, and I nodded. "Talk to me, Reign."

"He's Lynx," was all I responded with because that was enough for me.

"All right, I'll let that one go for the moment. Did you find your mother?"

Anger bubbled in my veins at the mention of my *mother.* She didn't deserve the title.

"Yes. She's a bitch." I explained how she had treated me and what she had said. I tried to not let the knife dig inside of me, but it was there. I then concluded with, "It's on her, not me. It was her choice to cheat on her husband. I just suffered the consequences."

"I see. What about your biological father?"

My nerves spiked. "Lynx is working on that."

He pressed, "What about Drew?"

Preparing myself to talk about Drew hadn't gone as planned. I still ached from the words he had told me in my dream. Regardless, I had already made up my mind that I was going to see him because I needed to. I needed to shut that door on my life so I could be open to the possibilities of my future.

"I'm going to see him." I told the doctor about my plan to do it on my own, even telling him about the dream and my fears that he would hate me.

He rubbed the bottom of his chin. "You really have come a long way, Reign."

I felt good about that, too.

***

As I stared at the house, the drowning feeling didn't come like last time. Nothing had changed except for the bushes getting trimmed along with the grass. I hadn't told Lynx I was coming here. I had wanted to as we lay in bed together that morning and he asked me what my plans were for the day. Consequently, I felt as if I were deceiving him when I really wasn't. I just needed to do this for me.

I knew Lynx would have wanted to come with me, but I also knew, if I asked him not to, he wouldn't. As a result, I didn't understand myself not wanting to tell him. I guessed it was to prove to myself that I could do it on my own, that I was strong enough to handle whatever was thrown at me without anyone's help.

I borrowed Andi's car, sitting in the same exact spot as last time, feeling a sense of déjà vu hit me as my gut wanted to start twisting. I fought it, though. I *needed* to talk to Drew. I needed to shut this part of my life down and move on. I didn't know how I would do that, but I needed to figure it out.

I was nervous; don't get me wrong. The uncertainty of the situation warranted it, but it was something that needed to be done. It shouldn't be too hard, considering he had a family now. I just needed to know one question.

Why didn't he come and find me? That was the one thing plaguing me. I felt like that one little question was what was holding me back from truly finding myself.

Drumming up the courage I must have had buried deep inside of me, I exited the car and walked up to the front door. Fear, uncertainty, and nerves cracked me everywhere. I was really going to see the boy—well, the man—whom I had thought was dead. I also felt a slight bit of excitement about it, even though the nerves were masking that part until it was almost nonexistent.

Sucking in deeply, I knocked on the front door. Each second that passed, the nerves electrified my system to the point my palms were sweating and my heart felt as if it were going to jump out of my chest and run down the street in a sprint.

The handle to the door slowly turned, and my breaths picked up.

How was he going to react to seeing me? Would he be happy or pissed like in my dream? Would his woman and child be here?

How did I not think of all these things until this moment? I should have run through every scenario so I could prepare myself. Shit.

The door creaked open, and there he was: Drew with sandy blond hair and the same eyes I had thought were gone from me forever. He was so much taller now, reminding me of Lynx. My heart squeezed at the thought of him and him not knowing I was there.

"Can I help you?" he asked in a gruff voice.

My words clogged my throat. He didn't recognize me. I had thought maybe he might. I hadn't changed that much, just filled out a little more. For the most part, I was the same. He had to remember me.

"Drew?" I questioned, needing him to confirm it.

My heart thundered as his brows knit together, almost in confusion.

I rocked back on my heels. The seconds seemed to tick like endless hours.

"No Drew here," he said and tried to shut the door, dismissing me.

I panicked, holding the now closing door open with the palm of my hand, frantic that he was going to shut me out.

"Andrew Lewis?" I asked again.

He shook his head as my stomach twisted in the most painful knot I had ever felt.

"Sorry, ma'am. I'm Devin James. I don't know anyone by the name Andrew Lewis."

My heart fell to the floor, shattering into a million, broken pieces of glass. This couldn't be. It just couldn't.

My face felt chilled as all the blood drained from it, the panic and anxiety crashing into me like wolves fighting for dominance.

"You're not Drew Lewis who was in the foster care system?" I prodded, not letting the pain of the situation show in the tremor of my voice.

"Hon, I'm not sure who you are, but no, I wasn't in foster care. I'm sorry, though. I'm not who you are looking for."

I stared into his eyes, seeing my Drew. This was him. It had to be. How did he not know who he was? This was too much, way too much. The crescendo of emotions threatened to pull me under, yet I fought to at least keep my head above water.

"Look, ma'am. I'm sorry, but you need to leave."

In one last-ditch effort, I blurted, "I'm Reign, from the Peterson's house."

His entire forehead scrunched as if he were trying to remember, and I believed he would.

"We lived in the same house together, went to school together. You were my best friend," I blurted out, hoping that something, anything would rattle his memory.

"I never lived with any Peterson's, and I'm sure I would remember you from school, Reign. I'm sorry."

I felt wetness prick behind my eyes as the confusion became all-consuming, and I replayed everything Trey had told me in my head. He didn't have any reason to lie to me. Why would he? Why would he do that? Why would he want to hurt me?

I bit back the tears. I would not cry. I would not. I was stronger than this.

"I'm sorry to have bothered you." I needed to get out of there and figure out what was going on.

I turned, needing escape.

"Reign."

I stopped. I knew that voice, knew in that moment the man behind me was Drew.

I turned only my head, willing the tears not to fall.

"I'm really sorry."

I nodded then ran to Andi's car. I threw it in drive and allowed my tears to fall as I headed home.

He didn't remember. He didn't remember *me*. *Us*. How was that possible?

I couldn't get air into my lungs. They felt utterly constricted as the weight of what had happened came crashing down on me. I wasn't even a memory to him, while I had thought about him for years. *I was nothing.*

I felt the change in my body like I had become more attuned to my emotions. I felt myself begin to swirl down the path that landed me in the hospital.

I tried breathing, but an hour into the drive back, I still had no answers.

When my cell rang, the display said *Lynx Calling*, but I didn't answer it. I let it go to voicemail. I wasn't together enough, so I dug deeper.

***

I pulled up to the old track that Lynx had brought me to several times. He had called four times, and I still hadn't answered. I needed time. I needed to process. I needed to figure out my head.

I grabbed a pair of tennis shoes from the back, laced them up, and ran. I ran and ran and ran. When I didn't think I could run anymore, I pushed myself to keep going. The blackness had threatened me in the car, so I knew I needed to do something. With each step I took on the tarred track, I tried to figure out what was going on.

I hadn't realized that not having Drew know who I was would hurt this badly, would make the spear to my heart twist and turn. I let tears fall and the anger pulse as the burn invaded me, and I pounded it into the pavement below. The surface was hard and unrelenting, just like the emotions threatening to take over and drown me.

I breathed in deeply, desperate to hold on to the small sliver of light I had found over the last few months. I reached for the love I felt from Andi, Lynx, and even Nurse Hatchet, drawing on their strength as I ran. I held on to them with everything I had. I wasn't going to let this take me back to that place of torment. No.

Not until I was completely worn out did I slow to a walk. My legs burned and my breaths were hard to take in. I moved to the car, knowing I needed to get back. I had taken the night off, but Lynx would be sending out a search party for me soon if I didn't return his call.

I sat in the driver's seat and grabbed my phone. Twenty-seven missed calls, ones from both Lynx and Andi. I hit the button for Lynx.

"Where are you?" he said in a panic when he picked up on the first ring.

I let out a breath from just hearing his voice. "I'm fine. I'm on my way back."

"Back from where, Reign? You scared the living shit out of me." His voice told me it was very true, and I felt horrible for it.

"I went to see Drew."

Silence on the other end.

"I know I should have told you, but it was something I needed to do," I continued.

More silence.

"Please don't be mad at me." The last words came out in a hiccupped cry that I couldn't control. Yes, the running had helped, but I was still a mess.

Finally, he said, "Babe, what happened?"

"Can we talk about it when I get back? I'm leaving now."

His answer was immediate. "No, tell me what's wrong."

More tears fell. "He doesn't remember me, Lynx. He says his name is Devin James, but Lynx"—I paused, swiping the tears from my eyes—"it was him. I know those eyes. I knew when he said my name. I don't know what is going on."

"Babe, you need me to come and get you. I don't want you driving when you're this upset." I loved how concerned he was for me, how wonderful it made me feel that he cared so much about me, that he loved me.

I needed that so much right then. I needed that rock he had become to me, but I wouldn't have him come and get me.

I brushed all the tears away and took several deep breaths, bringing myself under control. It was strange. I was very sad and pained, but the darkness hadn't come like I was used to.

I drew on all my strength. "I'm okay. I'll come right to you."

"I'll be waiting."

***

I pulled up to Lynx's house where he jumped out of the porch chair and stalked toward the car, Pepper at his feet.

I opened the door, and he engulfed me in his arms. I burrowed myself into him, absorbing his warmth, strength, and love.

"Come in, babe. Let's talk this out."

I shook my head as he led me to the front porch. Pepper curled up on the ground.

Instead of letting me go, he sat down in the chair and pulled me into his arms, wrapping them around me tightly. I curled my legs up, resting my head on his chest.

"Tell me," he prompted, and I did, every last detail. It didn't feel any better saying it. The only part that felt good was being in his arms while I did it.

"Babe, I need the name of the guy who got you this info, because while I was waiting for you, I did some searching of my own."

My stomach fell, and I sat up, turning to him.

"I'm so fucking sorry, babe. I should have looked right away, but I thought you had it handled. It's not good."

I tried to get up from his lap and move to the chair next to him, but he didn't allow me to, which in the end, I was grateful for since I needed him more than I realized.

"Whoever that motherfucker is that told you about Drew is a lying piece of shit."

My gut twisted.

"Babe, who you thought was Drew isn't."

"But he is! I saw it in his eyes."

"No, babe." He sucked in deeply, like the words he had to say were painful for him. It made me brace for whatever news he was about to deliver. "Drew had a twin brother. They were separated as infants. The man you saw today was Drew's brother, not Drew."

My world stopped on its axis. I couldn't move, too stunned, shocked, and appalled to do so.

Drew had a brother? A twin brother? Drew couldn't have known because he had never said a word to me, and he would have, especially as alone as we both felt for so long.

"Does Devin not know this?" My words came out so softly as I let the hurt pass. It felt as if I were back in that place where I had watched Drew die, like I was watching it happen all over again, the light bleeding from his eyes.

"No, babe. He knows nothing of Drew. If the asshole who was looking for your information would have been smart, he would've caught all of this. He wasn't, though. I'm so sorry, babe."

Tears spilled from my eyes to my cheeks.

I fell back to his chest. "So I really did watch Drew die that day?"

"Yeah, babe. I'm so sorry."

I lay there, letting the pain of seeing Drew die all over again spread through me. The full-out darkness didn't come, though. I wouldn't allow it to. After all, I had already lived through this once. I knew I could get through it again.

Chapter Eighteen

I stared out the window at the woods where the trees rustled slowly with the wind. It was like the calm after the storm of the day before. I didn't sleep much; even in Lynx's arms, it didn't come. I had hoped he hadn't noticed, but he had squeezed me every so often, letting me know he was there with me.

I was happy for it, yet I didn't want him to have to feel like he had to be there for me every second. While I loved that he did, I had realized having him with me was simply a bonus. I was finding it within myself to stand on my own two feet, and it was an amazing feeling.

Although the day before had been painful on so many levels, it had also been freeing. The reason wasn't good, and it didn't make me a better person. It was because the boy I had known did die all those years ago. He hadn't moved on with his life, totally forgetting about me like I was nobody.

I was somebody to him at one time. He had cared about me as I had him, and I knew he would want me to be happy. Whatever way that came, he wouldn't want to see me in the bowels of Hell that I kept entering. I thought he would have been disappointed that I let the outside world win instead of fighting.

The shower kicked on in the other room, and I felt compelled to go outside. Pepper followed.

Walking to the swing that Lynx loved to push me in and I loved being in, I sat in it and rocked slowly. Visions of Drew played in my memories, opening me wide up. Then I did something I had never done before. I felt the urge to talk to him.

Hey, Drew. I don't know where you are right now, because you know I didn't believe in that higher being stuff since He or She never came to help either of us growing up. I sighed. *But I want to believe that you are someplace good, someplace where you're happy and at peace, someplace where you don't hurt and only good things can happen to you.*

I miss you so much. One tear fell down my cheek, followed by another. I didn't try to stop them; it was no use. *I've missed you since the moment you left me, and I haven't been able to get a grip on the fact that you're gone. We were supposed to stay together, get out of that hell hole, and be our own family. It hurts that we'll never have that. I wanted that with you for so long.*

I would give anything to have you back, and I thought that I had. I thought that I had you for a brief moment.

Did you know you have a twin brother? I bet you do by now. I shook my head. *Identical. I thought he was you.* I blew out deeply. *The kicker was I saw what we could have had, what we could have been: a family with a kid you played with and showed how to be a great person, because that's what you were. You were so great to me.*

I'm so sorry about that night you saw me with him. *I wish I could have taken it away somehow, made you stay away from that room. If I could do something differently, something to make what happened go away, I would do it in a heartbeat. I never wanted you to see me like that. I was so ashamed, but I couldn't let him hurt you.*

You were my only light in all that hell, and I couldn't let that disappear. I would have done anything to protect you. Anything. I'm so sorry. So, so sorry. I know I let you down. Hell, I let myself down, but I didn't see any other option at the time.

Looking back, we should have just left, disappeared. But all those are "what ifs," and I've learned I can't keep on with the what ifs, because they'll never happen.

I know now, though, I have to move on. Don't think that I'll ever forget you, because that is just not the case at all. I will never *in a million years forget you, Drew. Ever. No matter what happens in my life, you will forever have a special place in my heart.* I paused, feeling a little uneasy about my next words.

I've met someone. If you're looking at me, you already know that, but I don't know how all that stuff works. But I love him, Drew. I do.

In my dream, you called me a whore, and that broke my heart because that's the one thing I'm not. Yes, I did things I'm not proud of, but being a whore with Lynx isn't one of them. I really hope you don't really feel that way about me. That would be devastating. So, I'm going with the belief that you don't.

I waited for the right guy to break through, to get to the real me, and I found him. He treats me better than I ever thought I deserved. He gets me, the core of me, and I think I get the core of him. We're not perfect at all, but we are perfect together.

I hope that you're happy for me and that you want me to find my sliver of good in this world because I think it's time that I take it and run with it. I'm tired of being down all the time. I'm tired of not smiling and always feeling like shit. These last few months have been a huge eye opener for me, and Drew, I'm ready to live. I want to have a life, build something that I can be proud of, right all my wrongs, and be a better person.

I want to have a family. My tears turned into sobs as I let everything hang out. *I want to have a family that I can love, cherish, and teach. I know I had shitty role models, but I learned what not to do. I also learned to protect and fight for the things I love and care about. I want my small sliver of the good, and deep down, I know you'd want that for me, too.*

I'll always love you. Never forget that. Ever. *But I have to do what's right for me, and I'm finally figuring out what that is. Love you. Miss you…*

I swiped my face that was a blubbering mess. In all the years I had thought about him, I had never once talked to Drew. It hurt too much. Actually, truth be told, I had never believed he could hear me in the first place. Why I felt compelled to do it at that moment, I would never know, but something about it was cathartic. Even with the bombs going off the day before, my shoulders didn't feel as heavy, like the weight had finally released the grip it had on me for so many years.

Did I dare say that I felt a little peace with myself? I had craved that for so long yet never thought it was remotely possible. However, talking to him and getting out my feelings had done that. It was as if the bottle that held everything in so damn snuggly had its top blown off, and I was able to release what was inside.

I didn't think I would ever get over Drew's death, but the weight of it wasn't as heavy.

"Babe?" Lynx's deep voice came from behind me.

I wiped my face one more time before getting off the swing and turning to him.

"You okay?"

I didn't answer. Instead, I went to him and wrapped myself around him, his arms coming around me securely. I let loose, crying until I didn't think anything was left. Lynx simply rubbed my back and kissed me on the top of my head several times, remaining quiet, just being there for me. I loved how he knew exactly what I needed.

I pulled away and looked up into his concerned yet saddened

eyes, stood on my tiptoes, and gave him a peck on the lips.

"I'm okay." I really meant those words. "Yesterday was hard, and I want answers." Oh, I so did. I was going to find Trey and demand why he had told me all that shit—why he couldn't just tell me that Drew was gone, and why he had to make up all that bullshit. I had a fire of determination brewing on that one. "I was talking to Drew."

Lynx's arm went a little stiff then relaxed. I didn't have a clue how all this guy-girl stuff worked, but I went with what Lynx and I had: the truth.

"I never talked to him before, and I surprised myself with how good it made me feel." I looked deeply into Lynx's eyes. "I'll never forget him, Lynx. He's a part of me." I needed him to understand that. I didn't think a guy would like to share their girl with anyone, but a part of me would always be with Drew.

"And that's perfectly fine, babe. You wouldn't be you if you did."

I smiled at that. It was sweet. Lynx was always sweet to me, but at times like this when he got me, it was all the nicer.

"I love you for you."

A tear I thought I had used up slid down my cheek. "Thank you," I whispered and nestled my head into his chest, breathing in his scent.

"I found some things out. I think we should go inside so I can show you."

My gut tangled with my heart. Lynx had told me the night

before that he was pulling every string he could to get all the information about Drew, Devin, and Trey. I wasn't ready to hear any more the night before, but right then, I was. I wanted answers, craved them. I needed to know why.

I nodded as he led me through the yard and into the house, taking us directly to the couch where we sat next to each other. On the small coffee table was a manila folder, and my anxiety began to pick up. While I wanted the answers, I was afraid of them.

He grabbed my hand, holding it gently. "You okay with this?" he calmly asked.

I wanted to scream *no,* but that was the fear talking. I wouldn't let being afraid of what I would find hinder me anymore. I could handle this. I *would* handle this.

"Yes." The confidence in my voice was surprising to me, and by Lynx's smile, he felt the same way. It was so nice to have a rock, someone to have my back while I picked up the pieces of my life.

He released me and opened the folder, exposing a picture of twin babies. They had matching, little baseball outfits on; except, one had a white hat, while the other had a blue.

"Cubs fans?" I questioned with a little smile.

"Guess so." He pointed to the boy on the right. "That's Drew Angles."

My heart skipped a beat. He was such an adorable, little baby with chubby, little cheeks and those same eyes.

Lynx then pointed to the boy on the left. "This is Devin Angles."

He was the spitting image of Drew, down to the way their noses were shaped. It was quite uncanny.

Lynx then started pulling out pieces of paper as he spoke. "Drew and Devin's parents were killed in a motorcycle accident when they were seven months old."

My heart broke for those little boys.

"From the report, they hadn't been out by themselves for a long time and were just out for a ride when they were hit by a drunk driver."

That was when my heart seemed to fully stop beating as Nurse Hatchet's story played in my head: her loss, hurt, and mourning for her parents. She had witnessed all of that, and as horrible as it sounded, I was glad Drew and Devin hadn't seen it with their own eyes.

"This is the kicker. Their mom, Debra, and father, Dennis, only had one living relative: Dennis's mother who was in her late sixties. She only took one of the boys: Devin."

More tears spilled from my eyes. I hurt for Drew who was left behind, unwanted.

"She stated she didn't have the energy for two toddlers, so Drew was put into foster care and given the last name Lewis."

"He was so young," I whispered softly, looking back at the pictures of the little boys.

"Yeah, babe. When the grandmother, Bev, died, Devin went into foster care and given the last name James after he was adopted."

I nodded.

"They never knew the other existed."

That couldn't be right. "Surely, the grandmother would have told Devin about his brother."

He shook his head. "She died a year after Devin went to her. He was only around eighteen months at the time."

"What about all of her stuff?" Clearly, it had to be somewhere.

He pulled out some other papers. "Auction."

I grabbed the paper and looked. The state auctioned off all of her belongings, leaving Drew and Devin with nothing.

I gasped. "Oh, no."

"Yep, so they have no recollection of even their parents, but you probably knew that from Drew."

Nodding, I said, "He always told me he didn't think he had real parents because there wasn't any trace."

"The only thing I can think is that the grandmother put that as a stipulation."

The picture of the boys caught my attention again, their little, smiling faces breaking my heart. "Why would she do that?"

Lynx put his arm around my shoulders, and he kissed my temple. "Don't know, babe. People do crazy shit for different reasons."

I knew that to be true, but it still sucked.

He released me, going back to the papers. "Devin was adopted." He handed me the paper, and I stared at it in awe. "Suzanne and Edger James. They kept Devin and just changed his last name to theirs. They adopted him when he was two and a half."

"Were they good people?" I knew better than most what happened when they were bad.

"Yep. They're still alive and only have Devin. I ran their names through the system and nothing came up for a Devin James or either of his parents. From what I can tell, they are on the up and up."

Relief filled me that at least someone in this fucked up mess was able to have a good life, able to have a shot at living happy. "That's good."

"The woman you saw, Kelsey, is his wife, and the little boy is Spenser."

I smiled at that. Devin had a family and had found his slice of the light. Happiness didn't cover the magnitude of what I felt for them.

Lynx cleared his throat and pulled out another piece of paper. "Brace yourself, babe," he warned.

I closed my eyes and breathed in deeply as he handed me a crisp, white sheet of paper. Tears gathered in my eyes.

Drew Lewis, 17, died of multiple gunshots in what is believed by police to be a drug deal gone wrong.

"What!" I screeched, still reading the words.

Police and emergency vehicles were called to the alley behind the Greenway Gas 'N Go at eleven forty-three a.m. where they tried to revive him. He was dead at the scene.

Cocaine was found next to the body

with prints matching those of Mr.

Lewis.

"This isn't true!" I shook the paper at Lynx, not mad at him, just mad.

"Babe, I know."

"That asshole got away with killing Drew?" It hit me with the impact of a freight train.

I had never looked to see if the Peterson's had gotten in any trouble. I had never looked to see if they had gone to jail. I had been so closed off I had never taken the time to find any of that information out. That was a sucker punch to the gut, filled with guilt. I should have. Dammit, I should have.

"He did, but he's dead now."

"Good!" I barked a little nastily. "The asshole deserved to die!" Then I wondered, "How?"

"Didn't pay a dealer for his blow."

"That fucking piece of shit!" I stood, needing to move. I paced and chewed on my nail. "He took him to that alley and put those drugs on him." I shook my head. "I'm glad he's dead. I'm not giving him any more of my thoughts." My thumb hurt, so I moved to my other and chewed. "What about the wife?"

He cleared his throat. "Still alive, but she had a stroke. She can't move from the chest down and is in a nursing home with around the clock care."

That information didn't provide me with any solace. She should have to live with mice shit covering her and only table scraps to eat.

"Babe," Lynx called.

I froze at his tone and turned to him, my heart racing.

"They can't hurt you ever again."

He was right. Needing to calm down, I started breathing and counting. *Inhale ... one. Exhale ... two.*

By number thirteen, I had myself together and came over to sit with Lynx. Then he gave me the death blow.

"According to the reports, the Peterson's cremated Drew's body, and there was a small ceremony at that time. I looked into the laws, and the Peterson's weren't required to have a formal burial. And since they cremated him, there is no record after they received the ashes. If I had to guess, the Peterson's just took the money given to them by the state for themselves. There is no record that indicates he has a place."

The way he had said the "has a place" part was a little creepy, but I got what he was telling me. There was no final resting spot for Drew. It was like he had never existed on the planet, like he had never belonged, was never with me. I was the only one left who remembered him and would be for all the years to come.

My eyes burned as tears sprang up. My chest ached for Drew, for the man he would never be, for the family he had never known. Crying quickly turned into sobs as I gripped on to Lynx. I needed his strength at that moment. I needed him to be able to hold me because my confidence was being crushed. Lynx being Lynx, he did. Even feeling so saddened about Drew, so hollow, Lynx filled me, allowing me to fall apart. I knew he would be there to catch me.

Chapter Nineteen

"Oh, my God." Andi pulled me into her arms and hugged me with everything she had. I reciprocated, feeling the love this woman had for me. I hoped she could feel mine, too.

I had just finished telling her all the sordid details that Lynx had shared with me the day before. At first, I didn't know if I was going to tell her or not, but deep down, I knew I needed to. Andi had been my sunshine for so long, still was, and I couldn't begrudge her the information. Also, it felt good talking to someone other than Lynx about it. Lynx was great—don't get me wrong—but sometimes, talking to your best friend was needed.

"I hurt for him," I told her shoulder as she pulled away, eyeing me carefully, no doubt looking to see if I was going under again. I couldn't blame her. There was always that possibility. However, I felt more confidence in myself that I could take the information and deal as best I could.

She said softly, "I know. It's written all over your face."

I gave her a soft smirk. She knew me, just like Lynx. I liked that a lot.

"I feel like there wasn't any justice for Drew, and it eats me up that no one except me will remember him."

Andi pulled me to the couch in her apartment, sitting next to me so we were facing each other.

"His brother knows nothing about him. I think I should tell him about Drew, but then I think *why do that when it would cause Devin pain?* What kind of person would I be to go into his life and disrupt it like that?"

"Oh, honey." As she gripped both my hands, I could feel her comfort and love deep in my soul. "What does Lynx think about that?"

Shock hit me momentarily at her question. She hadn't asked much about Lynx, and I had never pushed for fear of hurting her or her feelings for me. I knew they were there, and I held them with white gloves. She meant too much for me to let her down.

"He says it's my decision." At that, I smiled and shrugged. "He said that if I wanted to tell Devin, he'd go with me, but if I wanted to keep it to myself, that was my choice. Part of me feels like I should tell him about his brother and what an amazing guy he was, but then the other part says just keep it locked down so the loop of hurt stops with me."

"I'm behind you whatever you decide," she told me.

I had to ask, "What would you do?"

She sucked in a breath and thought a moment before she spoke. "I'm not you, so whatever I say here isn't going to be a right way or a wrong way. You know you have a choice here. You need to ask yourself this: Can you live with yourself not telling his twin? Can you live with letting Drew only live inside of you? If you answer yes, then you keep it to yourself. If you answer no, then you tell Devin."

I thought about her questions. They were logical and precise, everything I had expected from Andi.

"I need some time to think, but your questions are good. I just don't have the answers right now. It's all too fresh. I need to let it soak in."

Confliction rolled through me as images of the Drew I knew scattered in my head. I felt my lip tip up at the recollections of him. He was a good guy, the best.

She gave my hands a soft, reassuring squeeze. "All right, I have to make brownies for my parents' house tomorrow. Family dinner." She rolled her eyes, and I laughed.

Andi loved going to family dinners and sometimes took me with her. She always made the best brownies. Not to mention, I loved how she turned the subject around, letting me release all the buildup.

I quirked a brow. "Do you want me to help you?"

She full-out laughed. "Nope, just come and talk to me while I cook."

It was my turn to laugh. "Now that, I can do."

The afternoon was spent making brownies and talking to my best friend. It was comforting, and Andi did it all naturally.

***

The bar was busy, which was good. It gave me little time to think about anything except filling orders and cashing people out. It was a nice change of pace from all the heavy, emotional stuff over the last couple of days.

As I locked down the bar and finished with cleaning, my cell buzzed in my back pocket. I looked at the display, reading *Lynx Calling.* I answered immediately with a goofy smile on my face.

"Hey."

"Hey, babe. I'm outside."

"Be right out."

I hollered good-bye to the other bartender and a couple of the waitresses who were flipping the chairs up on the tables and went out to Lynx.

Walking out into the cool night air, I loved the feeling of it on my face. It gave me the same sensation I felt when Lynx pushed me on the swing: freedom.

Lynx stood next to his truck, his arms crossed, as handsome as ever. I had never believed in good things happening, especially to a person like me, but he was my happy, and I took him gratefully.

I walked right into his arms, hugging him as he kissed the top of my hair then my temple. I loved when he did that.

“Have a good night?”

“Yeah, tips were good, so that’s a bonus. I’ll have enough soon for a place.”

Lynx’s arm tightened, and I looked up. “What?”

“Babe, you have a place.”

I scrunched my brows in confusion. “I live with Andi,” I reminded him.

“And whose bed do you sleep in at night?” The *duh* light bulb went off.

“With you.”

He kissed my lips softly. “Yeah, with me. So, when you’re ready, which babe, needs to be soon”—he smiled that sexy smile and I melted—“we’ll move all your shit to the house.”

“Are you asking me to move in with you?”

His hands came to cup my cheeks as he pulled me in closely to him. “There’s nothing I want more, babe. I fucking love waking up to you every morning and falling asleep next to you. This shit is real, Reign.” He said no more, because his lips were on mine in a ferocious kiss.

Yes, definitely. This shit was real.

***

“Babe, come in here,” Lynx called from his office.

I was in the kitchen, doing the dishes from lunch. I dried my hands off and went to him, finding him sitting at his desk, his brow knit and anger written on his face. My stomach dropped. He looked up and schooled his features, but I was already on alert.

"I want you to take a look at this."

Slowly, I walked around his desk. Sensing my unease, he pulled me into his lap.

"It's okay, Reign. I just want you to see this."

I nodded and looked at the computer monitor.

On it was me working behind the bar, and on the barstool was Trey.

"Surveillance video of the bar." He pointed to Trey. "Is that the guy?"

Anger rippled through me like a storm in the ocean. "Yeah."

Lynx's body went taut. "Fuck."

My hands began to sweat, and my heart was beating a mile a minute at Lynx's tone.

"What's going on?"

"That's Trey Simmons. He's a fucking idiot." Well, I already knew that part. "No, seriously. He thinks he's more than what he really is, which is a very low-level thug."

"But, in the bar, everyone said he was the guy who knew everything," I retorted.

Lynx's eyes met mine. "That's what he wants everyone to think."

"But why would he make up some elaborate story about going to the hospital and then finding Devin? He obviously knew something."

"True, and I'm going to figure out what." He tapped my leg. "Up ya go. I need to go hunting."

I didn't move. "Hunting?"

"I'm going to hunt Trey down."

I swallowed. "Don't get into trouble."

"Babe, the only one who's got trouble is him." He stood and placed me on my feet.

"I want to come with you."

"No," he replied, and that lit the fire inside me.

He wasn't doing this on his own.

"No? This is my life, Lynx. I deserve to know the whys."

He brushed a stray hair behind my ear. "Yeah, babe, you do. I'll find him, and then you can talk to him."

I cooled. "Okay, but be careful."

He kissed my lips. "Always. I have a beautiful woman to come home to." Pepper barked. "And a dog."

My insides turned to goo. I went up on my tiptoes and kissed him hard and deeply, letting him know how much everything he had done meant to me.

The words I wanted to say got lodged in my throat as he pulled away, gave me a slight peck, and was gone.

I realized quickly that I was not a patient, wait-for-Lynx-to-go-do-crazy-shit type of woman. As the seconds turned into minutes and the minutes turned into hours, I cleaned every surface I could find in the house. I even cleaned around the toilet with an old toothbrush. After vacuuming and sweeping every floor, I had nothing left to clean. Nothing. Lynx had been gone for hours, and I became restless without the cleaning to take my mind off of it. What was worse, I didn't have a shift that night at the bar.

The thing that struck me most was me and the door. I had spent so many years checking, rechecking, and triple-checking to make sure my door in the apartment was locked, that I was secured within the confines. While there in Lynx's space, the urge to go to the door and make sure it was locked didn't arise within me. For the first time in my life, I felt safe, and I felt it with Lynx. Even though he wasn't there, I still had a sense of safety, something I had never had in my life. Just the thought had me smiling.

Finally, I thought I would try a movie to get my mind off of everything and calm down. I put in the *Fast and Furious*. I freaking loved Vin Diesel, and the action of the movie kept my attention, but Lynx was always right there in my mind.

I lay on the couch, and somewhere between one of the car chases, I fell fast asleep.

I woke to my phone ringing on the coffee table. The room was only lit by the blue screen, the TV having gone into sleep mode after the movie was over.

The display said *Lynx Calling*, so I flipped it open.

"Are you okay?"

"Yeah, babe. I'm on my way to get you. Be ready to roll in five."

Wait ... what?

"Where are we going?"

"We have someone to talk to. Five minutes, Reign. Love you." Disconnect.

Shit!

I raced through the house, throwing off my cleaning clothes and putting on some jeans and a hoodie along with my tennis shoes. Headlights peered through the curtains, and I looked out the front door window to see Lynx. I locked the door behind me and raced to him.

He hopped out of the truck and met me on my side, stopping me from opening the door.

"Trey is in the back of the cab. He's taped up and can't move or talk."

Shock wasn't even the word I felt. It was an all-consuming, holy-shit moment.

"You need to be cool with this, Reign. I found out today that asshole in there pissed off some pretty important people. We're gonna chat with him and hand him off to those people."

My eyes widened. "Are they going to kill him?"

"Babe, that's not our problem. He'll be alive when we give him over; that's all you need to know. Everything else will be neither of our concerns." His face was so straight, hard, unyielding. This was a side of Lynx I didn't see every day, the one that was trained to fight and kill. Maybe I should have been scared of him like this, but I couldn't make myself. I felt safe with him. He would never hurt me or let anyone else do so.

"I get it." I did. Trey had made his bed. All I wanted were answers to why he had done what he did. What happened after that wasn't on my shoulders. I learned from Wrestler McMann that everyone had their own problems, demons, and I only had to battle mine. I couldn't take on theirs, especially when I was working so hard on mine.

Lynx softened a bit and leaned down to kiss me. Then he opened the truck door, and I jumped in.

He wasn't kidding about Trey being taped up. His hands were bound with silver duct tape behind his back, and his knees were bent up and taped together around his ankles with a piece of tape over his lips. He also had a pretty nice shiner on his right eye.

"Hi, Trey," I said calmly, though on the inside, I was scared as hell for so many reasons I couldn't count them all.

He mumbled something unrecognizable before I turned in my seat and buckled my belt.

We drove for hours on the pitch dark back roads. I didn't ask where Lynx was taking us. I trusted him and didn't think letting Trey hear anything he wasn't supposed to would bode well for us.

As we pulled up to a shack of a house, I instantly had a chill race up my spine. It looked like one of those places they made horror films out of. The paint was worn and falling off, the dangling shutters hung by maybe a nail or screw, and the roof looked partially caved in. There was no way anyone lived there.

When Lynx put the truck in park, the unease coursed through my veins. I almost felt like I was on one of those crime scene shows and a bunch of cameras would jump out at me at any time.

"No one's in there. It'll just be the three of us," Lynx said, resting his hand on my thigh, obviously sensing my nerves going aflame.

Giving him a soft smirk, I placed my hand on top of his, giving it a squeeze. “What do we do?”

I might have lived on the streets for a year and done some questionable things, but taking a man covered in duct tape into a scary as hell house was something I had never done, especially when I just wanted to ask him questions and find out why. Nevertheless, I trusted Lynx, so whatever was about to go down, I would follow his lead, wherever that might go.

“First, get out of the truck.”

I giggled and immediately wiped my features clean. I should not be laughing at a time like this, but Lynx had a way of making me feel at ease during anything, even this.

“Right.” I opened the door and jumped down, the chill from the night making my skin prickle.

Lynx came around the truck and opened the door to the back where Trey was, grabbing him by the ankle and pulling him out. Trey plummeted to the ground and cried out from the fall. His eyes were locked on Lynx’s angry ones.

Trey began shaking his head back and forth, mumbling something through the tape. Lynx gave Trey a kick to the side, and I jumped. This was definitely not the Lynx I knew. This was darker, sinister, demanding, and it probably made me a sicko, but seeing him so strong over Trey was a huge turn on.

“Gotta carry the fucker,” Lynx said, picking Trey up around the waist and walking to the door. “Babe?” he called out.

I hightailed it to the door.

"It's open."

I turned the handle, and the door creaked open as if it hadn't been opened in hundreds of years. I searched the wall for a switch as Lynx brushed by me. A loud thud then sounded right before Trey's groans.

Locating the switch, I flipped it. Nothing. I tried again. Nothing. We were lucky the moonlight was flowing in, lighting up the room in a soft glow. Still, I wanted lights. I wanted to see what was going on. I didn't like the unknown.

"Babe."

I looked to Lynx.

"Over there." He pointed to a rotted old chest that had a lantern sitting on the top. "Here," he called out before tossing me a box of matches. Luckily, my reflexes were pretty good, and I caught them with ease.

I lit the match and then touched it to the wick, bringing the lantern to life. The space was something I would have stayed in when I was living on the streets. The plastered walls were falling down, and the hardwood floors looked so tattered I was glad to have shoes on. I inhaled the smell of mold or mildew. It must have been coming from the only sitting spot in the room, a dirty, stained couch. It was funny, because back in the day, I would have loved to have something as dirty as a couch to lie on instead of crawling under the viaduct to sleep. It was strange how life changed.

"All right," Lynx said, tearing off the tape from Trey's mouth as he continued to lie on the floor.

A yelp of pain streamed from his lips at the yank. Lynx then kicked his taped up legs, only for Trey to let out another sound.

I stood back, taking it all in and trusting Lynx.

"What the fuck, man?" Trey barked out with more balls than I thought he should have considering the menacing, murderous look on Lynx's face. Most men would cower in a corner. Hell, if I didn't know Lynx, I would.

Anger pulsed from every angle of Lynx's body, and his jaw ticked before he said, "The fuck is, you told Reign here shit that wasn't true. That shit caused problems. Now you're gonna tell us why the fuck you lead her to Devin."

My heart clenched at the mention of Devin, but I didn't let it show. I wanted answers. I deserved them.

"Fuck off. Do you know who I work for?" Trey antagonized Lynx, which I thought was a really, really bad move.

Two kicks to the gut had my hands instantly coming around my stomach, like that would protect me from the blows, as if they were really happening to me.

"I know exactly who the fuck you work for, asshole. Unlike you, I get my information right the first time." Lynx picked Trey up by the arm and threw him to the couch. It was amazing the strength Lynx had. "Also unlike you, I talk to people. I know a lot." Lynx's eyes glared into Trey's.

I wondered who this man worked for and if we were going to be in trouble because of it. I knew how the streets worked, and blowback occurred all the time. I didn't want that for Lynx and me. I wanted to know why Trey had done what he did, but not at the cost of us getting in trouble from big players.

"Fuck off," Trey repeated before Lynx slapped him across the mouth. Trey spat blood out onto the floor. "He's going to take you out, motherfucker," he chided.

"Oh, yeah? Okay, then tell us the information, and we'll all get out of here." Lynx surprised me by changing tactics as quick as a shark.

"Why?"

I stepped in, finally finding my voice. "Because I want to know why you would tell me about Devin when I asked you about Drew."

Trey's eyes swept up and down my jean and hoodie covered body. "It's a shame you cover that tight ass up."

The punch to Trey's jaw was a surprise to both me and him.

Trey spit on the floor and moved his jaw from side to side. "Motherfucker, once I'm untied, you are fucking done," he threatened, but Lynx ignored him.

"Tell me!" I yelled a bit more loudly than needed, but the tension between the two men was reaching epic proportions, and I needed it to be done.

Trey's lip curled in a way that made my skin crawl. "Babe, why do you think I come into that fucking bar?"

I shrugged.

"To look at that sweet ass and those amazing tits."

Lynx went to punch him, but I called out, "Wait," and Lynx

held back. “Continue.”

Trey chuckled. “I knew that pussy had to be good. You’ve got this one whipped with it.”

There was no stopping Lynx this time as every muscle in his body tightened to the point he looked as if he were going to explode. He laid into Trey, kicking and punching while Trey heaved for breath.

Lynx grabbed Trey by the throat, squeezing hard, and Trey’s face began to turn purple. He said nothing, so Lynx let Trey go with a gasp of air.

“Fuck,” Trey choked out, his voice raspy.

“So you wanted a piece of me.” I cut through the fog, trying to get to the damn point.

“Fuck, yeah. Every motherfucker in that bar does. Except, you don’t give it out. When you came to me, I saw an opportunity. I searched for the Drew kid and found the brother. He looked just like the picture you showed me, so I used it to my advantage.”

My stomach plummeted. “To your advantage?”

“Sure, you go to Devin, thinking he’s Drew; he rejects you; and I’m there to pick up the pieces. Easy.” Even with blood dripping from his face, he didn’t seem afraid.

Rage burned through my veins like molten lava. I clenched my fingers and swore there was static in my ears. “You mean to tell me, you gave me that load of shit so you could fuck me!” I charged him, getting a few good licks in before Lynx grabbed me around my stomach and held me back. “Let me go!” I demanded, still kicking and screaming. I was sick and tired of people thinking they could use me for sex. I wasn't a fucking toy.

A red haze filmed over my eyes. I wanted to annihilate Trey, let him feel what it was like to be used. My kicks and thrashings became more forceful as I allowed the anger to take me over.

"Babe." Lynx's lips came to my temple. I felt his soft touch, and it somehow penetrated through the haze, settling me as he set my feet on the ground, my breaths still coming in hard pants.

I wanted to claw Trey's eyes out. He had no idea what his shit had started, and only so he could fuck me! And I was the one who had been in the hospital? He should have been there. He was so fucking delusional.

"I would have never fucked a limped dick piece of shit like you!" I yelled at him.

He brushed his face against his shirt, smearing the blood from his cut lip. "Kitten has claws." He chuckled. Yes, chuckled.

My body went taut, and I again tried to get out of Lynx's grasp, but he didn't allow it.

"Babe, let's get this shit done," Lynx told me in my ear.

I knew he was right. I wanted this over with. The past couldn't be changed, but the future could.

I nodded, stopping the fight.

"You would have fucked me, because that would have been my marker. You'd have had to. If not, I'd have taken it from you."

It was Lynx turn to stiffen at my back. Everything at that point happened so damn fast it made my head spin. One moment, Lynx was behind me, and the next, he was on Trey, beating the ever-loving shit out of him. Trey was trying to shield his face, but not doing a very good job.

The rumble of a motorcycle came from outside.

Shit, someone was there. Who the hell could be there? Were these the ones coming to get Trey?

I rushed over to Lynx. "Lynx," I said calmly to get his attention yet didn't get anywhere. I screamed his name, breaking through whatever fog he had been under as he pummeled Trey who was bleeding out of multiple cuts and starting to bruise. "Someone's here."

He stopped and listened then moved away from Trey.

"Calvary's here." Mystery seeped from his words.

As the motorcycle noise got closer, I noted it wasn't just one but several. Lynx was so calm with this, while I was sucking it up, feeling my body begin to tremble. Lynx wrapped his arm around my shoulders. He wasn't even heaving breaths from hitting the hell out of Trey. Wow.

"What's going on?" Trey's words came out muffled because of the blows to his jaw.

Lynx gave me a squeeze. "Well, asshole, it seems you fucked with the wrong people who, in exchange for things being settled with your boss, get you."

The hair on the back of my neck stood, and my imagination ran wild with what they were going to do to Trey. I shouldn't care—he was an asshole—but I couldn't help myself.

“What the fuck are you talking about?” Trey asked.

“The Ravage MC. You fucked with them, and now they get to fuck with you.”

I watched as every drop of color leaked from Trey’s face, and his mouth snapped shut. It made me think these guys weren’t good guys.

“You see, they get a clean slate with your boss, and you get six feet under after they do whatever it is they do to ya.”

“Fuck,” Trey bit out. “Man, don’t give me to them,” he pled.

“Too late.” Lynx paused. “Besides, you pretty much said you were going to rape my girl, and on top of that, all the shit you’ve put her through already; so I’d never let you live to see another day. If it weren’t them, it would be me. After we hand you off, we are washed clean of your filth.” That sounded good—not the *never let you live* part, but the being clean of him. I wanted that.

The motorcycles sounded like they were right outside the door as Lynx pulled me with him to the front door. The bikes stopped and the lights went out.

Six. There were six of them, each swinging their legs over their bikes and taking their helmets off.

As they walked up, my heart seized. They were big and didn’t hide the guns attached to their bodies. The one who led the pack had salt and pepper hair slicked back and a very long beard of the same color. He oozed power and confidence. Hell, they all did, just like Lynx.

“Pops.” Lynx held out his hand as the man walked up and shook it firmly.

"Lynx," he said, looking around the space and taking everything in. He was thinking so much I could almost see the wheels turning in his head. His eyes came to me. "Hey." He lifted his chin then looked at Lynx. "Your girl?"

Lynx smiled. "Hell, yeah."

"Damn, all the pretty ones are already taken." Pops' lip tipped up. The joking camaraderie helped with my nerves, but then his eyes swung to the couch. "There's that piece of shit." Pops walked farther into the room as the other guys started piling in.

One with long, blond hair braided down his back, wearing a red, white, and blue bandana, scanned me, taking in every curve. "Damn, sweetheart."

A flutter went in my belly, not at him calling me that, just at having the male attention. I had stayed clear of it for so long I wasn't used to it.

A beefy hand came down on the man's shoulder, and when the man stepped into the light, I gasped. This one … He was mean, mean to the core. Looking at him, the hair on my arms stood to attention while a prickle came up my spine.

"Dagger, leave the girl alone."

"Come on, Rhys, I'm not fucking dead."

In walked a man with brownish-blond hair to his shoulders and a beard trimmed short to his face. "Nah, not dead, but if you chase any tail, Mearna will string you up by your balls."

The bandana man, Dagger, laughed. "Still getting used to that shit, brother." He shook his head, moving farther into the room.

Next came two men who were exactly identical. No shit. Same blond hair, cut exactly the same; same eyes; same sculpted facial features; same black shirt, jeans, and a leather vest thing. They were mirror images of each other. I couldn't help staring.

"Lynx," one said, lifting up his chin.

"Buzz." Lynx nodded. "Breaker."

"Long time, man." They all three shook hands.

"Yeah." Lynx was quiet for a moment, like he was lost in another time. "Shit's been crazy."

"You been doing okay?" the man named Buzz—what kind of a name was that?—asked.

Lynx gave me a squeeze. "Better than I've been in a long-ass time."

"Good, brother."

Breaker didn't say anything, just lifted his chin and then was gone.

Broad shoulders came to the door, and I had to look up. Sapphire eyes stared back at me. Even with the lack of light, his eyes glittered. His light, caramel hair looked as if he'd run his fingers through it many, many times, and he, too, had a beard cut short. Maybe it was a prerequisite—must have beard to be in bike club—or something.

"Cruz," Lynx greeted.

"Lynx, you've got some of our trash, I hear."

"Yep, we're done with him."

Cruz's face lit up in a wicked grin that put me on edge. "Play time." He clapped his hands together with a loud smack before walking toward the other men.

Lynx asked, "Pops, we good here?"

Pops turned slightly. "Fucking great. We've got this." He then turned around in what felt like a dismissal.

"Come on, babe." Lynx pulled me from the house and into the truck.

I didn't look back. I didn't want to know what those guys were going to do to Trey.

I hoped I never crossed paths with them when they were pissed at me.

***

"What's wrong?"

I had thought Lynx was asleep, so I was being quiet not to disturb him, but I was wrong.

"Just can't sleep." I hadn't been sleeping well since our talk with Trey, and that had been four nights before. It wasn't Drew who haunted my thoughts anymore. No, it was Trey, and that scared the shit out of me.

"Babe, what did we talk about? No lies. Talk."

I sighed deeply. "I keep having dreams of Trey coming to claim his marker."

Lynx stilled. I could almost hear his teeth grinding in the back of his mouth. "I swear to you that motherfucker will never touch you. Ever."

I believed him, but that didn't stop my mind from conjuring up different scenarios in my head. It was creepy as hell.

"I know."

"Nah, babe. He's gone. A memory. What he did fucking pisses me off, but it's done. We know why now; we have our answers. Now we move on."

I burrowed deeper into his warmth, loving the way his hot body made me so warm.

"Yeah," I breathed out, snuggling into him.

Chapter Twenty

"Pepper, come here, girl." I whistled to get the dog's attention. When she ran around the corner and darted to me, I threw the ball with all of my might, and Pepper chased after it.

We had been playing like this for over an hour, and neither of us were tired of it. Funny how something so mundane as playing catch with a dog could bring me so much joy. Lynx was right; her companionship meant the world to me.

The sun was shining, and birds were chirping. The light breeze made it a perfect day. The only thing that would have made it better would be if Lynx would get back.

He had said he had some jobs to take care of, but he hadn't told me anything about them. In some strange way, I got it. I understood he wouldn't be able to tell me things about his job, and while I feared for his safety, I never badgered him for information when he got home. If it was something I needed to know, he would tell me.

Pepper brought the ball back, tail wagging, and dropped it at my feet.

"Again?"

She barked.

"All right." I heaved the ball, and she took off after it.

I needed to come to a decision about Devin—whether to tell him about Drew or to let it go. I didn't know what the right thing to do was. My mind kept flipping and flopping, wrestling with the words *yes* and *no* constantly.

The smile on Devin's face came into my head with images of his wife and kid. He had everything and was happy. If I told him this, it would change his world, but in reality, nothing would different. Drew would still be dead, and he would grieve for a brother he never knew and suffer that pain the rest of his life. I knew that pain, carried it around for so damn long it dug into my soul. I didn't want that for him or his family.

Yet, didn't he have a right to know? To understand the guy Drew was, to know he had family, even if he was gone from this earth?

As I continued to throw the ball and Pepper brought it back, I felt something settle in my chest. I knew my answer. I knew what I was going to do.

"Babe?" was called from the back of the house.

I turned to see my man standing there in a dark T-shirt, torn jeans, and looking utterly handsome. And I loved him with everything I had inside. I had never thought I would have that or be able to give that of myself, but with Lynx, it came naturally, which made it all the more special.

I jogged up to him. “Hey.”

His smile widened. “Babe, I think you need to go back where you were and run back here.”

I quirked my brow, wondering what he was playing at.

“When you run, your tits do a little dance for me.”

Warmth crept up my neck and face. He had been doing this more lately, being open about his want for me, and I was doing my best not to let it fluster me, but my body did every time, giving me away.

I smacked him on the arm playfully. “Stop it.”

He pulled me into his arms and kissed me deeply and hard, sucking the breath out of me. When he pulled away, it took me a second to get my bearings.

I opened my eyes to see his smiling face peering down at me.

“You love it.” He pecked me on the lips.

I did.

“Whatever,” I said. “I decided what to do about Devin,” I blurted out, just needing to get it out of my head.

His smile fell as he walked us over to the rocking chair and sat me on his lap. We had talked a few times about what had happened with Trey, Devin, and Drew over the past week, but Lynx had never pushed me on anything. I appreciated that because I was always afraid I was going to get pulled under from the garbage that kept landing in my lap. Proudly, I had held myself together, though, fighting through the darkness and staying in the light, doing things like playing ball with Pepper or taking her for a walk. I would also go running or meet up with Andi to chat.

I refused to get sucked down, but that didn't mean it couldn't happen. Each day was a battle and a journey. Some days were a little harder than others, such as the days after learning about Trey, but I pulled through and lived.

Making this decision was a huge hurdle for me, so I needed to get it out.

"I decided I'm not going to tell Devin." I sucked in a breath and kept going before he said anything. "I know it probably makes me a shitty person for not telling him, but I know the pain of losing something, Lynx. Devin will spend the rest of his life playing the 'what if' game, and it won't bring Drew back. I don't want to be the one to cause him that torment or give him that demon that he'll never be able to chase away. He's happy and has a family. His life is good. I don't want to be the one to fuck that up."

Lynx rocked us in the chair, my head resting on his shoulder as the rhythmic sounds of the chair going back and forth fluttered in my head. He said nothing for so long I started to get worried and second-guess myself.

"You think I should tell him?" We'd had this conversation before yet only really discussed the pros and cons.

"Babe." He began stroking my back as he spoke. "Either choice is shitty, but you're right. You can't bring Drew back for Devin. Sure, you could tell him some stories, but it wouldn't be the same. It wouldn't be like siblings, like me and my sister. I get it. I support you and think you made the right decision."

I let out the air I hadn't realized I was holding and relaxed into his body. The relief that he didn't think I was a flaming idiot making horrible decisions made me love him all the more.

He gave me a squeeze. "All right, we've got somewhere to be."

I jolted up, startled. "Where?"

"Just trust me."

At that, I smiled.

The drive was only twenty minutes in when he started to slow.

Eyeing a cemetery, I grabbed his arm as the panic invaded my body. "What are we doing here?" The words came out breathy as my breathing picked up and nerves hit me.

"What's wrong, Reign?"

"I just don't know why we're here," I breathed out.

He put the truck in park. "I want you to meet my parents."

The panic fled out of me like I was a toilet someone had just flushed. I felt shitty as hell. There I was, panicking over my own shit, and I didn't even take into account Lynx. Damn, I needed to work on that.

"Really?"

"Yep. Come on."

We climbed out of the truck, and he took my hand, leading me through the stones of peoples' resting places. I caught a few of their names, but nothing that stood out to me.

Finally, we stopped. *Ken and Jodi Lynx*, the stone was engraved.

I quickly moved off the grass.

"What are you doing?" Lynx asked.

"I don't want to stand on them."

Lynx chuckled. "Babe, it doesn't work like that."

"You don't know that," I argued, not wanting to be disrespectful. I might have grown up in shit, but I had manners, especially for the dead.

He grabbed my hand and pulled me to his side so I was standing with him in front of the headstone. The stone was engraved with the birthdates and death of each with the words *Beloved Parents* inscribed. It brought tears to my eyes. Not for me, but for the man standing next to me. I squeezed his hand back, hoping I could, for once, give him the strength he so freely gave me at every turn.

His parents loved him, doted on him. He'd had everything, and it had been swiped away from him in the blink of an eye. I felt my heart tighten as I tried my damnedest not to cry, to be strong for Lynx. It wasn't easy, but somehow, I managed.

"Hey, Mom, Dad," Lynx started, and I squeezed his hand again. "I wanted you to meet my girl. Her name's Reign Owens, and she makes me happy." At that, I leaned into his shoulder, gripping it with my other hand. "You would have loved her," he spoke, the catch in his voice telling me this was hard for him. "Mom, you seriously need to be around to help her cook." I nudged him with my hip and felt my lips tip, gaining a small chuckle from him. "Damn, I wish you two were around."

I looked up at Lynx to see tears had fallen from his eyes before he swiped them away almost angrily. I let go of his hand and wrapped my arms around the strong man who had supported me throughout so many ups and downs these past few months, trying to give him the same comfort he had given me just by his mere presence. His arms locked around me in return, and I felt his body silently shake. I said nothing, just held him close.

It was long moments later before he wiped everything from his face and turned back into the strong man who could handle anything.

"We're gonna go. I just wanted you to meet her." Lynx looked down at me just as I looked up. He gave me a soft kiss on the lips. "Come on, babe." His body grew taller as he sucked in a deep breath and took my hand, leading me away from his parents.

As I looked around, I noticed he wasn't going in the direction of the truck.

"Where are we going?" I really didn't want to walk through a cemetery. It made me uneasy, but I followed him as we strolled through until we came to a clearing that only had a few stones. It must have been the newer section where plots hadn't been bought yet.

A pang hit me. Drew had never gotten that. I might never get that. I shook it off and continued.

Lynx stopped and tilted up my chin with his index finger so I was staring into the beautiful depths that brought me so much comfort. "You know I love you, more than anything on this fucking planet." Tears sprang to my eyes. When I didn't move, he said, "I do, you know. You are the center of my world, and I thank whoever put us together in that fucking hospital. My life wouldn't have been the same without you." This time, the tears fell. "I've done something."

My breath hitched as fear ricocheted through all of the love I had just felt.

"Come here." He pulled me three steps closer to him then turned me around so my back was to his front.

I looked out over all the tombstones, not getting it. "What?" I asked.

"Look down," he said, and I followed his directive. That was when time stopped, and my knees gave out. If it weren't for his arm locked around my stomach, I was sure I would have fallen to the ground.

A small stone lay in the grass, newly put in to the ground judging from the dirt around the edges. The name *Drew Lewis* was engraved at the top with the dates of his birth and death. Sobs began to rack my body from the weight of what the man behind me had done for me.

He had given me back something I had thought I would never have again. He had given me back Drew, given me a place to grieve his loss, a place where I could come and talk to him. While my heart broke for Drew, it was then filled with so much love for the man behind me.

I placed my hand over my mouth, trying to get myself under control, but I couldn't, so I just let the water fall from my eyes in rapid succession.

"I wanted you to have some part of Drew. I know he's not under the ground, but this is where he's laid to rest, where you can come and talk if you want to."

This man had to be the sweetest, most generous man I had ever met in my life. How many men would get a headstone for their love's first love just so they could come and talk to him? Not many, but my guy had. He cared enough about me to give me that.

I turned in his arms, snuggling into his warmth and hugging him with everything I had while my body shook, and I soaked his shirt. His hand absently rubbed my back up and down, which I loved.

He waited until I looked up at him before he spoke. "I wanted you to never have to forget him." He lifted his thumb up, swiping the tears from my eyes.

"I love you," I said softly, and I heard his quick inhalation.

I had never told him that. I had never told any man that, not even Drew when he had been alive. We had run out of time.

As I stared into the eyes I had come to love so deeply, I knew this was exactly where I was supposed to be.

"Love you, too, babe. I've been waiting to hear you say those words."

"I know. I wasn't ready. This moment right here, you being you, I couldn't let it go without telling you."

He leaned down and pecked my lips. “Thank you for that,” he whispered. “I’m gonna give you two a few.”

He started to release me, but I clutched on to his arms. “No, you’re not going anywhere.” His brow quirked up. “I want you to meet him.” I gave him the same line he had given me. “He was my only family, all I had until you and Andi.”

Lynx nodded as I turned in his arms, my eyes focused on the stone.

I blew out a huge breath. “Hey, Drew. I know, I know. Twice.” I shook my head. “I should have talked to you sooner, but I’ve been messed up, Drew. Really messed up. But I’m getting things sorted. This is kinda weird, but I told you about Lynx.”

His hand tightened around me. He must have liked that I had talked to Drew about him.

“This is him. He gave me you back.” At that, the water filled my eyes and spilled over once again. I could never in a million years repay this man for what he had just given me. There was no price tag to put on it. It was irreplaceable.

“I’ll take great care of her,” Lynx said, surprising me.

I craned my neck to see him.

“You’ve got my word, man.” As if I didn’t love this man enough, he had to go and say things like that.

When it looked like Lynx was done, I turned back to Drew.

“I’ll come back and see you. Miss you.”

I would always miss Drew, always. Regardless, I was ready to start my life, a real life with me living it and not just existing. I was ready for a life with Lynx.

Chapter Twenty-one

"Come on, babe," Lynx called from the hallway as I applied some gloss to my lips and fluffed my hair. I had spent way more time on my hair and makeup than I normally did, but I wanted to look perfect.

I had put on a skirt earlier, but Lynx had said, "Babe, it's my sister. Wear jeans and be comfortable." He didn't realize it was his sister I was meeting for the first time! I wanted her to like me. I really did.

This had been so far out of my realm of possibilities—meeting a man's family—that it didn't hit me until I had started getting ready. The nerves took over, and I tried to suppress them by making myself look as okay as possible.

A week before, after returning home from the cemetery, Lynx had asked me, if on my next day off, I would meet his sister and her family. I had said yes, but the gravity of it didn't hit me until about three hours ago. Since then, I had been a shaky mess. I wasn't feeling sad. No, just anxious and nervous that she would think I was too messed up to be with her brother, that she wouldn't accept me, or that she would think I was a horrible match for Lynx, all of which would break my heart. I kept telling myself it didn't matter, but deep down, it really did. I wanted her and her husband to accept me into the fold.

I made one more swipe of my gloss then put the lid on it. My eyes popped with my long lashes, and my skin looked almost flawless. My dark hair was in long waves, cascading down my back with a sweep of bangs in the front. I felt good about the way I looked. I had never put too much thought into it, even at the bar, but that day, it felt good, and I looked better. It helped bring the nerves into check.

"Coming," I yelled, walking out of the bathroom and slamming hard into Lynx. My head snapped up. "Sorry."

He took a step back and scanned me up and down, and I felt the heat rise to my cheeks as a wide smile stretched across his face. "Beautiful. Absolutely fucking beautiful." He pulled me to him and kissed me hard. When he pulled away, I saw my gloss on his lips and became frantic.

"You messed up my lips!" I tried to get out of his grasp to grab the gloss and fix my ruined job.

"Babe, give me those lips."

My stomach started to quiver as tingles raced up my body. I gave him my lips, gloss be damned.

After fixing my lips, we climbed into Lynx's truck and made the twenty-minute drive to his sister's. I couldn't get my leg to stop bouncing as the nerves flung around inside me like super bouncy balls. I tried holding it still, but then my hand just went up and down with it. My anxiety was through the roof, and I felt the urge to run, to go and pound everything out into the pavement, but that wasn't an option, so I counted in my head.

One ... deep breath. Two ... deep breath.

Lynx laced his fingers with mine, bringing them to his lips and kissing them softly. I sucked in his comfort and willed myself to calm down.

"Babe, you'll be just fine. I'm not gonna let you fall."

My head snapped to him at his words. He got it. He so got it.

"Love you." I had been telling him that at every opportunity, letting him know the feeling he had for me was mutual and returned. I didn't want him to ever think I took him for granted. I wouldn't. He was too important to me.

He kissed me again. "You, too, babe."

I felt my body begin to relax—not fully, but enough for my leg to stop its action.

Lynx slowed the truck in front of a ranch-style home with tan siding and brown shutters. You could tell they loved the place by all of the trees and bushes. Each one had their place like it was meant to be there. Each one was trimmed, and the dirt was covered with mulch.

Lynx parked the truck as he said, “Come on, babe.” He gave my hand a squeeze and hopped out of the truck, coming over to my side then helping me out. He intertwined his fingers with mine and led me up the concrete walkway.

I felt my insides shake. I didn’t know it was possible, but it was. I felt everything in me shake. I started breathing again, just as we got on the landing and the door swung open.

A wide smile adorned a beautiful woman with long, dark hair and deep, brown eyes. I saw some similarities to Lynx in her, like her nose. She was slender, yet her jeans hugged hips I would love to have.

“Brody!” she screamed, and I gasped. He had told me his name, but I had never heard anyone call him that before. It seemed surreal since he wasn’t Brody to me. He was Lynx.

She ran out and wrapped her arms around her brother, and he gave her a one-armed hug, not letting go of me even when I tried to pull away to give them a moment. He wouldn’t let go.

I had to admit I loved it. I loved that he liked having me close to him. That little gesture meant the world to me.

“Hey, Bay.” Lynx pulled away and introduced us. “Bailey, this is Reign. Reign, this is Bailey.”

The smile didn’t leave his sister’s face as she stepped close to me, and I instinctively took a step back. While I wanted her to like me, there were some things I couldn’t get past quite yet, and one of those was the touch of people.

I quickly held out my hand, compromising on the hug I saw in her eyes she wanted to give me.

She looked to Lynx who nodded, and she took my hand. "It's nice to meet you."

"Same here."

She released my hand quickly, making me wonder if Lynx had told her about me, if he had warned her about my issues. I really didn't know how to feel about that, if I should be happy he had taken that initiative or sad that he had talked about my problems with someone else.

"Uncle B!" a little voice came from behind Bailey before a little girl with light brown hair put up in the cutest, little pigtails pushed past her mom and came directly at Lynx.

He let go of my hand, scooped the little girl up off the ground, and held her in the air as she giggled.

"And who's this? This can't be my little Bray. No, this little girl is an imposter!" he said in a wonky voice that made the little girl laugh. "No, my little Bray is small. You are way too big!" He pulled her down against his chest, and she wrapped her arms around his neck.

My heart skipped a beat. Seeing Lynx with the little girl made something in me want, really want to have my own family. I had thought about it a lot lately, but seeing that had sealed the deal.

Lynx would be a wonderful father. Me, I would do the damned best I could. I wanted it. I wanted the happiness that little girl felt for her uncle and he for her. I wanted to see that every day.

My heart warmed and thumped hard in my chest just as Lynx turned the little girl to me.

"Reign, this little peanut is Braylynn. Braylynn, this is Reign."

She smiled at me. "Hi, Reign. You have a funny name."

"Braylynn Marie!" Bailey snapped at her daughter.

I cut in, "You're right. It's nothing like Braylynn. That's a beautiful name for a beautiful, little girl."

She giggled and squirmed in Lynx's arms. "Come on! Mommy cooked." She said it like it didn't happen often.

"I only cook when I have to," Bailey explained with the same smile plastered on her face. It wasn't fake or forced; it was genuine and I felt it. "I'm not horrible, but it isn't something I enjoy."

"Sis, you'll have to teach her how to cook, because Reign burns water," Lynx teased.

I smacked him on the arm, laughed, and then immediately stopped, feeling like I had done something wrong. Was it the laughing, joking, or that I was playing around with him? I didn't know, but Lynx pulled me into him, still holding Braylynn; kissed my temple; and said, "Babe, relax."

I breathed out and nodded.

We walked into the house, and it struck me hard. This was not a house; this was a home, a place where not only people lived daily, but a place where people *lived.*

The pictures on the wall in the hallway showed smiling faces and special trips. Braylynn's pieces of artwork were in frames like they were the most expensive paintings in the world.

It was a place where people had built a life and were living it every day. I wanted that. I needed that.

I was so stuck on the pictures I jumped when Bailey stood next to me and said, "I love pictures. Mal says I take so many every second of Bray's life is documented."

"Mal?"

"Malcolm, my husband. He's in the living room."

I nodded absently, looking at a picture of Bailey, Lynx, and what looked to be their mother and father because they were spitting images of them.

"That's our mom and dad. It's one of the last pictures we have of them." The sadness in her voice was immediate, and I felt like shit for staring.

"It's beautiful." I looked up and saw one with Bailey and a man in a raft. "This one looks fun."

Bailey's eyes moved to the picture, the smile returning to her face. "Mal took me rafting. I told him he was nuts, but I had one of the best times of my life there. You ever been?"

I shook my head. I hadn't been out in the world to have any of these experiences, and I felt that loss. I wanted that. I wanted some memories: happy ones, fun ones. I deserved that. Lynx and I deserved that.

"You should have Brody take you. He's great at pretty much everything." I admired the love for her brother that poured out of her. I also admired the pride in her words. If I had a brother like

Lynx, I would feel the same way. "I'm sorry about the hugging outside. Lynx told me that touching doesn't fly."

I turned to her, about to say something, but she cut me off.

"Don't say it's okay, because it wasn't. Lynx has been through a lot and knows more than he should." I smiled at that. "But I should have listened, and I'm sorry if I made you feel uncomfortable at all."

She was sweet, but I was happy that she got me. She didn't know me from the person walking down the road, but she was trying. I was going to, as well.

"I'm really okay." I sighed. "It took a long time for my best friend to be able to grab my hand. It's something I'm working through, but I'm just not the touchy-feely type." I hoped I didn't come out bitchy. I simply needed her to know I wasn't ready for that kind of contact.

"I'm a hugger." She shrugged. "I got lost in the excitement, but I'll do better."

"Thanks." I gave her a soft smile, feeling like she really did believe it. I was happy she was giving me that, even though it was hard on her. She was pulling herself back, and that meant a lot to me.

"Help me set the table?" She was letting me off the hook. In so many ways, she reminded me of her brother.

"Sure."

We passed by the living room where Lynx was playing with Braylynn.

Bailey stopped. "Mal," she called, and the man in the recliner turned. He was handsome with an olive skin tone and dark hair. He wore glasses that were wire framed, almost looking like the kind Santa Claus wore. "This is Reign. Reign, this is Mal, my husband."

"Hi." I waved my hand stupidly as Lynx looked up with a smile on his face. He loved that little girl with everything he had, and it showed all throughout his body.

Mal didn't get up from his chair; he just said, "Welcome, Reign. It's nice to meet you."

"Same here."

"Okay, Reign is going to help me in the kitchen."

I shrugged at Lynx. My help in the kitchen wouldn't be much help at all, but I followed.

The kitchen had white cabinets, cream walls, and a dark marble countertop. The floor was tiled in an intricate way that must have taken whoever had done it days. The large kitchen island was littered with food. I didn't know whom she was expecting to be there that night, but there was no way we could eat all of it.

Off to the side was a large, open dining area. The entire space was warm and inviting. The table looked as if the wood had been beaten over time, giving it a very rustic feeling. More pictures lined the walls, and I had to stop myself from going to look at them as the curiosity grabbed me.

"Will you put the plates on the table?"

I saw them sitting on the island. "Sure." I walked around the space and picked up the plates that weighed a ton. They must be stoneware or something. I only knew what that was because Andi's mom had a full set of them.

Bailey went to the stove where the scents of whatever was on it wafted throughout the room.

Taking a step, my foot caught on something that slid. I dropped the plates, trying to brace my fall onto the hard tile, and the shatter of the stoneware on the ceramic tiles was deafening as my shoulder slammed into the floor.

I let out a loud cry as pain radiated up through my arm and shoulder blade. My hand hurt, too, and when I looked at it, I saw blood. Shit, I had cut myself. I had ruined their plates and hurt my damn self. I looked to my feet where a dog with wheels and a red pull cord lay sideways. A toy. Crap. *Reign, you should have looked for toys. Kids, dammit.*

"Oh, my God!" Bailey screeched as she ran to me and kneeled down beside me. Her hands moved as if it were killing her not to touch me.

I gave her an out. "Can you get me a rag?"

She jolted up and ran to the counter as the blood poured out of my hand. Shit, it must be deep.

"What happened?" Lynx came storming into the room like a thundercloud ready to clap. His eyes looked different, almost removed as he stared down at me. The spark that I had come to love in Lynx wasn't there, and that scared me more than my hand bleeding.

"I'm okay. I tripped." I sat up on the floor, my shoulder hurting, but not showing it at all.

"Dammit!" Lynx yelled, spotting the toy on the floor. He went to it, picked it up, opened the back door, and threw it hard into the night sky.

Panic arose in me. This was one of his attacks. The sound of the fall and the sight of my blood must have set him off. Shit.

Bailey rushed up, giving me the towel, just as Lynx was there, pushing Bailey out of the way. I felt horrible as she stumbled backward before finding her footing.

Lynx was in a robotic state, like he was working on autopilot, doing what needed to be done, yet he wasn't really there with us. He was somewhere else.

"Lynx," I said softly, getting no response from him as he inspected my hand.

He pressed as I tried pulling my hand away from the pain, but he held it firm.

I sucked in deeply and tried again. "Lynx."

Again, nothing.

Scared wasn't even the word at that moment. Try petrified that I had lost my man. I had to get him back. It was my turn to help him. He had been my rock since I had met him, so it was my turn to pay him back. The fact that I loved this man made me want it even more. He needed to fall, and it was my turn to be strong and be his shelter.

"Lynx!" This time, I yelled until his emotionless eyes looked at me, but they weren't really looking at me. They were looking through me, which made the hair on the back of my neck rise. "Lynx, I need you to breathe with me. I'm gonna count."

He didn't respond.

I cupped his chin with the hand that wasn't hurt and pulled him close to me. "Breathe with me," I ordered. "Now! One" I sucked in deeply, waiting him to mimic me, but he was still lost. "Lynx, I said one!" I yelled right in his face.

He sucked in a breath, but his eyes still weren't there.

"Two!" I yelled again, and he followed. "Three!"

He did it again.

As I got to ten, I began lowering my voice as the fog he was under began to lift. It was the strangest thing to see him change right before my eyes from not being in the room to being right there with me as he blinked his eyes rapidly.

"Oh, shit." He shook his head. "I had an attack. I'm so fucking sorry, babe."

The fear radiating from him took me off guard. Lynx didn't have fear. He was strong and knowing.

"Did I hurt you?" He was scared he had hurt me; that was where the fear was coming from. Dammit.

"Lynx, I tripped over a toy and fell."

"And cut yourself." His attention moved to the towel on my hand that was now covered in blood. "Shit. Fuck. I need more towels, Bay."

Bailey, with tears falling down her cheeks, immediately got more and put them down next to me.

I felt so bad for her. Lynx hadn't meant to push her. I hoped she understood that.

Mal came to the door with Braylynn in his arms, but Bailey

rushed over and ushered them out of the room.

"I'll be okay, Lynx," I tried to reassure him, regardless of the pain coming up my arm and the cut. I wasn't going to tell him that, though.

"You're bleeding badly, Reign. You're going to need stitches if the wound is as big as I think it is, judging from that plate." He nodded his head to the shards with my blood on them. "You probably have shit in your cut that will need to come out."

I moved my hand to his cheek, bringing his attention back to me. "I may need stitches, but I'm going to be just fine. People trip and fall all the time. It's okay, Lynx."

"It's not okay. I never want to see you hurt. Ever, Reign. And then I just …" He ran his hand through his hair, pulling away from me, and I dropped my hand. "I'm so damn sorry."

"You have nothing to be sorry for. I'm happy I could help you. That's what we have, Lynx. You've helped me so damn much, and now I got to return it. While I hate that you have to go to that place in your head, if you had to do it, I was glad I was able to help you."

My heart bled for him. The pain all over his face was laced with embarrassment, something I never wanted him to feel.

"You listen to me, Lynx." I turned my tone from calming to demanding, catching his attention. "You don't hide that shit from me, just like I don't hide that shit from you. We are a team. We fight back the darkness together. You don't get to take on all my shit and then not expect me to take yours, as well. That is not how this works, Lynx."

"We need to get you to the hospital," he interrupted me.

I knew we did, but he wasn't listening to me, and I wasn't going anywhere until he did.

"Not until you get it through that skull of yours that we do this together. We build a life together. You think I won't see more of that same thing? I know I will. You think I won't have downs and want to stay in bed all day? I will. It is the vicious cycle that plays in our lives, and I refuse to let it win. I won't allow it to. We deserve better. We deserve our happy, and I'm fighting for it, so I need you to do the same."

His forehead came to mine as he continued the pressure on my hand. "I love you so damn much. I don't want this shit to tear us apart. My shit. I've gotten better, but it happens sometimes."

"Then we talk about it and deal."

"Okay." He breathed out as his shoulders slumped, and I knew I had my Lynx back.

"Now, would you take me to the doctor so I can get some help?" I said it as cute as I could, trying to lighten the mood, but Lynx wasn't fully to that point. I looked at Bailey. "I'm so sorry about the plates and dinner."

"Stop that right now. It's my fault for not checking for Bray's toys. I didn't …" She paused, the words caught in her throat as she cleared it. "I'm so sorry, Reign."

"It's okay."

"I'm taking her," Lynx said, picking me up in a bridal hold.

We passed the living room where Braylynn was sitting on her

dad's lap, crying.

"Wait," I told Lynx, and he halted. "Let me down. I need to talk to Braylynn."

"No, we need to go."

I fully turned to Lynx. "I know that, but she's scared, and I'm not leaving her when I know that. I spent my entire childhood being scared, and I refuse to do that to anyone, especially a child."

Lynx waited a beat then set me on my feet. I felt a bit woozy and the room spun a bit, but I made it over to her and kneeled down on the floor so our faces were level.

"Braylynn?" I asked, and she opened her beautiful, brown eyes filled with tears spilling over. "Hey, honey. I'm all right. Your Uncle B is going to take me to the doctor and get me all fixed up. There's no need to worry. Everything is just fine."

"Blood," she said.

"Yes, that's what happens when you cut open your skin. I'm sure you've had a scraped knee or two, right?"

She nodded.

"It's the same thing. I need to go get it checked out, but there is no need to be sad or scared."

"But …" she sobbed. "I didn't pick up my toys when mommy told me to."

Ah, so that was what it was.

"You know, sometimes we forget things. We get busy and things slip our minds. We don't do it on purpose, but it happens, and we take it as a learning lesson." I wasn't quite sure where all of this was coming from. I sounded like a combination of Wrestler McMann and Lynx. Scary.

"I'll pick them up, promise."

"That's good, but no more tears, okay? It's all going to be just fine." I tried to soothe her and felt the urge to touch her knee in reassurance, so I did. That was the moment I had a little five-year-old in my arms, her arms linked around my neck as the panic kicked in.

It took me long moments as I breathed and breathed.

"Let—"

I cut Lynx off, "No." He stopped speaking as I finished breathing and wrapped my arm around the little girl. "See? Going to be just fine."

She nodded her little head, her pigtail coming in contact with my lips, and it tickled. Finally, she dried herself up and let go.

"Now we're leaving," Lynx ordered as he picked me back up and carried me out of the house.

Chapter Twenty-two

I woke to Lynx taking very deep breaths in and out, my head lying on his chest, rising and falling with him. I could almost hear him counting in his head as his arms tightened around me. His skin had changed from normal to clammy with sweat.

I lifted my head, and Lynx's eyes shot open to me. He wasn't lost like he had been three days before, but he wasn't there, either.

"Lynx?" I called out as he exhaled roughly, his lips moving with each breath. "What's wrong?"

Over those past days, Lynx had kept his eyes on me like a hawk, barely letting me out of his sight.

I had needed twenty-one stitches in my hand after they had removed all the pieces of broken stoneware. The cut had sliced pretty deeply, but the doctors at the hospital had fixed me up as good as new. My shoulder and neck were banged up a bit, but nothing was out of place, just sore.

I had called into work, even though I didn't want to, because I wanted the money I earned. However, it was for the best. Besides, I would be back the next night. I would have to wear a plastic glove over my cut hand, though, so liquid wouldn't mess up the stitches. That was going to prove challenging, but I could handle it.

I had learned I could handle more than I had ever thought possible.

"It was the blood," he said roughly.

My heart ached for him. I put my hands under my chin and rested it on his chest. If he wanted to talk about it, I would listen to every word and give him my undivided attention.

"It was the loud crash, too, but when I saw you on the ground, bleeding, I was taken back to a place where blood was spilled everywhere. I was angry at the toy," he said softly. I didn't know what to think on that one.

"I was. That's why I threw it, probably smashing it to hell." He wiped his face with his hand. "I need to buy Bray a new one."

I gave him a small kiss on his chest in hopes that he would continue, that he would let me into this part of him. I had a lot of Lynx except this. He had never cracked that door open to me, yet right then, he was.

"I hadn't had an episode since the one when you got out of the hospital. I thought, for some stupid reason, it had finally released me, that I was finally free from being thrown back in time, but I'm not." He sighed loudly as he continued, "I don't think it'll ever go away, but Reign, I have to tell you I am so much better than what I was."

My heart constricted as everything I felt for this man steeled around my heart.

"I was really bad when I got home. Any sound would have me on edge. It's what landed me in the hospital so many times. You know what helped me?"

"What?" I asked.

His hand rubbed absently over my back. "Talking to other Vets who had gotten out and had the same problems as me, who had been through war, seen some of the same things I had. I hated that they had to live with it like me, but I was also relieved I wasn't alone. I had someone I could talk to who would get it, who would understand. And, babe, I know you've been through shit, but until you've been in a war zone, you wouldn't get it. I'm not saying that to be a dick, but it's the truth.

"War is its own entity. It changes you in ways civilians don't understand. It makes you a different person than you were before you went in."

I wanted to ask in what way it had done that to Lynx, but it didn't matter. The Lynx he was right then was the one I loved. Besides, if I didn't have to dredge up any of the bad shit, I wasn't going to.

"I am who I am, babe." He leaned up and kissed my forehead.

"I love who you are, Lynx: the good, the bad, the sometimes scary."

His hand stilled. "I don't want you to be scared of me."

"I'd never seen you like that, and it will take me some time to understand it, but I'm here with you. I'll do whatever I can to help you battle back your demons. I didn't fear that you would hurt me; I feared I wasn't going to be able to clear the look in your eyes. That was what I was afraid of."

"You reminded me of what I needed to do, and I thank you for that." Lynx kissed my head again then lay back down. "We may not be perfect, babe, but we're perfect for each other."

I smiled, remembering I had said those words. They were truer than ever. "Absolutely."

He pulled me on top of him and kissed my lips softly and sweetly. As we made love, we let our bodies tell each other how deeply our feelings ran for one another. I felt it down to my soul that Lynx was the guy for me. I loved him, and he loved me, warts and all.

***

"Damn, woman, that's scary shit right there." Andi placed her coffee mug back down on the table.

We had just finished eating dinner, the two of us talking about what had happened since the last time we had spoken. I had told her about Lynx and what had happened at his sister's. I needed someone other than Lynx to talk to. I didn't know why, but I did.

Lynx got me, and I got him, but there was just something about talking to your best friend that made it more freeing, more liberating.

"I know."

Andi tugged her bottom lip between her teeth. "You sure this is good? You both have so much shit you're dealing with. Are you sure it's wise for you to get in this deep with someone who has problems as bad as you?"

That thought had never crossed my mind.

"As far as I'm concerned, we love each other, ugly bumps and all. Yeah, we have problems, but so do other people." I grabbed my napkin, needing something in my hand, and I twisted it. "I think we understand each other better since we've both fought and are fighting to be free of it all."

"I'm happy for you." A genuine smile lit up her face. "You deserve this, Reign."

"I'm happy, Andi. For the first time in my life, I'm truly happy. I want to live, not just breathe air. I want to *live*. I want to do all those things I missed out on as a kid and so far as an adult. I want to experience things and figure out what I like and what I hate. I want a family."

Her eyes began to water. "You deserve that."

"I watched Lynx with his niece, and it was one of the most beautiful things I've ever witnessed. I want that for me, for us."

"Then you need to take it. Don't hold back."

"He wants me to move in with him."

She eyed me skeptically. "Hon, I hate to tell you this, but you already are living with him."

My brows drew together.

"Seriously, Reign, you sleep there almost every night and have clothes at his place. What difference would it be to move in the rest of your stuff?"

She was right. I had been sleeping there, eating dinner there, building a life with Lynx there, but something ate at me.

"But I don't want to leave you." My words were hushed. I didn't even know at first if she had heard me, but she had.

"You're not leaving me; you're building a life, a home with someone who means something to you. Lynx is a stand-up man. He laid Drew to rest for you. Guys don't do that shit unless they love you with everything they have inside of them. He does. Your moving in with him doesn't mean we are cut off from each other. It just means we do lunches, dinners, and text often. I love you, Reign, and I want this for you."

Tears sprang in my eyes, and my nose did that weird tingle thing before I knew I was going to cry. I didn't stop myself.

"I love you, too, Andi. You stuck by me through everything, helped me when I pushed you away, stood by me when I spat ugly words at you. You never gave up on me, even when I gave up on myself. You're my light. If it weren't for you, I wouldn't be sitting across this table right now, bawling my eyes out like a baby."

Andi's tears came in a steady stream as she rose from the small table and wrapped her arms around me. I reciprocated as we cried together. This was what friendship was, what sisterhood was—unconditional, unequivocal love, and I had it for her in spades.

Andi pulled back, grabbing a tissue box and bringing it back. We cleaned our faces and then she got us some more coffee before sitting down.

"Look at us, a big pile of tears and snot."

I laughed. "I'm all about the tears and snot these days."

Andi twirled her mug of coffee, staring down into the brown brew.

"What?" I asked.

"I met someone." Her eyes fluttered up to mine, and I smiled.

"You did?"

"I've known him for a long time, but I never really took that step."

"*Him*?" I asked, confused.

She laughed. "Yeah, you're the only female I've ever had those feelings for, Reign. His name is Matthew. He comes into the diner at least once a week, maybe twice. I flirted with him, of course. Better tips." We laughed. She wasn't wrong there. "He's asked me out several times, and I said no, but this last time, I said yes. We had a great time together, and I can't wait for you to meet him."

My heart grew for my best friend. She had been the light, the sunshine for me, and now she was spreading it to someone she cared about.

"I'm so happy for you."

"Me, too."

When my phone beeped, I looked down to see Lynx had texted me, *I'm here*.

"Lynx is here."

Andi rose, wrapping me in a tight hug. "You should take some of your bags with you."

I pulled back. "What, kicking me out?" I teased.

"Never, but it's the right thing for you."

I nodded, went into the room, and packed two big bags, stuffing them full.

Walking out to the truck, I was only balanced because the bags were level on each side.

As soon as Lynx saw me, he jumped out of the truck and rushed to me, taking the bags from me.

"I guess I'm moving in," I told him.

Lynx dropped the bags at my feet, picked me up in the air, and kissed me hard and deeply. "Best fucking news I've heard in a long time."

***

Wearing a doctor's latex glove wasn't ideal for working behind the bar. My grip on the bottles didn't feel right, and I would be lucky if I didn't drop anything. Plus, the pace at which I normally moved was slowed way down. No one complained, though, which was good, and I was pretty sure I got some sympathy tips along with it. Fine by me.

I closed out my register and stocked the back just as the text from Lynx came in, saying he was outside. I smiled, feeling extremely happy.

"Leaving," I called out as I moved to the door, heading for my man's truck parked in the front of the lot.

The pitch black night was only lit up by the parking lot lights casting a glow on Lynx. I wrapped my arms around him and kissed him deeply. Damn, I loved him.

"Have a good night, babe?" he asked, helping me into the truck.

"It was decent."

He nodded, shutting my door and getting in the driver's side.

"Tips were pretty good. I think the customers were taking pity on me."

He chuckled. "I bet."

Something was off with Lynx. He wasn't lost in himself, and he wasn't angry, but something wasn't right. It made my insides constrict.

"What's wrong?"

He smirked. "Sometimes, I hate that you know me so well."

"I do. Spill."

"I found your father," he said, rocking me to my core.

"Really?"

"Yeah, Reign. I've been digging. Your mother worked at a shit-load of places, or it wouldn't have taken me this long. Sometimes, she only stayed weeks at a job then moved on to the next. It just so happened that when you were conceived, she had four different jobs during that time. I extended it out, not knowing if you were born on time or what." I didn't know any of that, either, so I was grateful. "Some of the men who worked there twenty-one years ago moved on to different jobs, so I had to track each of them down. Therefore, it took me awhile, but I found him."

"Are you sure it's him? Because after Drew and Devin, I can't deal with it not being right." That wasn't exactly the truth. I could deal with it. I just didn't want to go down that road again. I knew I was stronger than before, but I still didn't want to go through that heartache.

Lynx put the truck in drive and headed toward his place. "He's in Seattle, Washington. His name is Weston Cheeseman."

"Cheeseman?" That was an odd name.

"Yep, be happy you were stuck with Owens." Lynx chuckled. "He runs a software company, has a wife of thirty-one years, two sons, and one daughter." He paused. "They are twenty-five, twenty-two, and nineteen."

The weight hit me hard. He was a cheater, too. He was with my mother while he was married and had children at home. That rock settled in my gut like a boulder.

"He wouldn't want to know I exist," I said softly.

We pulled into the drive, and Lynx cut the engine. I didn't move from the seat.

"He wouldn't want his wife and kids to know I'm part of him."

"You don't know that."

I raised my brow questioningly at him. "Seriously? You think he wants his wife of thirty-one years to know he stepped out on her when she had kids at home?"

"Babe, dig down deep. I can see it in your eyes. You don't know what this man would think or feel. You can't put that judgment on him right know, because you don't know." He was right, but I still felt it. "He's legit, babe."

"You're positive?"

He rubbed his hand over his face. "I did something." He paused as I waited. "I have a friend who owed me a marker." I knew about those all too well. "I had him get Weston's DNA."

"You did what!" I screeched, and it echoed throughout the cab of the truck.

"He didn't hurt him, just broke into his house and got me some of his hair from a brush and a fork he used to eat with."

I sat there, flabbergasted. "Is there anything you can't do?"

"Nope. I've paid my dues and helped many people out. This helps you out, and I'd go to the edge of the earth to help you."

My heart warmed through the shock.

"I took your hair from your brush and a fork from your breakfast one day and had DNA tests run. Babe, I wasn't going to tell you any of this if it didn't come out positive. I wouldn't put you through that unknown."

I loved this man more than words could say. He so got me.

"Thank you," I whispered.

He grabbed my hand and brought it to his lips. "Love you, Reign. Always know that."

I nodded.

"Got the results back today. Ninety-nine point nine percent positive."

My knee started bouncing. I couldn't stop it as the adrenaline started pumping through my veins. My father. My dad. Would he want to know I existed, or would it be better to let it go, like I had with Devin and Drew?

I fought back the wave of darkness that threatened me, keeping it only at my feet. I was strong. I could handle this. I *would* handle this.

"Do you want to meet him?" he asked, as if it were every day you found the father you never knew. He was so casual and at ease, and I loved him for it. I needed that. I needed to be reassured that it was going to be all right.

I dug down inside myself. "I do want to meet him, not that it would change anything in my life, but it would be nice to know. Then again, he has a family, and I don't want to be the cause of problems within it."

"You can't put that on yourself. He made those choices. He'll have to talk with his family. You have every right to meet him."

I remembered Wrestler McMann and I having this discussion about my mother and her choices. This was the same thing, but it still curled my stomach.

I challenged, "Isn't that hypocritical, Lynx? I mean, I'm not telling Devin about Drew, because I don't want it messing up his life; but I do this to Weston Cheeseman's family?"

"There's one huge difference, babe."

I sucked in a breath, knowing in my gut what he would say.

"Your father is alive; Drew isn't."

I let out the breath. It sounded as if a balloon was let go, and all the air squealed out of it.

Why did my life have to be so difficult? I had just found my sliver of peace with Lynx, and then another thing dropped in my lap. I was getting tired, really tired of having all of this, but I refused to go down. I wouldn't go down without fighting for what I wanted and what I needed.

"I want to meet him."

"Good. We leave tomorrow."

Chapter Twenty-three

I had never been on an airplane before and almost walked right out of the airport, but Lynx held my hand, giving me the strength I needed until I was able to dig it up myself. I was still pissed at him for springing this flight on me so suddenly. His let's-rip-the-band-aid-off scenario still knifed at me. I had thought I would have some time to come to terms with knowing the name of my father, yet the next day, I was flying to meet him.

"It's going to be fine," Lynx said next to me. I had made him sit by the window. There was no way I wanted to look that far down from the sky.

I tried breathing to stop the incoming panic attack, but I ended up needing to close my eyes and count. It helped with takeoff, and so far, being in the air was fine. It was like being in a car expect up thousands of feet with the clouds whizzing by.

"I'm still pissed at you."

"Good, focus on that and breathing."

I glared at him, and he laughed.

"Babe, he knows we're coming."

That got my attention.

"You didn't tell me this. What happened to always being honest?" I clipped out.

He clutched his fingers together. "I called after you decided you wanted to meet him. He's skeptical that you're his daughter, so I had to bring the papers with me."

"And tell him you had a guy break into his house? You can't do that. He'll have you arrested!" The panic overtook me then, the breathing not working. I put my head against the seat in front of me, trying to stop the swirling around me.

"It's all handled, Reign."

"How?"

"Don't worry about it. I've got this."

I turned to look up into those eyes I loved so very much. He was telling me the truth; he had this. He was taking this on for me and making it easier for me. Dammit, why did he do nice shit when I was pissed at him?

"Fine," I snapped yet grabbed his hand and held it for the rest of the flight, clenching it as the plane landed and jumped several times.

"I'm surprised you wanted to go on a plane," I told him after we landed.

"Why's that?"

"Doesn't it bring memories back for you?" I shouldn't have brought it up, but I was curious. I was still learning his triggers. One could show up at any time for either of us.

He rose from his seat, and I followed, grabbing our bags.

"No, I was on the ground, flying doesn't do it for me."

After getting our bags and rental car, we drove, following the GPS's directions.

Seattle was dark, rainy, and dreary. It did nothing to bring on a happy mood. I wasn't sure I could ever live there, not seeing the sun. The place was almost like I was inside sometimes: cold and void. I was uneasy, although I was certain it had a lot to do with meeting my father for the first time.

Lynx checked us into a hotel. Then we set off to the downtown area where buildings were as tall as the sky. I had never seen buildings so tall before. I felt so small next to them, like I was an ant in this wide world.

Lynx went into an underground area and parked the small car. I felt weird having to stand up to get out of a vehicle instead of Lynx having to help me down.

Once he led me to an elevator and pushed some buttons, my nerves shot out of my body like electrical charges. My body pulsed and my heartbeat was so hard it felt like it was going to push out of my chest. Even though Lynx had my hand, it was sweaty, and I felt hot overall.

Just like with Bailey, I had a myriad of sudden thoughts: What if he doesn't like me? What if he rejects me? What if he wants nothing to do with me?

I breathed out, remembering the "what ifs" didn't matter in the grand scheme of things. It was going to be what it was. He would either like the fact that I had come to see him, or he wouldn't. If he didn't, this would be the only time I would ever see him.

In a way, I felt bad for him not knowing I had existed and wondered, if he had known, would he have taken me in with his family, or would he have left me with my mother. Again with the "what ifs."

The bell on the elevator dinged, and I stared at it as the doors opened into a very bright, open space.

Lynx kissed the top of my hand and pulled me out of the elevator. *Cheeseman Enterprises* was etched into the glass on the wall with a large, dark, wooden desk below it. A beautiful woman with long, blonde hair looked up, her eyes scanning mine then doing a double-take on Lynx.

Jealousy raged through me. I wanted to pull him to me and yell at her, "*He's mine*," but no way would I do that.

"Brody Lynx and Reign Owens to see Mr. Cheeseman," Lynx told her as her eyes turned lustful.

Bitch.

"One moment." She picked up the phone, her eyes never leaving Lynx as she spoke into the receiver. Then she set it down and addressed Lynx, not me. "Through those doors. He's expecting you."

This was it, the moment when I met my father. My insides were in a twisted knot. I tried not to let them choke me down. I could do this. I was going to do this.

Lynx opened the door, and I walked inside. At the desk, a man's head popped up. His dark brown hair was combed to the side with lots of hairspray or something keeping it from moving. His eyes were blue, which matched his suit that had pinstripes running down the length of it. He rose, buttoning one of the buttons on his jacket, and came around the desk swiftly.

I halted, causing Lynx to run into my back. He rested his hands on my shoulders, giving them a reassuring squeeze.

"Mr. Cheeseman," Lynx said while Mr. Cheeseman stood in front of his desk, staring at me up and down.

I didn't like the appraisal. It made me more nervous and uncomfortable.

"Please, come in." He had a very deep voice, authoritative, like he was used to giving out directions and orders. I guessed you would have to be like that to run a company like this. "Reign?" he asked hesitantly.

I dug deep. "Yes. I guess I'm your daughter." I couldn't believe I had said it like that. This wasn't the time to joke, but it had just come out, and when I heard his soft chuckle, I felt my body relax just a bit.

"That is what I hear," he said.

Lynx reached in his pocket and pulled out a manila envelope, handing it to the man, who opened it and looked it over.

"I'll have you know that the housekeeper you had get this information from me has been fired."

I gasped at the news. "Don't take it out on him or her or whoever."

"Reign, to be in business, you have to trust the people who work with you and for you. She crossed a line. Whether it be for money or influence, it doesn't matter. You don't steal from someone, especially if that someone writes your paychecks."

I felt bad for the woman. She shouldn't have had to lose her job just so I could avoid being hurt. I hated that and felt like a shitty person for it.

"Sorry," I whispered.

"So your mother was Rebecca Jameson. I remember her. I'm sorry to say this, but it only happened once when I was weak. I told my wife about it immediately because I felt so damn guilty for it. Long story short, after about twenty years, she forgave me."

My gut twisted. "You think she'll forgive you for this?"

He smiled, and it was a very handsome one. "After the phone call from Mr. Lynx here, I spoke with her and my children. Life is too short. We'd like you to come to dinner tonight at our home, get to know us, meet your two brothers and sister."

Tears welled in my eyes.

"Mr. Lynx here didn't give me a lot to go on with your life. He only warned me that you weren't the touchy-feely type and to keep my distance."

I smirked. Lynx was always taking care of me.

"I'm guessing by the terrified look on your face that there is a lot you need to fill me in on … when you're ready, of course."

I didn't know if I would ever be ready to spill everything to this man. Sure, he was my father on paper, but to me, he was a stranger. It would take more than one meeting and a dinner to make me open myself up to him.

"Will you come?" he asked.

I cleared my throat. "Yeah."

"Great! Would you like to stick around and talk for a while, or do you want to go back and rest before dinner?"

He was giving me an out, and I was going to take it. I needed to recharge and get all my ducks in rows before meeting the family I had never known I had.

"I'm pretty tired. I'd like to rest."

He clapped his hands together, and I jumped.

"Sorry. Then I'll see you at dinner tonight. Lynx has the address."

Lynx nodded.

This meeting felt more like a business transaction than meeting my father for the first time, but I let it go. I needed some space and time before the next big meeting.

"Thanks," I said awkwardly as Lynx led me out of the building and into the car. He said nothing as my mind processed what was happening around me.

***

"No carrying any plates."

I laughed at Lynx's joke, just as the door to the sprawling home opened. The big, wooden planks were two feet taller than me, making me feel very small.

I had done what I had said I was going to do. I had decompressed and pulled myself together during our time at the hotel. I had even taken a nap, which had helped.

Now it was go time as a gorgeous, older woman stood in the doorway, her big, emerald green eyes wide in what appeared to be shock. Her long, brunette hair hung below her shoulders. Her shocked face turned into a huge smile that warmed her face and welcomed me in the process.

"Hi, Reign. I'm Chloe, Weston's wife."

I dug deep and put a small smile on my lips. "Nice to meet you."

"Weston said you were beautiful, but he was lying."

My heart stopped.

"You are absolutely extraordinary."

At that, I blushed. I had been called many things in my life, but extraordinary wasn't one of them.

"Thanks." I clutched Lynx's hand as he extended the other out to Chloe.

"Nice to meet you, ma'am."

"Oh, none of that ma'am stuff. I'm not that old now," she joked, lightening the mood. "Come in. The kids are here, and they can't wait to meet you."

The kids … While I had lain in bed before my nap, I had tried to come up with every conceivable idea that the kids of my father could throw at me. My mind had raced with all kinds of pretty horrible stuff. What I hadn't expected was to walk into the entryway of the house and see two boys and one girl around my age with wide smiles on their faces. They knew I was the result of an affair between their father and my mother. Surely, they were angry about that, so why were they smiling at me?

"Reign, I'd like you to meet Kyler, Colton, and Lindsey."

Each waved their hand as she said their names.

Kyler was tall, almost in line with Lynx, which I hadn't thought was possible. He was also the spitting image of my father. Colton was almost as tall as Kyler, but where Kyler had bulk, Colton was thinner, leaner, like he ran a lot. He had dusty brown hair that didn't match his brother or sister's dark tresses. Lindsey looked just like her mother, minus the few wrinkles around her mouth from smiling like her mother. She was so fresh faced and beautiful.

Weston walked in behind them, and my eyes went to him.

"Reign, Lynx, welcome to our home. I see you've met everyone."

"Yes. Nice to meet you," I said, pulling out my confidence. Where from? I didn't know and didn't care. I needed it, and I was grasping it with both hands.

"Please, let's go into the living room," Weston said.

I nodded as the three kids turned around and walked into a room off to the left. I inhaled deeply, suddenly needing the air, and the smell of cinnamon invaded me. It wasn't strong; it was homey, warm, and settled some of the nerves that were flaring.

Everyone stood in the room as Lynx and I entered, and I squeezed his hand.

Why were they all staring at me? Did I have something gross sticking out of my nose? I turned to Lynx, who kissed my temple reassuringly.

"Please sit," Chloe said, pointing to the love seat.

I sat with Lynx right next to me, his hand not leaving mine, giving me that moral support I so desperately needed. Everyone else scattered around, sitting on reclining chairs and couches.

The room was beautiful with butter cream walls lined with pictures of their family, all five of them happy. The fireplace was a focal point with large stones going all the way to the ceiling.

This house was like Bailey's: a home.

Weston clapped his hands together, making me jump.

"Sorry," he muttered. "Let's get the elephant out of the room first and foremost."

"Reign, I know all about what my husband did. He's paid dearly for it over the years." Chloe smiled at her husband with nothing but love shining through. I didn't know how she did it, but she did. "My children have just learned of this, as I liked to keep our personal business away from them." She looked at her kids, nodding to each one. I admired how she sat there with her back straight, exuding so much confidence. I would love to be like that one day.

"We're pretty pissed at Dad," Kyler said, his voice low. "And that's probably not going to change for a while, but that has no reflection on you."

It was my turn to have the wide eyes.

"Yeah, I can't believe my dad did that to my mom, but it's so cool I have a sister!" Lindsey exclaimed. I had to sit back in my seat a bit at her enthusiasm. "I've always wanted a sister. I begged my parents for one, and look, I got her!"

I wished I could share in her joy, but this was all too new for me, too raw. It hadn't penetrated quite yet, but I hoped that I would feel like I was in the same boat one day.

"I did something stupid, and I've paid for it, and I'm going to pay for it again." Weston looked at his three children. "I get that. I understand that. But there is no reason that you have to have anything less from us than us. We aren't perfect—I don't know who is—but we welcome you here with open arms."

Tears welled up in my eyes. He had no idea the gift he was giving me, no idea the impact it would have on my life. I tried to keep the tears at bay, but they fell, almost cleansing me in a way, cleaning me from my past and allowing me to move forward.

"I don't know what to say," I responded.

"You don't need to say anything, dear," Chloe said calmly. "We just want to get to know you, your life."

That struck a chord. I almost wanted to hide it all from them and pretend it hadn't happened, but looking at their expectant faces, I knew I would have to tell them some of it. I wasn't ready to share all of it, though. That would have to be for some other time.

Kyler spoke then. "I'm the oldest in the group. I work at dad's company, but I really love to paint. He says I can *paint in my spare time*." He used an even deeper voice for those last words. "But it's a paycheck." He shrugged.

"I'm the next," Colton said. "I run and train for marathons."

My eyes widened. "Those are, like, really hard," I said stupidly then bit the inside of my lip so I didn't say more.

Colton laughed. "Yeah, they are, but I love it. I also work at the company. Family business and all."

"My turn," Lindsey said with marked enthusiasm. "I'm going to start my freshman year at the University of Washington, and I'm super excited about that."

"Mom and Dad are, too. It will get you out of the house," Kyler barked, and Colton laughed. This started the back and forth, and everyone talked over everyone else.

I looked around the room filled with laughter and happiness. The only thing missing was Andi, and then it would be complete. I might have been through hell, but in doing so, I had become a stronger woman, one I was proud of. I was a woman who could stand on her own two feet, feel love, and give love. In that moment, I felt complete for the first time in my life.

Epilogue

One Year Later

"Lynx, we're going to be late! Let's go!" I called down the hallway.

Weston, Chloe, Kyler, Colton, and Lindsey were in town. I had visited them several times throughout the past year, learning about each other. However, this was the first time they were coming to me, and I was a ball of nerves.

A year ago, I hadn't thought this kind of life would be possible for me. I hadn't truly known the word happy. Today, I did.

Happiness was giving your heart to someone you knew would protect it with every breath they took. That was what I had with Lynx. Even after over a year of being together, he surprised me every day by just being him with simple things, like notes on the fridge to let me know he was thinking of me or texts at different hours. Every single one, I held so dear to my heart. I locked them all away inside me, selfishly hoarding them so I would never lose a single one.

I wouldn't say the road had been without bumps between us, because it had. I had my downs and he had some attacks. With each one, though, we rolled with it, helping the other come out of it. It wasn't easy. It was a constant battle. Nevertheless, it was one I was willing to fight for because Lynx meant everything to me. I loved him with everything I had in me.

"Coming." Lynx walked in, wearing dress pants and a green polo shirt, his hair a tussled mess. He looked totally edible.

"Yum …" I said.

I had overcome a lot of my sexual inhibitions, allowing that part of me to come out. It hadn't occurred overnight; it had been slow and tedious. But Lynx had been patient, letting me take my time. Now I could admit flat-out that sex was one of the most amazing things in the world. To feel that utter connection to another human being was undeniably the epitome of happiness.

"Stop that or we're gonna be late." He gave me a quick kiss, turned me around to the door, and patted my ass, which I loved, but I gave a mock glare for the fun of it. "You like it," he teased as we went out to the truck.

I had saved enough money to buy a reasonable car, but Lynx had other ideas, stating, "Now that we're living together, you're letting me take care of you." Then he had bought me a newer car so he didn't have to "worry."

After a long argument about me paying my own way, he had won, and I had gotten the car. One other thing he had won was me quitting bartending and coming to work for him to do his paperwork. I hadn't been for it, but after a while, he had won, and now I worked from our home. Yes, home.

It wasn't a house. I loved this place almost as much as I loved the guy I lived with. I even had pictures everywhere of all the places Lynx had taken me and the adventures we'd had.

The drive to the restaurant was quiet, my nerves settling once I knew we weren't going to be late. Andi and her man were meeting us there along with Bailey and Mal. In a way, it was the meshing of our families, and we were doing it in a small, Italian restaurant just outside of town. I had rented the back space so we could all be together and take as much time as we wanted.

As we pulled up, Bailey and Mal headed for the truck. I opened the door and slid out, smoothing my velvet green dress down just as Bailey pulled me in for a hug.

I didn't freeze up or push her away.

Over the last year, I had become accustomed to her hugs. She gave them away freely, and I loved every second of it.

"Hey, Mal." I gave a slight wave to him.

We still weren't in the hugging phase, but I was working on that. Even with all the time that had passed, there were certain things I still couldn't do. Although, I had to say the people who had pushed those boundaries just a bit—Bailey, Chloe, and Lindsey to be exact—were the ones I had been able to do more physical contact with.

"Let's go. Weston just texted me. They're in there," Lynx said after greeting his sister and brother-in-law.

The smile that graced my face was full of joy and promise. That night, everyone I cared about, everyone I loved, my family, were going to be together in one space. I had never thought I would have that. I had never dreamed of having it after I had lost Drew, but now I did, and I was so damn excited to see everyone.

When I entered the back room, Andi was the first to come to me and wrap me in her arms. I had met her man Matthew several times, but there still wasn't that comfortable feeling with him. Andi loved him, though, and that was enough for me.

"Hey, girl."

"Hey. Thanks for coming."

Andi pulled away. "I wouldn't miss this for the world."

We smiled just as Weston and Chloe came up. Things between us weren't perfect, but what in life was? The fact that we lived so far apart was a hindrance at times, yet we had come together more than I could have dreamed, something I was grateful for.

"Reign, my girl," Weston said, taking my hand and kissing the top of it. Letting him do this had taken a while, and we weren't in the hugging phase, but it was a way he showed me how much I meant to him.

Chloe, on the other hand, pulled me against her, hugging me tightly. "So good to see you."

"Same here. Thank you for coming."

"All right, move out of the way," Lindsey said, pulling Chloe from me.

She and I had something unique. It was kind of a sister thing, but more of a friend thing. I could say with all clarity that she was one of my best friends. We talked every day on the phone, and if we couldn't, we texted. Out of all five of them, I was the closest to her, which was one more thing I loved.

Lindsey pulled me to her, hugging me and swaying me from side to side. I relished in the hug. I had missed her. Skype just didn't cut it. The real thing was so much better. When she pulled away, it was a little too soon for me, but I kept that to myself.

"Hey, little sis." Kyler came up then, holding his fist up for me to bump. I secretly loved him calling me that, but I felt the urge to give him shit about it.

"Little, my ass." I bumped his fist as he chuckled.

"Hey, girl," Colton said, staying in his seat around the table.

"Hi." He and I hadn't really talked much, but I kept in touch with him and cheered him on in one of his races. That was a fun experience.

"Let's sit," Lynx said, and everyone found their chairs.

I looked around at all the people who had come together for me. I had to be a little selfish in that moment because I had never thought I would have this. I had never thought I would experience people around me who loved me, cared for me, and would do everything in their power not to hurt me. I would do the same in return.

"May I have your attention please?" Lynx said, rising from the seat he had just sat in. "I want to thank each of you for coming. Reign has wanted this for some time, and we appreciate that you guys"—he nodded to Weston and the family—"were able to come. This is a very special night for my girl, and I know it means the world to her to have you all here. It does to me, too."

Lynx turned to me, pushing out his chair. "Reign, I love you more than life itself. You're my light, my partner, my everything. I want to wake up to you every morning and fall asleep with you in my arms at night. I want you to burn dinner so we have to go out." Laughter came from the table. "And I want you to be a permanent fixture in Pepper's and my life."

I got confused for a moment, thinking I already was a permanent fixture. Then my pulse picked up.

That was when Lynx did something I had never believed possible for a kid who had never been wanted, who had never had anyone, who had done things she wasn't proud of to survive, and then who had tried to take her own life.

He lowered down to one knee, and tears welled in my eyes. I wanted to pinch myself to see if I was sleeping or dreaming, something.

"Reign Owens, will you be my wife? Will you burn my food, take walks with me and Pepper, and spend the rest of your life with us?" He reached into his pants pocket and pulled out a box as tears flowed over my cheeks and onto the floor. He opened the box to reveal a beautiful diamond, circle-cut ring.

I looked into his eyes where all the love he had given me shone so brightly. "Thank you," I whispered.

"What?" he asked in shock, and I hurried up and spoke, thinking he thought I was saying no.

I placed my hand on his cheek. "Thank you for giving me a life I never thought possible, for being my rock and letting me grow into myself, for being the man I need in my life. I love you with everything I am and everything I have to give. I would love to marry you and burn your food." Sobs racked my body as I heard the women in the room sniffling and the guys chuckling.

Lynx smiled his gorgeous smile and took the ring out of the box before he placed it on my finger.

I had never had anything in my life as beautiful as this except my love for Lynx.

He then scooped me up, and I wrapped my arms around his neck, holding on with all my strength.

Life was a journey of ups and downs. Unfortunately, I'd had way too many downs, but I dealt with them, grew from them, and learned from them. I wasn't perfect, never claimed to be, but I was the perfect me.

Readers,

Depression, PTSD, and other deep issues covered in this book take different lengths of time to combat—some take a lifetime, meaning some people are never free. In this book, time is skewed and sped up to flow with the story line. Please keep that in mind at all times and note that I understand it completely.

This book is dark. It deals with tough issues that many of us don't talk about because we're afraid of being exposed and cut open raw, but to heal, we must lay it out there. We must go there to find our sunshine and hope like hell that we do. Depression and suicide numbers are on the rise, and we need to be aware.

This book was extremely hard for me to write. It is deeply personal and pushed my boundaries as an author and a human being. I also found that it was very therapeutic to write. I hoped you enjoyed it and felt the tug of Lynx and Reign's story.

Please make sure to stop by and leave a review on whatever outlet you purchased *Needing To Fall.* It is much appreciated.

Thank you for taking the time to read,

Ryan

Need Help? Are you or someone you love in need of assistance? Please seek it immediately. Here are some contacts. There is help. You are not alone.

Suicide Prevention Lifeline 1-800-273-TALK

https://www.afsp.org/preventing-suicide/find-help

https://www.nimh.nih.gov/index.shtml

http://www.suicidepreventionlifeline.org/getinvolved/locator

http://www.ptsd.va.gov/public/where-to-get-help.asp

http://veteranscrisisline.net

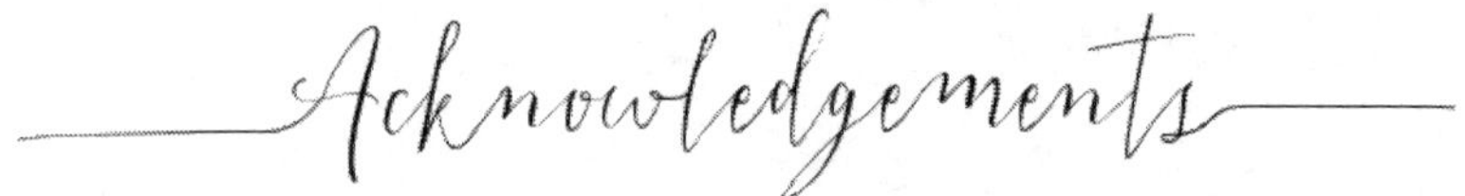

To my family, I love you more than words can express. You are my rock, hope, and light.

I had a shining star in writing this book. She pushed me hard. She had me digging deeper in parts of this book than I wanted to go. Her bubbles littered my work, and I loved every damn one of them. If it weren't for her being there and being my own personal cheerleader, this book wouldn't have come to light. For that, I can never repay her. It was therapeutic for me. I'm the lucky one to call her my friend. CC, "It's not a sprint; it's a marathon."

Ashley, thank you for all your help and lending me your ear.

My betas, Terri, SM, and Mia, love you, ladies. Thank you so much.

My readers, I appreciate every single one of you. Without you, I wouldn't have the opportunity to do what I love doing. You are MY ROCKSTARS.

Bloggers, thank you from the bottom of my heart for taking your time to read and help get the word out about my books. I appreciate each and every one of you.

About the Author

Sign Up for my Newsletter:

http://tinyurl.com/RyanMicheleNewsletter

Website : www.authorryanmichele.net

Facebook: www.facebook.com/AuthorRyanMichele

Twitter -- @Ryan_Michele

Pinterest: http://www.pinterest.com/authorryanmiche/

Goodreads: www.goodreads.com/RyanMichele

Instagram: author_ryan_michele

Google+: google.com/+RyanMichele

Other Titles by Ryan Michele

Ravage MC Series

Ravage Me (Ravage MC #1)

Seduce Me (Ravage MC #2)

Consume Me (Ravage MC #3)

Inflame Me (Ravage MC #4)

Captivate Me (Ravage Me #5): Coming 2016

Satisfy Me:

Rattle Me

Ravage MC Box Set

Ride with Me by Ryan Michele & Chelsea Camaron

Raber Wolf Pack Series

Raber Wolf Pack Book One

Raber Wolf Pack Book Two

Raber Wolf Pack Book Three

Raber Wolf Pack Box Set

Stand-alones

Safe

Wanting You

Blood &Loyalties

Needing to Fall